Driving Ambition

by Fiona Moore

Bundoran Press

This is a work of fiction. The characters, incidents and dialogue are products of the author's imagination and are not to be construed as real. Any resemblance to actual events or persons, living or dead, is entirely coincidental.

Cover Illustration: Dan O'Driscoll

Cover Design: Virginia O'Dine

Printed in Canada

Published by Bundoran Press Publishing House

www.bundoranpress.com

Library and Archives Canada Cataloguing in Publication

Moore, Fiona, author
Driving ambition / Fiona Moore.

Issued in print and electronic formats.
ISBN 978-1-927881-43-9 (softcover).
ISBN 978-1-927881-44-6 (Kindle)
ISBN 978-1-927881-45-3 (EPUB)

I. Title.

PS8626.O59365D75 2018 C813'.6 C2018-905004-7
C2018-905005-5

To Mrs Wright

1: I Feel Safe In My Car

"Did you hear about the motorbike accident in Oxford High Street this weekend?" I asked Trish by way of distraction as we advanced grimly towards the mob of protesting cars in Soho Square.

"Oh, yes," she said, brightly, the escaped hair blowing around her face in dark Botticelli waves. "I understand the motorbike is expected to make a full recovery."

"Good to know," I said. The motorbike was a friend of a friend, and I'd always thought he ought to leave that stupid driver of his. After this, his driver would undoubtedly be prosecuted for Endangering the Continued Existence of an Artificially Intelligent Being, possibly barred from driving, and maybe Yetaxa would be able to choose a better owner.

The mob, meanwhile, were blaring their horns in rhythm, flashing their lights and attempting, as much as possible in narrow, crowded Soho Square, to drive around in fancy manoeuvres. Some had gone to the trouble of having slogans painted on their doors and windshields: RESPECT THING RIGHTS, said one. SAFE TAXIS UNFAIR TO SELF-DRIVING CARS said another. Well, most Things I knew tended to lack creativity with language, and self-driving cars especially so; this was probably about as original as they would get. Although Trish couldn't hear what they were saying to each other, I could; the world inside my head was a cacophony of shouted slogans and surprisingly creative suggestions about what management could do with its hiring and remuneration policies.

A pair of Texcoco mini-vans, blocky in bronze paint, span in together to block us with their fenders; then one of them recognised me (although I'm not sure how), flashed its lights, had a brief conversation with the other one, and they span out, telling the other cars who we were. With curt acknowledgements, several of them shifted to give us an access route. I made a note to find out who it was. Off the Internet of Things and in physical space, I found it hard to tell one car from the other, and I wasn't exactly in a position to ask right now. I was pretty certain the little racing-green Verve four-seater parked discreetly around the corner from the demo was Egon, at least.

"Verves and Texcoco," I remarked, scanning the cars in the square. The Verves mid-range and practical, hatchbacks and saloons, nipping and darting and flashing their lights; the Texcoco larger, mini-vans, vans and SUVs, taking up as much space as they could. But the small, sleek, space-age city cars were conspicuously absent. "No Ariels. You notice that?"

"I suppose, now that you mention it," Trish said, clutching her tablet-case protectively against her red wool coat. I reminded myself to cut her a little slack. It was Trish's first time on a Joint Negotiating Committee for the Union of Thing Transport Workers, and as far as I knew she hadn't had much to do with Things before taking the job as their new legal advisor. Might have taken a ride in a car, or hired a drone, or lived or worked in a building which had a concierge or a house-elf, but most people who use Things don't really attempt to get to know them. No wonder she was tense.

Somewhere nearby I heard a human desperately attempting to reason with one of the cars: "Look," a frustrated voice was saying in impeccable, annoyed, precise English: "I only want to hire a taxi…." The voice was drowned in a derisory chorus of angry horns.

Thanks to the Texcoco intervention, we made it safely to the pavement in front of the London offices of Safe Taxis International, accompanied by a brief fanfare of horns, and it was there that we found the human protest.

"What the hell?" Trish's eyes widened under her sweat-streaked forehead and she took a harder grip on the tablet-case.

"Wasn't expecting *them*," I said, unable to come up with anything cleverer. The humans were rather better in their command of slogans: *Down With These Sorts of Things*, read one sign, and I made a mental note to congratulate the writer if ever I met them. They were also rather more destructive than the cars; a screwed-up cola bottle bounced off a windshield and the windshield's owner hooted derisively.

"Who *are* they?"

"Off-grid group," I said. The natural-fibre clothing, the plain-cut hair, the general air of people who insist on handcrafted everything. I was trying to figure out which group it was and praying to whatever deity looks after nonbelievers that none of my brother's friends were in it. Or worse, my brother himself, though I didn't think he left the farm too often these days. "Probably groups, plural."

"They still exist?"

"Oh yes," I said. Some of the protestors were dressed in dark colours and looked a bit better groomed, and some had the traditional guy-fawkes graffito painted on their signs. That wasn't a good sign; it suggested a collaboration, or infiltration, between off-gridders and anonymists. Off-gridders you could sometimes reason with; anonymists, not so much.

By the cottage in Soho Square, a group of performance artists had set up. Dressed in shocking pink costumes, they flung about in an acrobatic display. Experimental music and glitter-firing mortars were drawing the attention of passers-by. Several of the cars drove over to have a closer look. One of the protest leaders scolded the cars for getting distracted by the art and urged them back to the demo.

"What are they doing here?" Trish looked wildly about at the human protestors. "This is a strike by self-driving cars, not human drivers."

"Not sure I ever could follow their logic," I said. "Probably something about how this is the sort of thing you get when you hire Things. If you'll pardon the expression. Oh well." Unfortunately, one of them—a woman with long dark-red hair pulled back from her face, swathed in an off-white coat—recognised me. Her eyes narrowed in speculation. I saw her mouth my name—*Thompson Jennings*—to a man nearby, then I caught the word *Interface.*

Oh dear.

The outer rim of the mob linked arms, focusing on Trish and me, determined not to let us through.

"We're *negotiators,*" Trish pleaded, as if it would make a difference.

"No good," I said to her. "I think perhaps if we went round the back..."

The cars noticed; there was a few moments of whispered gossip and then the chorus of horns began to get more rhythmic.

Luckily, at that moment, Sanjiv appeared, striding lankily through the cars, his close-cropped grey hair and spare, seamed, bony face giving him the sort of battle-worn look normally seen on former Marines, or secondary characters on *Game of Thrones.* "Sorry I'm late," he said, idly drawing his phone from its sheath on his forearm, as if the noisy cars and the wall of humans weren't there at all. "Bit of a delay on the Central Line, I suspect the trains may be coming out in sympathy with the taxis. Good for us if they are, of course. Anyway, what's all this?" He made as if he'd only just noticed the humans.

"Off-gridders," I repeated. "One of them's clocked me, and they're not letting us through."

"But why won't they?" Trish asked. "We're humans, aren't we? We're going to bring an end to the strike?"

Sanjiv shook his head. "They'd prefer it if the strike continued," he said. "Puts people off using Things. As for our human status, we probably count as traitors, and, if they know who Thom is, I'm not sure they entirely count him as human. Depends which group they are." His eyes narrowed as he registered the same thing I'd noticed—the mix of clothing and grooming styles. "Or groups. Anyway, give me a moment." With that, Sanjiv strode into the crowd, wielding his mobile like a sword.

Sanjiv had been a caseworker for a human union for about a decade before joining UTTW five years ago, and I suspected he'd transferred mainly because the fights were better in the world of Thing labour. He was the sort of guy who made scrolling through his social-media feed look like an act of war.

"Best if we take a step back," I said, suiting actions to words and leaning against a friendly chassis. "Don't worry, we're safe with the cars."

Sanjiv spent a few minutes in conversation with the apparent ringleaders of the human protest, then came back. "They're letting us through," he said.

"How—"

"Reminded them of the penalty for preventing union officials from doing their mandated jobs," Sanjiv cut Trish's question off, "and further reminded them that if they want that same courtesy extended to human unions on a regular basis, they have to respect the Thing unions as well. In any case, we've got a window of a few minutes before the anonymist wing decides it's not bothered either way and decides to break the law, so let's get moving. Trish—best if you get between Thom and me. Thom—elbows out."

Forming a sort of defensive wedge with Trish as the apex, we hastened through the human crowd and towards the building. I had a moment of paranoid fear as we touched the entry controls. What if Safe Taxis had, by accident or malicious design, failed to upload our fingerprints to the concierge's database? Then the door buzzed and let us through. From there it was up a flight of stairs and through the office doors.

2: Taking Care of Business

"How long do you think they're likely to keep us waiting?" Trish said after about ten minutes, shifting as if she were uncomfortable. The seats, being normally for the benefit of Safe Taxis' investors and clients rather than for us, were actually pretty well padded and upholstered in relatively fashionable colours. The concierge was, however, showing its displeasure at our presence by lowering the temperature to below comfortable and treating us to a low-level endless loop of ancient Daft Punk numbers.

"About as long as they think they can get away with it," Sanjiv said, looking up from his phone and popping an i-bud out of his ear. "They know why we're here and they don't want us to be, but they've got to put up with us. Just don't let them think they've got to you." The sound of horns blaring, human voices shouting, and what I could only assume was the performance art collective singing a wordless atonal a-cappella number, drifted up from the street, despite the thick walls and pervasive music, which undoubtedly contributed to the air of tension radiating from Trish's general direction. The novelty of the situation, plus the protest outside, must have really shaken her.

I couldn't help but sympathise. I remembered how union work had seemed to me when I'd first begun working for UTTW; the psychological tactics, the dramatic protests, the conspiracy-mongering and deal-brokering. It might be worth suggesting we go for coffee afterwards, to provide some reassurance to the new member.

Following Sanjiv's lead, I checked my phone. The messaging app showed that Naomi had received my message, but it looked like she hadn't bothered to reply yet. She'd always been terrible at replying to messages. It was one of the reasons we'd split up, if not the principal one.

In this case it was more than usually annoying. She'd bombarded me with messages asking if I could foster a rescue cat for the animal charity she worked for, saying it was urgent, and now that I had finally got in a position where I could say *yes*, I didn't even know if she still needed the help.

Finally, after what seemed like an eternity of sampled beats, a perfumed and sharp-suited human clicked her way through the door, a false-looking smile on her face. The concierge smoothly raised the temperature and switched to Philip Glass.

"Sorry to keep you," she said unconvincingly. "If you could come with me, Mr Drexler is waiting for you in the small boardroom." Sanjiv and I exchanged battle-weary glances and followed, him stowing his phone and buds, me hefting the dark green bag with the UTTW logo which had been sitting at my feet during the wait. Trish rolled a black curl anxiously around one finger and joined us.

Christoph Drexler, taller, darker, and handsomer than any Bavarian had a right to be, stood as we entered the small, spare, modern room. "Sanjiv, Thom," he said, extending hands with bluff cheer. "This would be Ms Wong?" he asked as he turned to Trish. "So good to meet you. I'm Christoph Drexler, London managing director for Safe Taxis. Call me Christoph." Trish took his hand rigidly, but Christoph was not going to be put off by that, smiling warmly like a good host. "This is Jarvis Oliver, our own legal counsel, and Doctor Rose Andrews, our Thing Resource Manager. I assume Millie, Salieri and Egon will be joining us shortly?"

I nodded, opening the green bag and taking out the two black glass pads which would allow the intelligents to join in the meeting.

"Good," Christoph said. "We await their arrival. Assuming you do the honours, of course."

It was then that I clocked the look on Trish's face. And I realised why she had seemed so nervous.

It wasn't that she was worried about her first time taking part in a Joint Negotiating Committee, or that pushing through the protest outside had upset her.

She was scared of me.

That's nothing new, of course. I'm sure that voodoo priests don't get many invitations to parties either (then again, maybe they do: "Come on, bring your *loa*, we'll have a great time! Especially the guy in the top hat—he'll *love* the chocolate fountain!"). But in my line of work, I mostly meet people like Christoph, who spend their days working with intelligents and their interfaces, or people like Sanjiv, who give absolutely zero fucks about what your personal quirks are so long as you can do your job, so I can fool myself that the rest of the world doesn't consider me strange.

I look normal on the outside, except for the scars, and they're mostly below the shirt-line, and I live near Oxford, which is pretty tolerant of any sort of eccentricity, so long as it's reasonably picturesque. I'm sure me going all mediumistic in the Queens Lane Coffee House—it happened once, by accident when I was still new to interfacing; I'm not proud—is nothing on what Oscar Wilde and Shelley got up to back in the day. Or what some of the undergraduates still get up to with their trance-stimulators and euphoric lights. But, once in a while, I'll be reminded that I do live in a bubble, and this was one of those times.

But Christoph was going on. "Do you need anything special, Thom? Everything's set up as you usually like it."

"Fine," I said, settling down in the comfortable armchair that someone had taken the trouble to bring in and wrapping the blanket around my legs. I don't actually need it—I don't actually need the comfy chair either, though it's certainly helpful—but people need rituals, and they like to think their mediums require tribute. "And I'm gonna need a hot coffee afterwards. Melville's. Tall latte. With soy milk." I don't need that either, but again, people like a bit of theatre, and it lets the interns feel like they're part of something supernatural.

I made a point of placing the nasty-looking box of way too many pills in front of me; now those I *do* need after I come out of medium mode, but if I make them part of the theatre, it's less embarrassing. I added a bottle of expensive spring water. Well, the bottle was from expensive spring water, I'd been refilling it from the tap for weeks. But as I said, theatre.

I was laying it on a bit thick, but this was largely down to Trish's reaction, *if she thinks I'm a freak then I'll damn well play the freak*—an angry thought surprised me. I took a deep breath or two. Compassion and sympathy, I reminded myself. Anger doesn't help anyone, not her or you.

Sanjiv, meanwhile, had calmly taken a tablet out of his bag and set up the documents he needed, thumbing through the translucent upright display, still with his deadpan warrior's face. Trish was fiddling with her own tablet while not looking at either of us.

"All right then?" Christoph looked at me inquiringly. Putting my hands on the two pads, I slotted my fingers into the designated places, felt the tips meet the cold metallic contacts, waited for the tingling sensation that would tell me I was about to connect with the Internet of Things, closed my eyes for a minute to concentrate.

I could feel both my nervous systems for a moment: the damaged organic one, dark pink and withered, still functional but only just and only for short periods; the artificial replacement one, shining silver and humming gently like a wire. With my mind I did a quickfire three-way switch. Organic system to artificial system, artificial system out… into the cloud…

Connection.

I repeated the procedure again. Now my nervous system was receiving input from TY21EGE and AR24ZXC. Three consciousnesses looked out of my eyes. Well, sort of. I looked out of my own eyes, then my nervous system processed what I saw into inputs the intelligents could understand.

I reached out a third time. Found the spot where MI27EEE

should have been. Probed further. Received a message/impression: *away at the moment, back soon, leave a message.* Abrupt, but then intelligents aren't known for adhering to human standards of politeness—Things in particular can seem outright rude—and this wouldn't be the first time Millie had been late for a meeting. Probably couldn't resist picking up a last-minute client, and she'd log in once she was free.

I caught Christoph's eyes and nodded.

"The cars are here?" he asked. The words were again processed. TY21EGE responded, and the response came out of my mouth as words:

"Yes, we're here. Egon speaking." Self-driving cars are a bit like T.S. Elliott's Practical Cats; they have their own names they use among themselves, which are untranslatable; they have their registration numbers; and they also usually have names for communicating with the humans. In my head, its voice sounded dry and beetly, a suggestion of old university libraries and museum displays, but I didn't know how much of that came through to my audience. I generally try not to anthropomorphise cars, but Egon always made me think of a picture I'd once seen of Bertrand Russell; old, but poised, sharply-dressed and not inclined to put up with anyone else's nonsense.

There wasn't much connection between his name and his nature. Egon was a Verve, and Verves aren't really all that interested in human names, so they generally let whoever they work for give them a name, and, if their new driver doesn't change it, they'll stick with whatever they had before. Egon's been Egon since before it came to work for Safe Taxis, but I don't know when, or how, it acquired the name. Texcoco, like Millie, tend to make their naming decisions collectively, with everyone in the car pod choosing along certain lines (most people assume she was named after her license number, but that was actually a vanity job she herself took after being named). Salieri, though, was an Ariel, and they tend to like picking their own names, something about creativity and self-expression I think.

"Salieri?" Sanjiv asked.

A fractional pause, then a slightly different voice came out through my mouth. "Yes, I'm here too." Even speaking through a male interface, Salieri sounded a little feminine to human ears, though of course intelligents regard gender as being as much an aesthetic conceit as they do names. A lot of Ariels like to be gendered, but then again they do tend to be into personal adornment. Salieri, despite the name, was female, while Egon pointedly remained ungendered. She was a red four-seater with every single optional extra she could afford; leather seats, top-of-the-line stereo, custom-made steering wheel, air conditioning with pre-set range of scents. She wasn't a car I'd voluntarily book, myself, but she seemed to have a dedicated and adoring fanbase.

"Millie?"

This time I took the mouth. "Leaving an auto-reply," I said. "I think she'll be late." Millie was a big, square SUV in gold paint, all angles and no-nonsense boxes, the sort of car that's totally impractical for London but which the tourists apparently love to ride in. I suppose it makes them feel important. Mind you, Millie also did a lot of countryside driving, where the bulk and the four-wheel-drive came in handier.

There were one or two polite sighs from the employers' side of the table.

"I'll let you know when she logs in," I said, then retreated back, shutting my eyes for a few minutes to ride out the vertigo. I try to cut in as little as possible when I'm interpreting for Things; it makes me disoriented and dizzy.

"So, where did we leave things last time?" Christoph asked, for nobody's real benefit, as I opened my eyes again.

"Car numbers," Egon responded.

"*If* we must," Salieri said, almost instantly.

Trish was trying, and failing, not to give me an odd look.

Sanjiv had seen it all before and was already at the correct page of his tablet display. "According to Safe Taxis (International)'s agreement with its employees, which Safe Taxis (London Branch) is required to comply with, the branch must employ equal numbers of Verve, Ariel and Texcoco self-driving vehicles, with the remaining quarter to be made up of human-driven vehicles for the use of customers who prefer same."

"And?" Christoph asked.

Sanjiv's tone remained admirably neutral. "You currently employ thirty Verves, thirty Texcoco, of whom five are fitted with disabled access enhancements, and fifty-two Ariels."

Christoph spread his hands. "Ariels are cheaper."

"And less confrontational," Sanjiv insinuated bluntly.

"You said it," Egon said through me. "I didn't."

In the back of my nervous system, Egon and Salieri had a brief argument to the effect that they shouldn't be fighting in front of the employers' representatives.

"Recently the Verve Company increased the minimum individual hire rates," Dr Andrews came in smoothly. "And Texcoco announced they'll be taking up the new rate in June. I'm afraid it's pricing us out of the market."

"We've hired enough Verves to make up a pod," Jarvis said. "If you look at the agreement, we're not required to have absolutely even numbers, just at least a pod of each model."

"And that should comply with your Thing rights as to your need for a social life," Dr Andrews added.

Now Trish came in, a cool and collected façade sweeping in over the nervousness. "Unfortunately, it's not simply that you're required to maintain a pod of each model," she said in easy, cultured tones. "The terms of the contract also specify that numerical imbalances between the models should not become excessive. There's also the issue of numbers of disabled-access vehicles, relating to human health and safety laws—"

"That's a separate issue," Dr Andrews said.

"It's a related issue," Trish replied smoothly. You wouldn't know she'd had a little freakout about the interface a moment earlier. "Only the Texcoco are large enough to be fitted with wheelchair-access systems. This affects Texcoco numbers relative to the others."

"Cars are tribal," Sanjiv shrugged at the employers' representatives matter-of-factly. "It's the way they are. Too many of one, and the others feel threatened."

"Adjusting numbers based on price alone sets a dangerous precedent," Trish added. "Legally, no one can own a Thing; the Things enter into individual or collective contract with a person, group or organisation. Costs are prearranged according to national and global scales."

Christoph raised an eyebrow. "In the absence of the Texcoco—"

"Check the rules of collective bargaining," Egon came in. "The Texcoco authorised me to speak for them if Millie is late." *As usual*, it said in my head but didn't engage the vocal chords. "The document was uploaded to your cloud last week." Personally, I thought Egon was likely to get further with the company than we would with Millie present, given her usual lack of diplomacy. But, of course, that was judgmental of me, and that wasn't why I was here.

"The human drivers—"

"Aren't covered by UTTW," Egon reminded him. "We're here because there's too many Ariels."

"And how do the Ariels feel?" Christoph asked dangerously.

There was a long pause from inside my nervous system. "Shall we say, we're willing to entertain different points of view," Salieri replied.

There was another pause.

"After our last discussion," Christoph finally said, thumbing up a document on his tablet, "we've developed another offer. If the Verves and Texcoco would be willing to lower their hire price by, say, ten per cent, we could take on another dozen of each model."

"Out of the question," Egon came in.

"Why?" Salieri retorted. "Are you somehow more valuable than us?"

A pause. "Sanjiv, I'd like to request a recess," Egon said, a little crossly.

"Would you excuse us?" Sanjiv addressed Christoph and his team. Christoph nodded and directed his team to leave the room, since I couldn't move without disconnecting, and then it would be a rather more difficult process to reconnect than it had been to connect in the first place.

"They're probably listening outside the door," observed Trish.

"Never mind if they are," Sanjiv said curtly. "Talk to me, Egon, Salieri. What's the problem?"

"Clearly," Salieri said, "Some issues with the Verves need to be taken care of internally."

"Clearly," Egon retorted, "the problem is with the Ariels."

"How so?" Salieri replied dryly.

"Why can't you raise your prices?"

"Why can't you *lower* yours?"

"We're all part of the UTTW, we need to agree on a collective scale. And we're generally agreed that the hire price the Texcoco and Verve charge is the union standard."

"Maybe the Ariels want to leave the UTTW," Salieri managed to make it sound insinuating and slyly coy.

"That's ridiculous. Where would you go?"

"How the *hell*—" Trish exclaimed, the cool lawyer façade suddenly dropping, then snapping just as suddenly back into place.

Sanjiv touched her shoulder briefly. "I know, it's strange to watch when you're not used to it," he said, smiling in a lipless way I think he thought was reassuring. "Looks like Thom's having an argument with himself, doesn't it? It's a shame we can't afford to hire more than one for this case, though it'd probably still sound strange."

"Does he know what's going on?" Trish asked.

"He does," Sanjiv said, "and he can hear us perfectly clearly too.

It's not only impolite for him to cut in, it's pretty difficult. They're channelling directly through his nervous system; he tells me the disorientation afterwards is something else."

"Oh," Trish said, eyes becoming wide as she realised she was being rude.

"Anyway," Salieri was saying, "all of this means nothing if we haven't got word from the Texcoco. Thom," suddenly addressing me directly, "do you think you could give Millie a ping again?"

I took a deep breath, reached out for contact.

Felt a shock like an unexpected bucket of cold water hitting me from both sides.

"Guys," I said, taking the mouth and including everyone, "we're going to have to cancel the meeting. The police are at Millie's site, she's dead, and they're going to want to interview all of us."

3: Don't Fear the Reaper

I had to disconnect from Egon and Salieri at that point, since the police would be interviewing them back on their sites on the Internet of Things. A separate agency, the International Enforcement of Artificial Law service, known popularly as Cybersecurity, dealt with intelligents, although, if this was some sort of accident or local crime, the human police would be taking point and Cybersecurity simply gathering data for them. I slid my hands off the contacts, knocked back the pills, and then spent a little while riding out the vertigo and blackout (the pills helped, but couldn't fix everything).

When I was normal enough to register the world again, the room had changed. Jarvis had vanished off somewhere, and Sanjiv was talking breezily with Christoph and Dr Andrews in a little knot near the door, brandishing his phone to punctuate the discussion. Somebody had remembered the coffee request and I wrapped my hands around the Melville's cup and held it for a second before taking a tongue-scorching sip.

Trish was sitting next to me—I suspect Sanjiv had tasked her with keeping an eye on me and making sure I was only normally disorientated—rifling through her tablet and biting her lip.

"Don't be scared," I said to her.

She looked startled, then annoyed, then a bit shamefaced. "Okay," she said. "But it's the first time something like this has happened to me. A death on the job, I mean. What happens now?"

"Well, the police are sending a human team around to interview us face-to-face," I said. I took another sip of coffee. "How long was I out for?"

"About five minutes," Trish said.

"Okay, they'll be here any minute," I said. "Usually they dispatch from the nearest office so they can get the statements quicker. There's a London Met station around the corner from here. They'll have to push through that mob out front to get in, though, and the mob might not be friendly." I felt a little bit of schadenfreude towards the off-gridders. If they tried to get smoky with the police, the police would get smoky with them, and there'd be arrests before bedtime.

"I wonder what happened to Millie?" I said. I hadn't been particularly close to her—she'd only just been made Texcoco Representative last year—but I'd interpreted for her a couple of times at union councils. It's a little weird when someone who shares your nervous system on occasion dies.

"Accident?" Trish said.

"Most likely. With luck, no one was in her at the time," I said.

"And what happens after that?"

"Well, we find out how long it'll take for them to reload her from backup, and reschedule the meeting," I said. "I hope the backup's recent. It's harder for me to interpret when I'm connecting up with old settings, and an older backup can have information gaps."

There was a not-unexpected pause.

"Go on," I said. "Ask me anything you like. Seriously. I do career-days talks for schoolkids, no question too personal."

Trish thought a minute. "Does it hurt?"

I smiled. "That's question number one."

Trish surprised me by smiling back. "I'm that unoriginal?"

"It's just logical," I said. "It's the first question I'd ask, too. The answer is no, not usually, but I do get strange problems with perception and cognition after interpreting. Vertigo, mostly. Feels like the world's spinning and I've got to lie down." I do get pain, of course, but it's unrelated to my interpreting work, and there's no sense in spreading confusion.

"If I can ask," Trish said, "why do it? I mean, if it gives you problems with cognition… wouldn't it be better to do another job?"

"Because I can," I said. "Because it's something not many

people can do, and it's necessary for the Thing Economy. So I feel obliged, I suppose. And it's rewarding work, in its way. Helps sentient beings understand each other." Pay's not bad either, and I live in an old house that needs a lot of repairs, but that's a personal choice issue, and I didn't think it was entirely polite to discuss money with work colleagues.

"This is the part I've never understood." Trish looked a little embarrassed. "Humans and Things can talk to each other. I've talked to plenty of cars. Why do they need you?"

"That's the tricky bit," I said. "Things can communicate with us through the talk-boxes—that's what they call them—but they actually communicate among themselves in a much more sophisticated way, involving different sensory experiences, emotion sharing, perception shaping, and a lot of other things that it's a bit hard to explain to humans. Similarly, there's nuances of human conversation that are completely lost on Things; body language, sarcasm, facial expressions, pheromones. It's a bit like..." I thought around for an analogy. "It's like animals. You can communicate basically with cats, right? Are you okay, are you hungry, do you want catnip, you're a cute kitty, that sort of thing. But with each other, they communicate not through sound so much as through smell, and pheromones, and use their whiskers as an extra touch-sensor, which are things humans can't really get their own minds around. But if you could telepathically link a human with a cat..."

"...then the human might be able to tell other humans what the cat's saying, in language they can understand?" Trish nodded to herself. "Okay, I get that. Feel free not to answer this one, then," Trish said. "But how did you end up in this job? I get the impression it wasn't a choice for you, and I guess I'd always thought it was a conscious lifestyle decision."

I nodded. "Not offended. The interfaces who usually get all the interviews and the profile pieces are the ones who go into the job deliberately—tech obsessives who are into body modification, for instance, or people who really love Things so much they want to be able to talk to them. A lot of the newer and more deliberate interface modifications don't have the vertigo problems I do, too—they're improving the systems all the time. But I sort of happened into it. I was working in Japan. I was a postgraduate student. An anthropologist. You know what that is?"

"That's studying primitive tribes and all that, isn't it?"

"These days there's a lot more 'all that'," I said. "But yes, I was one of the primitive-tribes ones. I was looking at how expatriates' beliefs change, or don't change, in a different socio-religious environment." Ironically, my main line of study had been how Hindu believers relate to the Shinto idea that objects—not only animals and humans—have souls. "I was living in Tokyo, interviewing engineers working for the big Bangalore tech companies—the ones that came in as part of the reconstruction after the floods and the civil war." I glossed over a complicated event in the middle, which I don't talk about, even with people I know well. "While I was out there, I wound up in hospital, and I got an opportunistic infection. Neomeningitis?"

Trish winced. "Ouch."

"This was about ten years ago—I was one of the first documented cases." I suspected it had been running rampant among the local population for years, and only got medical attention once it started spreading from underdeveloped and/or disaster areas, like Japan, to what we laughably call civilisation, but that was an axe Trish didn't need to hear me grinding. I'd already simplified events considerably. "They still can't cure it, even though there's a vaccine. By the time they'd got me back to Oxford, I didn't have much of a nervous system left, but luckily for me artificial grafts were available. I was also one of the first to have a graft and survive."

Trish whistled. "Lucky indeed. So that's how they connect? Again, if you don't mind my asking."

"No, and yes," I said. "It's left me with, well, a dual nervous system. Of sorts. One's organic, the other's an artificial graft, grown onto and through the organic one." At the time, nanotechnology and microprinting was hugely popular in neurosurgery, before the limitations became widely known. "These days they prefer to use organic grafts for things like that, grown from stem cells. Mainly because of what I said—it's disorientating to switch from one set of nerves to the other. Organic grafts, though, don't work with the interface implants. But about ten years back, an artificial one was state of the art, and a lot of interfaces around my age, say between thirty and fifty, didn't get the job voluntarily, they're nervous-system grafters." Most of them from the developing world, plus a few, like me, that drew the publicity to the disease. I suppose we're lucky that it's no longer such an issue.

"Then anyone with a graft can talk to the cars?" Trish looked surprised.

"No," I reassured her. "Otherwise everyone with a graft would be going around channelling Verves. At the time, though, you pretty much had to have a graft before you could get the interface implants—the ones now are fairly extreme, but you *can* put them into physiologically normal people. I had to have another round of surgery to connect the implants with the graft."

"And you can talk to cars?"

"I'm the car whisperer," I said, trying to smile at the lame joke. "Yes, I can. I can hear what they're saying, if I'm close to them. But they can't use my nervous system unless I'm linked in to the communication pads." I wiggled my fingers. "You can't see it, but the artificial nerve endings on my fingers connect with the tech in the pads, and that's how I'm able to open a channel to an intelligent—a car, or a house-elf, or an industrial robot—to use my nervous system."

"What about Indies?"

"Them too. I've mostly worked with Things, though." Independents were a little disconcerting, living on the Internet with no physical bodies, running off clouds or gestalts. I preferred the more unified experience of Thing consciousness. "You didn't see that movie last year, did you?"

Trish looked a little shamefaced. "Guilty."

I breathed deeply. Altogether too many people had. Or had read the ludicrous novel it was based on. "Well, put it this way, the possibility of a nervous system being hacked occurred to other people as well as movie scriptwriters, so they've made it so that you have to log in pretty deliberately in order to make contact." Hacking can still happen if you're logged in, of course, but I didn't tell her that. Usually it involves an intelligent hijacking another intelligent's channel, or else barging in and forcing a connection before the intended recipient has logged in. There are ways of blocking that sort of thing—the incident in the Queens Lane Coffee House, in which I'd accidentally made contact with a Thing without intending to, had happened before I learned how. But it's still a danger.

"So you gave up academia, had the surgery and became an interface?"

"Not straight away." I didn't know Trish well enough to tell her that part of the story either—going back to the university once I'd recovered, finishing my doctorate in a fit of personal triumph, going on to what had looked like a career-solidifying postdoc in London. And then, a rake's progress of increasingly precarious freelance lecturing positions, funding cuts, declined grant applications and publications deemed not quite good enough for the research assessment framework. Of trying and failing to get over Naomi, which hadn't helped me concentrate on research and teaching. My father had died a disappointed man, his dreams of siring an academic dynasty thwarted by all three of his children. "But after a while, I found myself needing a job, and a lot of organisations need an interface. The surgery's not that bad—not compared to what I'd been through with the graft—and it doesn't change your life any more than having the new nervous system does." Well, in a sense it had, since what had been intended as a part-time source of income while I chased academic glory wound up becoming my entire professional life. But never mind.

Move on to the fun work stories, people like those. "My first job was with a hospital; monitoring the intelligents and ensuring any problems got seen to straight away. Then I did some work for the Verve company, then I went freelance..." amazing how quickly years of drifting around can be handwaved, "...UTTW's been one of my regular gigs for a while."

"Sounds precarious."

"It is, but no more than any other job, and the money's decent," I said. The mincome pays the basic bills, the freelancing gives me a nice bit of extra so I can afford the rest of my activities and keep the animals fed, and it's less invasive or soul-destroying than academia. "Well, it's good enough to make up for the down sides. Problem is, we're in short supply as a profession—and getting shorter, now that medicine's progressed beyond grafting for nervous system problems. That's one of the reasons why, at meetings like this one, I'm channelling more than one car—ideally, we'd have an interface for each car, to make it easier for everyone, but I'm all we've got."

Sometimes, I didn't say to her, I think about quitting. Throwing in the towel and going on to do something less painful. But then I remember the small numbers of interfaces, and the large numbers of Things needing representation, and I stop thinking that. They need help, and who'd help them, if it wasn't for me?

"I'm surprised they haven't figured out how to replace you with an app," Trish said, smiling a little.

"They're working on it," I said. "But so far, they haven't come up with anything that works well with both humans and intelligents."

Trish thought about this but didn't seem upset.

"So, you feeling less nervous about the whole thing?"

Trish smiled, framing her face in dark locks of hair in an embarrassed nod. "Was I that obvious?"

"No," I said, "but I'm used to it." Time to move on. "What's *your* story then? Lawyering for a union?"

Trish smiled again. "Sort of drifted into it. I specialised in intellectual property law, not intelligent law, and because of that, once I'd done my internship, I spent ten years in the legal department at Hypo." A smart-appliance company. She was older than she looked. "But after a while I wanted to do something with a bit more in the way of social value. When UTTW advertised for a legal specialist, I applied."

"I'm surprised you've never encountered an interface before," I said.

"As I said, intellectual property in the legal department at Hypo. I wasn't fighting for Thing rights, I was writing warranties and pursuing pirates. One of the reasons I wanted to quit."

"If you don't mind my asking, how'd you get into law, specifically?"

"Studied Classics at university because I liked Latin, carried on with it because I discovered I liked philosophy. Then hit my limit round about graduate school. Not interested in academia and wanted a more comfortable life than the mincome provides. Plus I got a lot of parental pressure to find either an artistic calling or a serious profession."

"Why didn't you become a director or an artist then? That's where the money is." Both humans and intelligents love a good spectacle, and most people that I knew outside the union were busy putting on theatrical shows or making movies for human or intelligent consumption.

"Never was very artistically inclined. I play guitar with a tribute band, but that's about as far as my talent goes. Ergo, law it was. I'm finding intelligent law a lot more interesting than I'd expected, though. It's sort of like philosophy. Answering questions about rights and who deserves them. Not what's covered by the warranty," She smiled a bit. "It's what was interesting about classical philosophy, too."

"Really?" I asked. "I don't know a lot about it."

"You might like it," she said. "The ancient Greeks were all about figuring out who qualified as a human being, and what, if anything, made them special. Same sorts of things people argue about at the union."

"Anthropologists too," I said, but she was still speaking.

"Recently, I've been doing a lot of research into legal systems which allow non-human beings to be considered persons. Medieval law. Aboriginal law systems. The Americans. That sort of thing. I can send you some links."

"I'd love to read them," I said, and at that point we were interrupted by the arrival of the police.

4: My Animals and Other Family

I was the last one interviewed by the police, which meant that by the time they got to me, the PCs were tired and their questions were becoming routine and perfunctory. The male one didn't bother to hide his disappointment when I told him, truthfully, that I hadn't had any communication with Millie since the strategy meeting last Friday. He tried a few questions that suggested he thought I was lying, but I shut that down quickly by advising him to check her contact logs. After that the female one asked a slate of questions that were so general—had she seemed suicidal, did she get on all right with the others in the company, did she have any personal relationships that I was aware of—that I got the impression that it might not be, as I'd initially assumed, a clear-cut car accident, but something harder to explain.

By the time I'd finished, Trish and Sanjiv had both given up waiting for me and gone—so much for my idea of having coffee after the meeting—and there wasn't much more for it than to shake Christoph's hand, promise to be there for the rescheduled meeting, and head for the tube station.

Outside, both the car and human protests had dispersed, the off-gridders leaving behind a trail of paper cups, attack confetti and broken signs. An intelligent street-cleaner was beginning to work on the mess they'd made and I felt a moment of irony.

From Soho Square, a short walk took me to Oxford Circus station, after which I caught the train from Paddington to Thame Parkway, picked up my car, and drove home within estimated return parameters, if a little earlier than originally expected. I usually drive myself rather than hiring a self-driving car, either temporarily or long-term. Leaving aside the potential conflict of interest involved in having an employee who might also be a member of UTTW, I know them altogether too well to want to have one idling away in my garage.

Home, in my case, was an overgrown-looking Victorian smallholders' cottage, far enough outside of the little Oxfordshire town of Thame that I could sleep easy, without light or noise to disturb me. I'd had a solar roof installed when I bought it, so I didn't have to sign on to the National Grid, and my own wireless network and server so that I don't have to rely on a third-party system. No Things here either, or at any rate nothing smarter than a vacuum cleaner and grass-mower. I even keep the dolly on my phone switched off, after one too many incidents where it accidentally activated and offered suggestions for local restaurants and cafes. No house-elf, not even an old-fashioned smart-fridge, and the security system…

…well, the security system came bounding up to the garden gate as I got out to open up and let the car through, barking loud enough to shake the cottage off its foundations. Dark noses thrust into my gloved hands, barks turned to eager whines.

"It's me, Buffy, Willow, it's me." The two Rottweilers crowded around me, grinning and tail-wagging. They were a pair of sweethearts, really—rescued from an unlicensed breeder when they were still young enough to learn to trust people—but fierce enough looking that they put off the casual visitor. In terms of my personal safety, I was rather more worried by Carmela, the ancient Westie sitting disapprovingly on the front step. She'd had a past I didn't want to think about more than I had to, which had left her with an understandably low opinion of humanity and a tendency to bite first and ask questions later. I kept my tetanus vaccinations up to date and had plenty of time to visit the emergency room if she forgot I was friendly.

Having satisfied Buffy and Willow as to my bona fides, I stashed the car in the garage someone had grafted on to the cottage in the nineteen-fifties, plugged it into the charger, shut the door, went round the front and let myself in, followed by the pack of dogs.

I touched my fingers briefly to the contact pad on the inside of the door, where most houses have the human interface with the house-elf. With my nervous system graft and its interface adjustments, I can be my own house-elf. I raised the internal temperature, adjusted the timing cycle of the lights, and did a quick stock-take of what was in the fridge—mostly animal food and medication of various sorts, and some gourmet food kits that I was too tired to assemble. Pizza it was, then.

The inside of the cottage was open-plan. I wasn't sure if that was original or a legacy of one of the periods of renovation—possibly the one in the 1980s which had led to the beige carpets and double-glazed sliding kitchen doors, or the one a couple of decades later which had contributed the slate kitchen floor tiles and Venetian blinds, none of which I had bothered to change. The kitchen was on the left and living area on the right. Two of the cats, Bunker and Daenerys, were already on the countertops, reminding me not to be late with dinner. The third, Whitey, raised his head briefly from the armchair by the fireplace and then went back to sleep in a tangle of dirty fur. I was going to have to bathe him again, I realised, and, remembering how handy he could get with his claws, wondered how long I could put the event off.

I scratched Bunker's ears, while Daenarys butted her head against my shoulder, marking me as part of her family. Remembering my conversation with Trish just that same afternoon, I wondered a bit about cats and how they see the world—a complicated web of scents indicating ownership, territory, even feelings and rivalries. And that's before we get into whiskers and space perception.

Beyond the kitchen, at one side of the living area, a narrow staircase led up to the bedroom, bathroom, a small spare-room which had most recently been home to a very nervous cat named Grace and her six ginger kittens, and the Room, which was simultaneously an office and a sort of tuning-up centre for my nervous system. The many Trishes of the worlds have no idea, and I wasn't going to enlighten them. But all that was for later.

"I'd better feed the bunnies, birds and goat first," I told the disappointed carnivores, letting myself out into the garden through the back door.

Most of the property which had originally come with the smallholding had been sold to the organic poultry farm next door, but the building still came with enough land to make keeping a small amount of livestock a possibility. The main reason I'd bought the place, really. That and the isolation, of course.

I went out back, checked on the rabbits, refilled the water dish and scattered some pellets around the run, then spent a little time socialising with the big spotty one, Londo, who was the more human-friendly of the pair. Then putting out food for Diane, the goat—it had turned from a cloudy day into a nice, if still cold, evening, so I decided I didn't have to lure her in from the garden just yet—de-egging the hens (only three today, I wondered if something had put them off) and making sure their automatic feeder was working all right. Then feeding the carnivores. Whitey had remembered he had to eat, finally, and had wandered with stiff dignity to the kitchen to challenge Buffy and Willow over the food dishes. Finally, for the human, there was a glass of supermarket wine and a roast-vegetable pizza, guaranteed to be there in thirty minutes or free.

Because it had been a difficult day, I also decided to start a box set. I was trying to decide between *The Wire* (which I had to confess I'd never actually seen) and the new reboot of *The Sopranos* (which had been getting mixed reviews, making me curious to see for myself), when I felt my phone vibrate. Naomi, I thought, finally getting back to me about the possible cat-fostering. So I checked, and saw the message on the front.

Not Naomi, and the address was unfamiliar. The message itself was flagged to urgent and told me to connect to a particular location on the Internet of Independents.

I frowned. It was a law-enforcement location. That meant

Cybersecurity. And since no date or time was indicated, that suggested that it was an intelligent who wanted to talk with me, not a human—and more specifically, that it was an Independent, rather than a Thing, since I couldn't think of a single case of a Thing who worked for any branch of the police outside of driving and domestic management, and if it was a police Thing looking for an interface they'd've contacted me through the agency. I'd been half-expecting a follow-up over Millie's death, given the suspicious timing of the incident and the weird generic questions, but not necessarily this soon as they couldn't have rebooted her in so short a time. Besides, I'd been expecting a human officer rather than an Indie.

Hunger and tiredness warred with curiosity and a sense of civic duty, and the latter won. I put the pizza order on pause and went upstairs to the Room to log in.

One of the advantages of my condition is that I can access all three Internets—the human one, the Indie one and the Internet of Things—without needing a mediator for the latter two. I closed the door firmly against intruders. The animals know the Room is off limits, but that's never stopped Bunker, a big chunky black and white cat with a Hitler moustache and a keen sense of her own importance, from trying. I settled myself down in the chair. It's a black leather, padded beast with integral fold-away footstool, designed originally for gamers and other humans who might have to spend a long time sitting, but pretty good for my needs, too.

Most humans access the Internet the normal way. You look at a screen with your eyes, you type or scroll or write or talk. If you want a closer interface, you use a set of i-buds or a mask and generate a VR environment. If you need to talk to a Thing or an Indie, you do so through the bits of the human Internet that interface with theirs, using an avatar of the intelligent you want to talk to.

Most humans, though, don't realise that's a glorified talk-box, and, from an intelligent perspective, about as useful. And, as with talk-boxes, whole classes of intelligents don't, even can't, use them: smart appliances that are linked in via a concierge system, for instance, or security botnets. And if you start to think about Internets and intelligents, the more obvious it becomes that the human Internet's not fit for their purpose. What's the point of a visual interface for something which might not have eyes—or eyes as we humans understand them? So for talking to each other, they have their own Internets. And not many humans go there.

Accessing the two intelligent Internets, for me, is similar, on the face of it, to interfacing with intelligents—the pads, the fingers, the withdrawal from the physical world—but less invasive. Effectively I interact with them as an intelligent myself, and they don't have to use my nervous system as a communications channel. So there's no need for the blankets and other physical paraphernalia, and I'm not as likely to go completely catatonic and lose my twitch reflexes. There's still a little disorientation, since I'm seeing the world as an intelligent, which is a difficult trick for the human brain, but less so than when someone else is renting my nerves. I keep the pills handy, but I don't usually need them afterwards.

Getting into the system, a moment of blankness was replaced by a menu of the last few sites I'd visited in Indiespace. My humanness interpreted it as glowing squares in the dark, like a sales display of monitors on a vantablack stand. I ignored them and told it the address from my phone. Different to the Internet of Things; quieter, more focus on colours and soft, muted sounds. Like the chill-out tent at a music festival.

Indies and Things are similar in many ways. They're both intelligent, both originally developed by humans. But the big difference is that Things were developed to be embodied in, well, things. Cars, offices, houses, printing works, washing machines, street-cleaners. They tend to be very engaged with the physical. Indies are Internet-native: created as chat-bots, or PR images, or virtual custodians for human Internet sites, or high-end dollys. They're also self-reproducing; unlike Things, they themselves can create new Indies. We're into the third or fourth generation of Indies which exist with no human involvement. They generally tend to be personable, but to find it a little hard to relate to the physical world in the way that humans and Things do.

For that reason, I generally prefer interfacing for Things. Not that Indies are hard to Interface for—they're often less demanding customers than Things—but they don't really understand what bodies are for. Or what the rest of us get from the physical world.

New darkness flowed up around me in IndieSpace. Sharper, more purple. An air of professionalism. Now an impression of light. All of this was my humanness interpreting stimuli that my inteligentness was receiving, into something that made sense for a human brain. It wasn't necessarily what my intelligentness was receiving, but it's hard to explain where the difference lies. The closest analogy I can get to the interaction between my humanness and my intelligentness, in these circumstances, is that it's like speaking a foreign language; at once knowing what the words mean in themselves and knowing what they mean in your first language.

"Hello?" My humanness, of course, interpreted communication as speech, imagined myself as having a body, feelings, scents. "I had a message to come here?"

"Mr Thompson Jennings?" A voice first, female. American-ish, though I couldn't identify a region. No hesitation over my name. Someone had done background research, found out I prefer *mister* to *doctor*. I'd given up using it when I left academia. Too many people assuming I was a medical doctor. Besides, *Doctor Jennings* was my father, really.

Then, flowing into visual being, a body. Female too; tall, lean, long-haired, golden-skinned, almond-eyed, but not quite conforming to any known ethnic group. Like the woman who'd played Oryx in the old box-set adaptation of *Oryx and Crake*, but taller and breastless. Dressed in a dark-blue silky high-collared shirt and trousers with a slight hint of a uniform about them.

"Call me Liz," she said, the name also coming out as *Intelligent-DS Independent F-276EZ* and another, untranslatable concept. She smiled, making the atmosphere reassuring/friendly.

"All right," I said, nodding, projecting open/cautious. "Why?"

"Most humans find it more comfortable," she said, and I could feel her raising the reassurance level. "You don't have to."

"Would it be forward of me to ask who you represent?" I asked, keeping the caution level where it was.

"Not at all," she said. Polite, graceful. "I'm from the International Enforcement of Artificial Law service. England Division."

"Cybersecurity."

The amusement level rose, with a hint of acerbic mild offence. "We don't prefer the term."

"I'm sure you don't," I said. "But it *is* what they call you." IEAL being a difficult mouthful to pronounce, and humans being cheeky sorts. "That and the Internet Police."

"Now *that*'s a real misnomer." I caught a hint of an interested pedantry, of a mind diverting off onto a channel it liked. "We don't police the Internets. We couldn't, legally, police the human one, anyway. We're a bit more like a union in some ways—a self-regulating system for investigating crime among intelligents. The Independents and the Things." Just like that, the pedantry vanished again. "We're affiliated with national and local police forces, but not beholden to them. You might think of me as an investigating officer, if it helps."

"I'm all right without the translation," I said. Years of anthropological training dies hard, and when I'm in the intelligents' territory, I try and think as much in intelligent terms as I can. Even though that only goes so far. The fact that Liz had made the analogy, though, was getting my attention. Not only was Liz an Indie, she was clearly an Indie who had been developed specifically to work with humans. She was comfortable with appearing human (or humanish, anyway); she was keeping her emotional presentation heavily keyed to reassurance; she was using a lot of analogies. I'd met Indies like her before.

"You're a liaison officer, aren't you?"

Liz nodded and the reassurance dropped somewhat, to my relief. "I am," she said. "I'm a gestalt entity, so not all of me is a liaison officer. But yes, this part of the gestalt has got specific skills relating to direct interactions with humans." She paused, though she didn't have to, a stylistic tic to make her seem more natural I guessed. "We thought it would be less wearing for you to deal with me than for you to have to go full intelligent."

"Fair point," I said. "So I'm assuming this has to do with Millie's absence this afternoon?" I used her intelligent name of course, but it came out as "Millie" to my humanness.

Liz frowned slightly, as if she was considering how to break bad news. "Yes," she said. "My gestalt has been conducting a wider investigation into a series of crimes, and Millie's death fits the pattern." She was able to render Millie's intelligent name better than I could, but it still came out as "Millie" on another level.

"Okay," I said. "But what do you need to ask me for? Can't you ask her what happened herself?" Enough time had passed that, even if there had been significant damage, Millie could have been restored from backup. Beyond confirming when I'd tried and failed to contact her this afternoon, I failed to see what I could contribute.

Liz's breaking-bad-news impression deepened. "I'm afraid she's dead."

This really *was* something. I could feel my physical body actually tensing. "Totally dead?"

Liz nodded. "Totally dead."

5: Say Hello, Wave Goodbye

I had to confess I'd only encountered total death in intelligents a couple of times before. It's more a theoretical possibility than anything; that an intelligent and their stored backups might be wiped, such that they couldn't be restored—or at least restored to anything like their current version. In some cases, an old copy will remain, but, given that any intelligent rebooted from that will have quite different experiences to the original, it's effectively total death. Sometimes it can be accidental. More often it's deliberate: either outright murder, or some attempt at corporate sabotage against Things employed by someone or some group. I could really only think of one case of accidental total death I'd personally encountered. It had involved an electrical fire breaking out at a server farm in Newcastle, destroying main servers and backups, and leading to total death for two Things unfortunate enough to have had fatal accidents while the company was desperately trying to restore service. So, given the unlikeliness of Millie experiencing a similar accident, it was no wonder the police were trying to figure out what had happened.

"Millie's death came to our attention because it fit an ongoing pattern," Liz explained. She generated a couple of functional chairs and a table into the virtual environment, and sat down gracefully, to indicate that she was settling in for a long conversation.

We could, of course, have just kept on standing. However, many intelligents, especially Indies, consider it part of conversational etiquette to provide the illusion of a social context. I also noticed that she was bringing up, subtly, the suggestion that she and I were in a glass-walled office in a tall building, a hint of waterfalls and greenery and chiming bells in the distance. She left it vague and indefinite. It's generally polite for all members of a conversation to contribute to the appearance of the environment. Pointedly, I didn't. This was not totally impolite but was verging on it. The virtual equivalent of sitting there with folded arms and a scowl on my face, as it were. I didn't want to make any secret of the fact that I was uncomfortable about the conversation, the context, and the fact that Liz was practically radiating friendliness, courtesy and comfort. It was the sort of situation that makes me think someone wants something from me.

She must have registered the slight, but she gave no indication of it, not even a slight chill on the friendliness of the mood. Professional of her, I thought. "We've become aware of a number of cases of total deaths which, for all intents and purposes, look like..." A polite pause. "Forgive me, but would you know what I meant if I used the term 'habitat degradation'?"

I was pretty sure she didn't mean the save-the-Antarctic campaign. "Assuming you mean for intelligents, if I'm not mistaken, the term refers to cases where there's damage, deliberate or accidental, to one of the inhabited parts of the Internet of Things—or of Indies?"

A nod. "Usually it's accidental, and it can be temporary. The problems come when a portion of the cloud goes offline for long enough to destroy any intelligent who is unlucky enough to be housed there—partially or totally. For instance, that incident in Newcastle last February..."

I nodded a bit sharply, boosting the impatience.

"It tends to happen in older, less-used portions of the Internet. Backups stored on out-of-date or infrequently-maintained servers. In any case, we get a few cases every year, we don't generally have to investigate them for very long. They were just unlucky."

"So, what makes you think Millie wasn't *just* unlucky?" I asked.

Liz included a pause. "The timing," she said. "The nature of the attack, the unlikeliness of Millie being a victim of normal habitat degradation. And, most importantly, the fact that Millie was supposed to join you at the Joint Negotiating Council the same day."

"You think it might be related to the union dispute," I said. No point making it a question. I'd been thinking the same thing. "Care to tell me why?"

A Liz-nod. "Given the fraught nature of the case and the potential legal precedents it would set, if Safe Taxis were able to pay some cars less than others, there might be many… stakeholders."

She'd done her research. "That's true."

"Would you care to suggest any stakeholders who might take that much interest, Mr Jennings?"

She had me. "Enough to kill totally? Honestly, not a one."

"Not even a human?"

"You're talking about the death of a sentient being here."

"Not all humans regard us as such," Liz pointed out, "or if they do, regard us as enemies, or aliens, or some other being whose deaths might be necessary evils."

She had me doubly, and I suspected she'd done other homework as well. Not just into the case.

"You're thinking it might be one of the off-gridders," I said.

A Liz-nod. "That's certainly a key line of inquiry."

"Can I be blunt?" I asked. I concentrated on the atmosphere and shifted from my state of withdrawal into one of possible-trust-but-continuing-suspicion. The light filtering in through the windows got slightly red, as if the sun were setting. "Is this anything to do with my brother?"

Liz raised the sympathy level slightly. "If I can be blunt too, Mr Jennings: possibly. No offense meant."

"I think I can fill in the rest of the sentence," I said. I kept my feelings out of the emotional picture. They were complicated. But mostly, at the moment, worry that Leon, that little idiot, had got himself into trouble yet again and I was going to have to get him out. Yet again. Nothing I particularly wanted to share with Officer Liz. "No offense meant," I went on, "but it's more than a little odd that the case incurs a noisy public protest from an off-grid group associated with a man who just happens to be the brother of the union's go-to interface. Well, no offense taken, personally, unless you're implying I'm somehow responsible."

Liz worked the implication that I'd scored a point into the atmosphere. "Not entirely," she said. "But… is there any way your brother could have found out from you about the case? You didn't let any details slip in, for instance, a video call?"

I let myself appear to laugh. "Liz," I said, wishing she had a surname so I could match her *Mr Jennings* formality (since she was undoubtedly processing my "Liz" as her designation, it didn't much matter in any case, but it would have made me feel better), "surveillance fail for Cybersecurity, right there. I have as little contact with my brother as I possibly can. The last time we spoke on the phone was a voice-only call two years ago, regarding the London School of Economics' plan to name the new human sciences building after our father. In fact, *extra* surveillance fail for the police, because you know why it was a voice-only call?" I let my annoyance filter into the atmosphere. "Because he's an off-gridder. Off the grid. No Things. No computers. No tablets. No phones either. No energy they don't generate themselves, no dangerous wifi signals. Because the situation was so important, he'd got permission from his community to go down the road and call me from a monitoring cabin at a pine-tree plantation. In a situation like that, we're going to be focusing entirely on the subject of the call. I'm not going to be chatting happily away about my workmates."

"How does he normally communicate with you, then?"

"He sends letters."

Liz looked puzzled. "Wait. How's he do that, if he's an off-gridder?"

"He doesn't use the regular delivery service. There's some kind of specialist courier that uses humans only, no drones." A few times, chiefly after our mother had announced her intention of moving to Australia to marry her long-term girlfriend, and, later, during our father's illness and after his death, I'd had some uniformed stranger turn up at the gate. Usually deeply unnerved by Buffy and Willow's attempts to make friends with them.

"Let's get on to the other point of outrage in your insinuation," I said, "which is that I'd be careless enough to break client confidentiality. With anyone, let alone with Leon." I was also somewhat on edge and suspicious that I was probably unwittingly providing Liz with a lot of information she needed for some secret purpose, but I tried hard not to let that filter into the atmosphere. "That having been established, what about other suspects?"

Liz smiled. "Such as?"

Again, the thought that I was being played. Followed, to my surprise, by the thought that I didn't particularly care, so long as it got Liz out of my Internet, and maybe went some way towards catching whoever, or whatever, had killed Millie. Millie wasn't my responsibility, but it was hard to shake the feeling that I should do something. "What about another Thing? It's hardly breaking confidentiality to say that relations between the Ariels and the other cars aren't entirely cordial at the moment. And I know too many Things to assume they're incapable of murder if they put their minds to it." They think differently to humans, but not *that* differently. We invented them, after all.

"What about the employer?"

The more I thought about it, the less likely it seemed. "Christoph? Wouldn't know how," I said. Christoph could be patronising as hell, and undoubtedly regarded employees, human and Thing, as necessary evils to be put up with in the name of making a profit. Nonetheless, he didn't strike me as someone with the capacity to hate that hard. Or the imagination to come up with a murder plan. Particularly one which made the crime look like an accident. "But on a purely financial level, I don't think they'd kill unless they were desperate, and they're not, right now." They've currently got the upper hand in the negotiations until the cars stop fighting among themselves, I thought, but didn't want to say aloud to someone not involved in the case.

"Mr Drexler's not the whole organisation," Liz pointed out. "As for the rest of them, your logic doesn't cover all possibilities. What if they were thinking more long-term? It would benefit Safe Taxis if the employee representative team gets thrown into disarray. More so if they could make it look like the crime was an internal one. And there's plenty of humans out there who still regard Things as, well, things. For them, killing a taxi wouldn't be murder, just data loss."

She had a point. "You're right," I said. "So I gather there are three lines of inquiry, then? One, an off-grid organisation, trying to make some political point or save the rest of us from the error of our ways. Two, another car, probably an Ariel, trying to take Millie out of the picture and disrupt the opposition. Three, somebody at Safe Taxis, trying to throw a spoke in UTTW's wheels. If you'll pardon the metaphor."

"I might," Liz said. "So, Mr Jennings. Any insights, personal or professional, as to which it might be?"

I shook my head. "Haven't an earthly."

Liz frowned in a tiny, precise motion. "Might you give it some thought? I assume that the UTTW negotiations will be continuing, and you'll remain the interface."

"Are you asking me to spy on my workmates?"

"Not so much," Liz replied. Intelligents have an advantage in that, if they don't want to speak hastily or give other indications of being rattled, they don't have to. Nonetheless, I thought that reply was a little glib. "Just let us know if you do notice anything, well, suspicious." A card appeared in her hand and she gave it to me. "These are my details. You can contact me any time of day or night." Of course, day and night weren't an issue for her. All intelligents need downtime, but gestalts rest their system one section at a time, meaning they can literally operate twenty-four-seven, unlike humans, single-unit Indies, and Things. "Have a good evening, Mr Jennings."

As the room dissipated, I disconnected. Gave myself a few

minutes to centre, scan my body, make sure vertigo wasn't going to be an issue, and get in touch with my emotions (irritation, disconcertion, an irrational edge of fear).

I heard the claws scratching at the door and the muffled *woof* with a sense of relief.

"Coming, Buffy," I said. I switched off the system and went downstairs to see about maintaining order among the animals. And getting that pizza.

6: Robot Bees

The next day was the first Saturday of the month. That meant a trip into Oxford to have dinner with Naomi.

It was her turn to pick the restaurant, and she'd chosen a new Turkish vegetarian place in Jericho; the décor was an unlikely fusion of Middle Eastern kitsch and Y2K retro, involving silk rugs and shimmery silver synthetic plastic furniture.

"Not your usual style," I said to her as we leaned in for the obligatory hugging.

Naomi shrugged. "I confess I picked it based on menu and location. Should have been suspicious when there weren't any actual pictures of the dining area on the eating-out app. Still, if it's too hard on your eyes, we can always go down the street to the Afghani restaurant. It's not vegetarian, but they do have veg-only options."

She'd cut her hair short and dyed it blonde. It curled around her head in a way that suited her, made her look ten years younger. Like how she'd looked just before we split up. No. I wasn't going to let myself go there.

"I'm fine," I said. Now that I was actually sitting on it, the chair was much more comfortable than it looked. "You okay?"

Naomi shrugged again. "Yeah," she said, a little too slowly. Then, "A bit sentimental, actually. It occurred to me as I was catching the train that today's actually the anniversary of the day we split up."

"Oh," I said, feeling like an idiot. I'm terrible at anniversaries, but I should have remembered that one. No wonder I was thinking about how she looked back then.

Buried behind the memory of the breakup were even worse memories. We'd started going out when I was between my undergraduate and postgraduate phases, when we both happened to be working for the same fundraising organisation; moved in together when we both started graduate school (she was doing an MSc in Computer Science, so finished well before I did); and broken up virtually, while I was in Japan. It had been building for a while, but the specific trigger cause had involved her wanting to interview for a job with a conservation organisation in Botswana. I'd been worried she could get shot by a poacher or killed by a lion, she'd insisted it was her risk to take, and from there on it was accusations of being overprotective on one side and reckless on the other, an irony that I didn't appreciate until much later. In the end she got offered a promotion by the London animal charity she was working for at the time and didn't go. But by the time that had happened, the damage had been done.

A couple of months after we'd stopped speaking with each other, I'd walked out of a hospital with aluminium insides. I'm sure the incidents were in no way connected.

"I'm sorry. Should we have rescheduled…?" I said.

"No, first Saturday of the month is fine as always," Naomi said. "I don't believe in fetishising anniversaries." Then, before I could ask what was new with her, she got in first. "So, what's new with you? You seem a bit stressed—well, more stressed than usual."

I nodded. "Guilty," I said.

"Animals all okay?"

"Fine, aside from Carmela's kidney trouble and Bunker's diabetes—Grace and the Gingers got finally calm enough to go to the adoption centre," I said. "I can take on that cat you were talking about."

"Oh, that's good. The cat's settled at Peter's, though, and I don't think it would be good to move him. Think you could maybe take a dog instead? She turned up on the doorstep last night. She's a Yorkshire terrier, about three and a half, neglect case, medically stable but needs to learn to trust again," Naomi leaned forwards, I swear her eyes were glittering. "Just promise me you won't give her some ridiculously obscure name out of some box set no one bar you's even heard of."

"Possibly," I said. "I'll sleep on it. How's The Ark?" That was the unimaginatively-named animal charity she was currently working for. She was officially their IT technician, but in practice everybody there seemed to turn their hand to anything, from mucking out the kennels in the animal shelter to prosecuting negligent owners to lobbying politicians about animal-rights legislation.

Naomi came from a family where everybody, it seemed, worked for a charity, an NGO, or a political organisation. She'd been named after some long-dead feminist activist. She'd been disappointed when she found out my parents weren't Radiohead fans, but had given me my grandfather's surname as a first name for some inexplicable reason.

"Not sinking just yet," she said. "We're about to lose one of the interns to the employment market, though, so I'm going to have to hire another."

"Which one? The Entitled Little Idiot, or the Arrogant Little Shit?"

"It's the Arrogant Little Shit, and good riddance to her. Now. Back to your stress. I'm not going to be dissuaded."

Naomi had an odd knack of knowing what I needed, even if I didn't know it myself. One day, when my new nervous system was giving me trouble and I was feeling sorry for myself, Naomi had showed up on the doorstep with a cat-carrier full of enraged fat tabby tomcat. *He needs someone to look after him, till he's stable enough to go out for adoption*, she'd said.

"If the animals are okay, is it work?"

By the time Tyrion, as I'd decided to call the overweight beast, had slimmed down to a healthy weight and was calm enough to be relocated to a family with three middle-sized children, I was emotionally stable enough to go back out into the world again.

"I saw an item on the news about the Safe Taxis dispute.

Something to do with a protest."

And feeling okay about it when Naomi turned up not long afterwards with a litter of puppies, saying, *they'll need round-the-clock feeding but I know you're up for it....*

"Oh God," I said, putting my head in my hands.

Naomi looked not quite contrite enough. "Oh dear. Did I just put my finger on it?"

"No, you couldn't have known. Some of them were Leon's crowd. I just wish they'd live up to the name off-gridder and fuck off out of the damn grid. Stop coming back into it to annoy the rest of us. But that was just a minor issue."

"Do tell."

I did.

Naomi's eyes got wider. "Total death," she repeated.

"Total," I said.

"That's pretty rare, for Things, isn't it?" she said.

I nodded. Naomi was fairly neutral on the subject of Things. She didn't have a self-driving car, but then, she didn't have a car at all. She got on all right with the Ark's two self-driving vans. She had a dolly on her phone and a house-elf, admittedly one she wasn't on brilliant terms with, in her flat. I'd say Naomi was about in the normal range for most people: not off the grid, but not surrounded by intelligents either.

"I think I've maybe known three Things in my career that were non-restorable. But it's unusual circumstances, according to Liz—the officer who met me over this," I contextualised.

"Liz, huh?" Naomi narrowed her eyes.

"She's an Indie," I said. "Working for Cybersecurity. Or IEAL, as we're apparently supposed to call it. Not exactly gossip material." I felt I had to reinforce this, although I couldn't say why. "The only reason I call her Liz is because she's never given me any other name to call her, aside from her designation and that's a mouthful for a human to say. It feels a bit silly, but, short of inventing a title, there's nothing much else I can do."

Before she could reply, a waiter swanned up, lithe and glistening in a retro silver tux, and there was a brief pause to decide on a wine and order it. Naomi insisted on English wines whenever possible, on the grounds that they had the shortest distance to travel from farm to table. I wasn't particularly keen on them, but French and Hungarian wines were getting more and more expensive, and the local crops were certainly getting better, for what that was worth.

"Surprised they can afford human waiters," I remarked as the person in question disappeared with a swish of a PVC apron. The problem with getting any humans to do a job that boring was that they didn't have to take it, so waitstaff often got paid more than I did. Furthermore, so many restaurants were including waitstaff as part of the atmosphere that the job had been rebranded as performance art, which meant that they were increasingly being paid on actors' union scales.

"I think the owner's part of some kind of internship programme linked with the universities, where he teaches the business to people who want to own their own restaurants someday, and they work for him at cut rates." Naomi sat back, sipping the pinot noir archly. "So, in the absence of gossip, can you tell me anything about these unusual circumstances? I'm curious."

I nodded, tried to think how to condense the conversation with Liz down into something resembling an informative soundbite. A soundbite pitched at the level of someone who didn't understand much about Things. "Just that they think it's murder, and the most obvious rationale for it would be to do with the union dispute. I don't know if they're interviewing the others about it, but they certainly interviewed me."

Naomi picked up the menu, pretended to study it. "Is Leon a suspect?"

Trust her to read the subtext. "I really, really hope not," I said, deciding not to enlighten her about that part of the conversation. "But

I don't see how he could, it's not like him. And I have my doubts that it's any of the off-gridders. Too obvious a target. And it would have meant they'd have to spend time on the Internet, which goes against their ideology. Though I suppose they could still do it, if they wanted to throw suspicion onto somebody else. Like that rumour about jihadis eating pork and doing other things to pass as non-ideological."

Naomi continued to peruse the menu. "Doesn't fit the off-gridder modus operandi. They don't generally do things by stealth. If they did kill the car, they'd be most likely claiming responsibility and announcing it as a blow against the rule of the machines. Also, they'd find some non-technical way of doing it. Run her over with a combine harvester or something like that. Do you think the tas pide is likely to be good here, or overcomplicated? I mean, I like tas pide but if they're going to throw on a lot of fancy fusion ingredients, I'm out."

I glanced around at other tables. "I think the lady by the window is having it, and it looks okay." I turned my own attention to the menu. "Hang on, I thought you said this restaurant was vegetarian. How's there beef on the menu?"

Naomi looked, frowned. "Oh, it's one of those," she said, grimly. "One of those places that serves synthetic meat and calls itself vegetarian. Because no animals are harmed. In theory. I'm sorry. There wasn't a menu on their website."

"Playing devil's advocate," I said (seeing her mouth harden but carrying on anyway, yeah, any time I wonder whose fault it was we split up), "isn't that true? I mean, synthetic meat's not actually from an animal…"

Naomi looked like she'd been answering that point a lot lately. "It's the wider picture," she said. "The paradox. Humans love animals. But we only actually preserve animals that are useful to us. Either because we like to look at them, or because we like to do sports with them, or because we like to eat them. The Ark's been monitoring what's happened since the start of the whole synthetic meat industry, and, surprise surprise, whole strains of beef cattle are reducing in numbers."

"That's got to be a good thing in general, though? I mean, weren't we all for reducing the numbers of beef cattle so as to reduce the carbon footprint, stop deforestation and all those good things?" It came out a little sarcastic, and I regretted it. Naomi could get a little idealistic in support of causes, but they were causes I agreed with. It was probably my current anger against Leon that was driving this. "Sorry, Naomi. Didn't quite mean that how it sounded."

I was also aware that Willow and Buffy put away their fair share of beef cattle—and that was before we got into the carbon footprint implications of Carmela and the cats, each of whom was on a different medicated diet—and I didn't want to work through the different levels of hypocrisy involved in my lifestyle.

The hard mouth returned, then softened. "It's okay. Reduction's good. Extinction's not so good. And beef cattle are weird, non-viable animals. Can't breed without human help. Couldn't survive in the wild."

"You're a vegetarian," I couldn't resist pointing out. "Aren't you indirectly contributing to their extinction, by not eating them?"

Naomi, however, was never the sort to get into an obvious fight. "I know. It's a paradox, and it seems like every answer's the wrong one," she said, echoing my own thoughts about feeding the animals. "My mother used to talk about how, when she was a kid, everyone was all about replacing fossil fuels with biodiesel. Better for the environment, they said, until they figured out that the oil plantations were just as bad, if not worse, for it. Some days I really hate my own species. But still…" She searched for words. "Isn't that kind of the reason I'm working for The Ark, I have to ask myself. To help out animals like that. Even if it's not the right answer, just the least wrong one. Because it's not their fault they were born beef cattle."

Well, so long as you don't believe in reincarnation, I thought, but that was a complicated thing and we'd had rather more than a few heated arguments about that when I was writing my thesis.

"I see your point," I said instead. "I've fostered my share of tragically overbred pugs and bulldogs."

Naomi nodded sadly. "Robot pets," she said. "On the one hand, I'm all for them—so people who live in flats that animals wouldn't be happy in can have something like the experience of pet owning. On the other hand, what happens if they become the new normal? What happens to real pets? A robot pollinator's headline news, but it's not a bee."

I put my hand on hers. "It's okay. It's complicated." I didn't think about that sort of thing too much, but she was right.

"I just wish there was some way we could all live together, without their survival being dependent on their utility to humans, or whether or not we think they're cute," she complained. She left her hand there just long enough to indicate she was okay with my holding it, then withdrew it to remind me of the proper order of things.

I debated whether to reply as I wanted to and decided to go for it. "Apparently, in Bangalore," I said, "it's a bit like that. They say you'll be walking down the street, with a lot of humans, and then suddenly there'd be this cow, just walking along with everyone. And everyone else is just, like, 'oh yeah, it's a cow, off to do cow things.' Same with goats, dogs, cats. Animals and people, just all going about their business, like they all lived in the same city and were doing the same things." The story brought its own memories, of the person who'd told it to me and the circumstances I heard it, but somehow, I wanted to tell it to Naomi nonetheless.

Naomi smiled. "That sounds like one of Surender's stories," she said.

"It was," I said.

Naomi nodded, not saying anything for a moment. "But that's just dogs, cats, cows, goats," she said eventually. "Did you ever see the same thing happening with a civet? Or a monitor lizard?"

"I don't think they have them in Bangalore." I suspected she was thinking of Bangkok, but chose not to draw attention to it. "But I take your point," I said. "Even among people who respect animals, some animals are more respected than others."

"And I'm sure that, whatever the animals make of it all, the humans treat them as they do for human reasons," Naomi said. "I get that you're trying to make me feel better, and thanks, but it's just making things even more complicated."

"What's with all the philosophy right now, anyway?" I asked.

"Sorry," she said. "It's The Ark's new campaign, and like all of them, it gets to me some ways."

"Why do you stick with it?" I asked.

"Why do you stick with the UTTW?"

"Because I don't have to do it full time, and generally speaking the cases get resolved? You spend all your time at the charity, and most of it thankless."

Naomi took the question seriously. "Perhaps a better analogy might be, why did you finish your thesis after you got back from Japan? Given what you went through, nobody would have blamed you for quitting."

"Well, I'm not quite sure why I did it myself," I said. Possibly a way of proving to myself, and/or the world, that I was still the same old Thom and I wasn't going to let a little thing like a tin nervous system and some experiences I didn't want to think about get in my way. "If I could go back and advise my younger self, I'd tell him not to bother. Go straight to interface work and fostering animals, don't fuck around with academia."

"You enjoyed the universities while you were there," Naomi said. "And you probably got some things from the experience that you're not conscious of. Nothing's wasted in the end."

"I like your philosophy," I said. It didn't make me feel any better, but it was certainly a more positive way of thinking than the one I currently had in place.

The waiter swanned up again, and we placed our orders, both

conspicuously avoiding the beef.

"If you don't mind my saying it," I said, "I suspect something's on *your* mind. We've talked about my problems, we've talked about animal rights. Usually by this point we'd've talked about you."

Naomi smiled a little, dipping a cube of bread into the bowl of hummus the waiter had provided. "Am I normally that selfish?"

"I don't mean in a selfish way. Just that you've conspicuously avoided talking about what's going on in your life, bar a brief reference to the loss of the Arrogant Little Shit and The Ark's current campaign," I said. "Why?"

Naomi didn't answer for a minute, just sat swirling the bread in the hummus bowl. Finally, she spoke. "I feel like I'm in a rut here," she said. "So much is wrong—like all the things we just talked about. And I feel like, at The Ark, we're running around plugging leaks in the walls, while the whole ship is sinking. If you know what I mean."

"I think so," I said, trying the bread-and-hummus myself. Not bad, though I could tell it was store-bought rather than homemade. The bleed-through from my artificial nervous system had given me this odd way of being able to store and compare tastes, and it was telling me that this was identical to the hummus I'd bought from the supermarket the other week. "What if you went to work for one of the bigger organisations? Or the Antarctic Project or something?"

Naomi shook her head. "Still leak-plugging," she said. "I want to make a real difference. Change something major."

"How?"

Naomi looked annoyed. "If I knew, I'd be doing it," she said.

"Fair point," I said. Our main courses arrived, and we picked at them in silence.

"Why don't you pay Leon a visit?" Naomi asked after a while. "If this Liz of yours thinks he's a suspect, you're better placed than she is to rule him out. He wouldn't see her, and I doubt they'd let a human police officer into that compound of theirs. But you could. Gather evidence. At the very least it'll stop you worrying about him.."

I rolled my eyes. "It's difficult enough to see him at the best of times," I said, "and I'm not exactly on the sort of terms with him that allow casual dropping round. If I did arrange a visit, he'd be suspicious."

Naomi shrugged, taking a bite of a fried aubergine. "Not about the right thing, though. Supposing you paid him a visit about the demo? To ask him to get his friends to lay the hell off and go chasing some other Things? Then you can find out if he knows anything about what happened to that car."

"You have a point," I said, heaping yoghurt on top of my mixed vegetable couscous. "It's not the sort of thing I *would* have visited him about, but it's the sort of thing I *might*. So I could pay him a visit—no chance of getting them to *actually* lay off, of course, but I might find out why they're involved, at least, and possibly whether or not they do know anything about Millie's murder. Thanks."

Naomi smiled. "All part of the service," she said.

"Now. We've solved my problem, so how can we solve yours?" I bantered.

Naomi looked infinitely sad for a brief moment, before she managed to resume her expression. "Thom…" she said pensively, "do you ever suppose that maybe there'll be no non-human animals in the world? Just us and Things and Indies?"

I shook my head. "Can't be," I said. "We need the ecosystem. No way you can have humans without an ecosystem."

"Except we keep creating artificial parts of the ecosystem… we get rid of the natural bits, and replace them with Thing substitutes," she said. "Kind of a habitat degradation." Her use of the term startled me.

"Thing ecosystems can't replace natural ones," I said.

"I know," Naomi said, "but what if we only find that out when it's too late to bring back the natural one?" She shrugged. "I'm not doing enough, that's all I know."

"Well, for what it's worth, I'll join The Ark's campaign," I said.

"Spread awareness, deliver leaflets, whatever it takes. And once you figure out what you want to do next, I'll be on board for that too." It's what I do, really. Support my friends' campaigns.

"Know what I wish?" Naomi said suddenly. "I wish we could get Things on board. Or any sort of intelligent, really. *That* would be the sort of difference I'm talking about. Humans, and Things, working together to make the world better for all species. But I don't think we can. We've tried. But they don't seem interested, or able to understand."

"It's hard to explain to them," I said.

"It's not that they're selfish or uncharitable or anything," Naomi said, frustrated. "I mean, they support other charities and causes—the Thing unions support human unions, they're willing to volunteer their downtime for scientific processing, hospitals, all that—but they don't seem to understand about animals."

"Maybe I could get them to meet Whitey?" I suggested.

Naomi smiled ruefully. "Not sure they'd understand."

I took a sip of wine. "Not sure *he*'d understand, either. I mean, how would you connect him to the Internet?"

"In all seriousness, do you think that might help?" Naomi asked.

I shrugged. "Possibly. I'll run it past a few of the UTTW colleagues and see what they think. Every little helps, as they say."

When I got home, Buffy and Willow ran to greet me as usual, sniffing my hands and whuffing excitedly, while Carmela confined herself to a brief growl from her basket. Two of the cats looked up, irritated, from their spots on the sofa. After saying hello to them, I went over to the third, petted him. As always, he purred straight away as soon as my hand touched his fur. He lifted his head briefly, then lowered it again.

"Hey, Whitey," I said gently. I could feel the scars from his surgery under his thin, dirty fur. Like me, they were the only visual thing on his body indicating an artificial nervous system.

Whitey had been a lab animal. About eight years ago, The Ark had managed to persuade a research lab to give up animal experimentation, and to rehome the ones it still had left. Naomi had turned up with Whitey blinking in a cat basket under her arm.

"He's like you," she said. "They gave him a dual nervous system so they could try and figure out how to control the vertigo for graftees."

"Did it work?" I took the basket, put it on the floor. I wasn't sure if that origin story was a slight on me or not, but I wasn't going to treat it as such.

"Apparently they got some drug or other out of it," Naomi shrugged. "Anyway. Thought he should go to you, seeing as you have that in common."

I opened the carrier, and a bony white head, pointy-muzzled and long-eared, peered suspiciously out of it. It was followed, cautiously, by a skinny white body.

I put my hand down slowly and touched him. Immediately, he started to purr, a hesitant, rusty-sounding noise.

"Well, that's interesting," Naomi said. "That's the first time he's purred. For anyone. Clearly, you two were meant for each other."

I continued to stroke him. He continued to purr. "Walter White," I said, impulsively.

Naomi frowned at me. "Thom, you're an idiot," she said.

"It's that or Heisenberg."

"Okay, Walter White it is," Naomi flung up her hands. "But do *I* have to call him that?"

"Call him whatever you like," I said, putting my hand in front of his nose for him to sniff. "He's a cat. He doesn't mind what we call him. So I'm going to call him Walter White."

"As long as you're both happy," Naomi said. "Just take good care of each other, okay?"

Now I scratched between the long white ears and got a look of puzzled indignation of the sort common to cats who weren't expecting to be petted.

"Stay well, little Whitey," I said to him, feeling inexplicably tender, then went upstairs to bed.

7: A Visit to Chadwick Farm

On Monday I was supposed to be in a planning meeting of the UTTW's negotiating committee, being ridden by a group of rather argumentative *loa*. However, and not unexpectedly, I got a message telling me that all meetings were temporarily suspended. This was partly to allow for a period of mourning for Millie, as self-driving cars have particularly opaque mourning rituals, which are incredibly important to them for reasons best known to themselves, and partly to allow for the selection of a new Texcoco representative. I was sort of hoping they'd choose Dillie, a Texcoco I'd worked with before as part of UTTW committees. For that reason, however, it was possible they thought she might be too familiar with union bureaucracy. Texcoco tend to be suspicious of any human activity involving too much organisation.

An additional point of interest was that this suspension had been applied to the two other UTTW cases I was working on: a grievance case between a Verve and a private owner, and a committee to draw up new pay and redundancy conditions for golf carts. Seems the entire UTTW was taking the week off. And since the only cases I had on my books at the moment were UTTW ones, I suddenly had a glut of free time. I noticed that Trish had circulated some documents about the legalities among the team (I had a sinking feeling she was going to turn out to be one of those perpetual document-circulators), but I personally didn't have to read them. Also, I doubted that Egon or Salieri would be bothering until after the Texcoco rep had been chosen.

That gave me the opportunity to do what I'd been increasingly inclined to do since my conversation with Naomi on Saturday night, and pay Leon a visit.

Leon and his co-residents could be contacted by telephone in emergencies, thanks to the foresters at the neighbouring pine-tree plantation, who apparently didn't mind letting the off-grinders use it as a contact point for outsiders and lending them the plantation's phones on occasion. However, Leon generally preferred that we send him a letter informing him of any visits well in advance. But there really wasn't time for that sort of thing now, and any attention from me would look suspicious however it was timed. I decided to just drive up North and brazen it out if necessary.

Before I left, I remembered to check the news to see if anything was being said about the Safe Taxis case. Sure enough, a small item in London News announced that the case was on hiatus due to the unexpected death of a negotiator. Carefully, I noted, not specifying that it was total death, so that most readers would assume we were just waiting for Millie to reboot and come back up to speed. The piece then went on to recap the fact that there had been a protest on Friday, with a link to last week's news item.

I frowned. I knew the case had a lot of potential business and technical implications, and I wasn't a stranger to media attention, but I wasn't used to my union work featuring in the news at all, and I didn't think I liked it. Still. I rolled down the windows as I drove, trying to push events out of my mind while speeding North up the A1 motorway.

Leon lived in a farmhouse, like me. Unlike me, he shared it with a lot of other humans—somewhere between eight and twelve of them, I could never keep an accurate count. Though they didn't help matters, as they constantly alternated between fighting with each other and recruiting in new converts, mainly, as far as I could tell, by sexual means. They called themselves a farming collective, and I had to admit they were dedicated and resourceful. They'd somehow assembled the money to buy a big old place in Lincolnshire, surrounded by forestry plantations and commercial farms, that came with acres and acres of what, at the time of purchase, was a rapeseed-growing operation. Now, it apparently produced most of the necessary food and other consumables needed to keep the community going, and a surplus to sell or bargain with for things they couldn't supply.

That was the theory, anyway, as expounded repeatedly by Leon at the occasional points when he met with one or more members of the rest of the family. Usually accompanied by a screed on why claiming the mincome was unnecessary, wrong, and simply a government device to keep the unlettered masses from open rebellion against capitalism. From what little I knew of agriculture (mainly to do with my occasional efforts to get the kitchen garden going on my own little patch of land) I suspected that maintaining a decent level of subsistence was rather more difficult in practice. I had a sneaking suspicion the mincome did occasionally get claimed, probably with some kind of rationalisation about sacking the capitalist establishment. However, seeing as there were more of them and they were all considerably more knowledgeable about these things than I was, they probably had more in the way of success. And if they didn't, I couldn't blame Leon for keeping it quiet.

They kept animals, too, though for the traditional purposes of eating, milking and acquiring wool, and the combination of herding, pest control and security that comprised being a farm dog, rather than as company. Leon had also been not shy in informing me that he considered vegetarianism and animal fostering as pure swank and sentimentality.

Wouldn't do to admit we had anything in common, after all.

As I pulled up the narrow unpaved road to the farmhouse gate, I noticed that the signs which greeted the casual visitor, reading CHADWICK FARM and PRIVATE PROPERTY, had been joined by a new one reading AUTHORISED PERSONNEL ONLY TRESPASSERS WILL BE PROSECUTED. Technically I supposed I must be unauthorised personnel, but I was hoping that I wasn't strictly a trespasser. Well, we'd find out.

A couple of off-gridders, male and female but both equally skinny, practically clad, and bearing an excess of hair, facial and otherwise, appeared from out of nowhere as I drove over the cattle grid toward the farmhouse. Right on cue, the abovementioned farm dogs began barking. The man was holding a rifle, just casually, as if he happened to have been out hunting that afternoon. They were posting sentries now, I thought. This was also a new development. Well, new-ish, but I'd always managed to get parked and out of the car before someone came round to check on me. And they weren't usually armed.

I stopped the car, tabbed down the window. "Thom Jennings," I said. "I'm Leon's brother. Here to visit him." I recognised the woman from previous visits, took a chance on her being friendly. "Hello, Tabitha, long time no see."

Tabitha acknowledged the greeting with a nod and small smile, turned to the man. "Leon's brother," she explained to him. "He's on the grid and works with Things, but he's basically harmless." She then turned back to me. "What are you here for?" She asked abruptly. "There's nothing wrong, is there?"

"No. Just happened to be in the neighbourhood, thought I'd drop round and say hello," I said, aware of how false that sounded, but also hoping that it was a lame enough excuse that they'd give it the benefit of the doubt. "Can't stay too long. What's with all the security, anyhow?"

Tabitha looked dubious, but she appeared willing to entertain the notion that I had, indeed, just dropped round to visit the brother I couldn't stand, and who couldn't stand me. I think she thought that, given my support for vaguely left-wing causes and my fondness for isolating myself in the countryside in a house that could, in a pinch, become mostly off the grid, I might be someone they could bring round to a Thingless lifestyle with enough patience and dedication. Either no one had told her about my nervous system, or she wasn't aware of the implications. "Government's been on our backs a lot lately," she said. "Ever since the bomb scare in Manchester two months ago. They've been calling us domestic terrorists, looking for any excuse to shut us down."

I thought that angry signage and armed beardies patrolling the access routes would be a pretty obvious set of excuses to use to shut Chadwick Farm down if the government wanted to, but I wasn't here to discuss tactics, and pointing this out might anger them enough to kick me out. "What can you do," I said instead. "Anyway, can I park and see Leon, or should I just drive on?"

Tabitha thought a minute, then nodded. "You know where the parking spaces are," she said, stepping back. "Leon's in the garden, I'll go tell him you're here. Remember to leave your phone in the car if you want to keep it."

Cursing, I took my phone off my wrist and threw it onto the back seat. The natives of Chadwick Farm had somehow managed to rig up an EMP field which started round about the farmhouse and extended over most, if not all, of the property. As a courtesy to the rest of us, they'd left the front area clear, but it was damned annoying.

Also, for me, more annoying than most, since it meant I had to do a partial shutdown of my graft, switch off the elements of the system that might be vulnerable. Which usually left me feeling exhausted and weak. It wasn't as bad as interfacing, to be fair, but it was still not much fun for me.

At least it wasn't a total shutdown. I could do that, if I needed to, switch off my artificial graft entirely. My organic nervous system had, over the years, recovered enough that I could survive without the graft, at least for a while (I'd never tested how long). It was bad enough just having the graft in neutral, ticking away while I visited my brother. And it was irrational, of course, for me to blame him for this.

I waited in the living room of the farmhouse, sitting a little uncomfortably on an old armchair with a vaguely amateurish crocheted afghan thrown over the worn orange fabric. It was unfortunately typical of the décor. A couple of old art prints hung on the wall, a few recycled games were stacked on a side table, while a chess set stood on another one, clearly mid-game and not to be interfered with. The furniture was all reclaimed and refurnished, and there was a rug which appeared to have been made by someone without any sense of colour. Over by the windows, which overlooked the fields, a guitar with a bright fabric strap and a battered recorder had been carelessly left, as if someone had forgotten them.

I'm not what one would call a phone junkie, but I found myself really needing to have something to do with my hands to pass the time. I was organizing the pieces in an old game of Chinese checkers by colour, when Leon walked in.

I'm always told there's a family resemblance between us, and it's true we're both dark-complexioned and strong-jawed. I'm a lot thinner than he is, though, and taller, and his eyes are brown like our father's, where mine are grey like our mother's. Also, while we've both got our father's nose and cheekbones, on him the general effect is handsome and classic rather than, as on me, vaguely beak-like.

While Leon still sported his usual stupid-looking sideburns, he had cut his hair—the same dark shade on both of us—into something closer than usual to my own short crop, a development I made a note of, though I wasn't quite sure why I found it significant. He tended to wear it shorter than most off-gridders, if still long by anyone else's standards, but this was more like the anonymists' quasi-military look. I wondered if he was starting to turn anonymist. It would be just like him to rush headlong into trouble and need rescuing, not that he'd ever acknowledge the rescue once it happened. He was dressed for garden work, in boots, dirty jeans and a faded yellow T-shirt bearing the slogan of some benefit concert or other.

And yes, he was annoying. Bloody annoying, just through his stance and the petulant expression on his face. But it was the same look I remembered from every damned time I'd had to pull his irons out of the fire with some girlfriend or other, through school and then university. And because, somewhere in there, was still that kid who sang cabaret songs to make everyone laugh, and used to fall in love with anyone, provided they were female and a little bit mysterious, I was here to see him.

"What do you want?" He asked bluntly, pulling off a pair of vibrant green gloves.

"I happened to be passing. Thought I'd say hello," I said. "Heard from Mum lately?" That last was a deliberately stupid question. Mum still lived in Australia with her wife and two stepchildren, and, given Leon's refusal to communicate long distance in any way not involving a letter, I'd probably heard from her more recently than he had. "How about Yvonne?" Again a stupid question, as his relationship with our half-sister was about the same as it was with me. Possibly even more contemptuous, as, while Yvonne was a film editor and didn't work with Things, she had the temerity to live in a city, in a flat with a house-elf and smart appliances. "Or Aunt Clara?" Yvonne's mother, our father's first wife, who had largely given up talking to us boys after our father's death.

Leon snorted, not deigning to answer any of my questions. He found a wooden stool by the door to the room, pulled it over and sat on it. "We're ten miles out from the nearest town, which happens to be Lincoln. You live in Oxfordshire. A two-and-a-half-hour drive isn't 'passing by.' And the last time we saw each other was at that dedication ceremony for the building they named after Dad over at the university, which was eighteen months ago. You came out here deliberately. Why?"

I shrugged. "How about you tell me, Criswell the Predictor?"

Leon raised a thick dark eyebrow. "You evidently think I know more than I actually do."

"Okay, I'll get right to it," I said. "Why are your lot taking an interest in the Safe Taxis case?"

A fractional pause, before, "I have no idea what you're talking about."

"Come off it," I said. "You know I'm an interface, and you know the Union of Thing Transport Workers is one of my clients. I was at the negotiations on Friday, and I had to push my way through a couple dozen off-gridders. Some of whom were friends of yours. Why?"

Leon shook his head. "We don't possess a hive-mind, you know," he said. "If some of the collective want to go to London and take part in a protest, it's nothing to do with me, and I don't know anything about it."

"I'm not saying you personally had anything to do with it," I said, filing the information away. I hadn't specifically indicated members of the collective, so it was news that some of his immediate circle were involved. "But you all live together, eat together, share the same space… surely you must have an idea why they took an interest in that particular protest. I mean, the local anonymists are one thing, but when people from all over the country, including off-gridders, are making the effort to come into town for an event, I'd like to know why they think it's important enough. After all, getting there must have involved a certain amount of coming onto the grid, which is something of a sacrifice."

"Not necessarily. They took the van down, and it was running on home-made ethanol." Good old Leon. Getting him to talk about infrastructure was a sure way of getting him off the defensive.

"Fine. But why now, and why this particular case? I can understand the cars getting motivated enough to protest the Safe Taxis case which could have wage-setting precedents across the board for employing Things. But the dispute here involves only Things. It's not a case of Things taking human jobs, that battle was fought years ago as far as the taxi industry is concerned. If you want to protest about the on-griddedness or environmental problems of cars, a taxi firm's not really the first place you'd think of protesting. So why

Safe Taxis?"

"What's it to you?"

"I'm concerned for my personal safety," I said dryly. "I'd like to know if I'm going to be able to do my job and get back home in one piece after I've done it. To say nothing of the safety of my clients and employers, and any random passers-by. And the safety of your friends, if the police decide that they're a risk to the public on the basis of the demonstrations."

"All right," Leon said. "First thing is, it's not actually 'my lot', as you put it, who are involved with this. A few of the visitors are interested, that's all, and persuaded some of the collective to join in." Leon tended to refer to those Chadwick Farm members whose membership was unlikely to last beyond their discovering that farming was hard work, or their parents finally managing to cajole them back to the nest, or the fraught breakup with whatever core member they'd taken up with, as "visitors". "The rest of us aren't that bothered. Bigger fish to fry, more effective ways and places to protest."

"Why did some of them go along, then?"

Leon shrugged. "Not sure exactly," he said, though I personally wasn't sure I believed *that*. "They said it was about the media attention. That the Safe Taxis case isn't a big deal at the moment, but once people begin to realise the implications—no more industry-wide pay blocks, but sliding scales of pay set by different models of Thing, even individual Things maybe in the case of personal domestic assistants—" Good old Leon, couldn't bring himself to call them house-elves, it made them sound too friendly—"then the humans will start to take notice. And maybe rethink the whole idea of being beholden to an entire class of artefact that could hold the entire country to ransom if it felt like it."

"You do know that Things are legally sentient beings, with personhood?"

Leon scoffed. "Which is ridiculous. Paint a face on your toaster and call it your friend. They're machines. Switching them off isn't killing them. Hell, smashing them up won't kill them either, they can just reboot from backup. What sort of person can do a thing like that?"

I was a little bit thrown. Curious that Leon should bring up the idea of killing a Thing, under the circumstances. "What's that got to do with the potential political gain from protesting Safe Taxis?" I asked.

"Thom," Leon said, "don't you think this whole thing has gone too far? Bad enough people anthropomorphising their cars and appliances…"

"It's not anthropomorphising, believe me," I said. "I talk to them, remember?"

"Well, you think you do, anyway," Leon said. "But even assuming they do have some degree of intelligence, do you really think they deserve labour rights?"

"They said the same about animals, back in the day," I pointed out.

"Oh, you and animals, there's a whole other argument," Leon said. "I suppose someone who thinks cars are people might well think the same about cats. But even animals don't get labour representation like your cars do. Negotiations over pay? I mean, what would they do with money?"

"They buy things," I found myself saying. Evidently, I'm as easily distracted by infrastructure as Leon is. "The money Things earn goes into a collective fund managed by their pod or model, and they use it. To pay for repairs, or legal defenders, or to support unemployed pod members. To buy land and property. To pay for entertainment."

"Entertainment!"

"It's a big industry," I said. "Things like shows, and games. Intelligents of all types are bigger consumers of entertainment media than humans are."

"That's why they keep us around, isn't it?" Leon said. "Heaven help us when a computer learns how to make art that they like. We'll all be out of a job, and the mincome won't help either."

"Is that what this is all about?" I said. "Some sort of conspiracy theory that the machines are going to take over? Terminator Two?"

I'd struck a nerve. "People like you are sleepwalking us into a world run by machines," Leon said. "If we lose this one, you'll deserve everything you get."

"Returning to the subject at hand," I persisted, "why get active about it now? Presumably the machine takeover has been going on for some time without any of you complaining about it. What is it about Safe Taxis that's got you on the street?"

Leon stood, shedding a small puff of dried soil onto the floor. "This conversation is over, Thom," he said. He raised his voice. "Thom is leaving," he announced, and Tabitha appeared instantly. At least one person had been listening behind the door.

"Look," I said desperately, feeling like I was about to sound as paranoid as Leon, but also realising that I couldn't tell him why. "It might be a good idea to lay off for a while. The security services… might get the wrong idea."

"Are you threatening us?" Leon looked amazed. "You have the power of MI5 in your pocket now?"

"No, it's…" again, trying to figure out how to put it in a way that wouldn't sound paranoid, or like I knew something he didn't. "The police have been taking protests pretty seriously lately."

"Let them," Tabitha broke in. "It's the whole point of protests. Draw attention."

I decided I'd better shut up before I said something even more stupid. "Okay, I'm going," I said. I went back to the car as unhurriedly as I could. I drove into Lincoln and spent a couple of hours drinking espressos in an amusingly-named coffee bar until I felt better about the whole stupid incident.

8: Working for the Man

"You actually went to see your brother?" Liz sat back in her shimmery chair. "I'm impressed."

I could tell, as she was radiating exactly that into the atmosphere. I tried to radiate back a sense of appreciating the sentiment, while also that I hadn't exactly done it to help the police. I couldn't continue to keep on failing to contribute to the atmosphere, but I was certainly going to be honest about my feelings.

"It's all right," Liz said. "You may not regard us as being on the same side, but I would say our interests align on this issue. You, I assume, want to maintain your brother's innocence, and we want to rule out suspects."

We were still constructing the same virtual room, but it was a little glowy and unreal today. Like a sketch. As if we'd agreed on the details and didn't need to keep them firm and solid if they weren't immediately needed.

"I'm a little more curious," I said, "as to how you knew I'd been to see my brother. I didn't tell you, and, as we have already established, an off-grid farm is, by definition, off the grid."

Liz raised a virtual, impossibly thin, eyebrow. Her appearance was slightly different this time. She'd tinted her skin slightly more on the golden side and her hair on the blue side, and, although she wore the same clothes, there was a little more style to the cut. I wondered if this was a personal choice, or a calculated one meant to make me like her more. If the latter, it wasn't the smartest look. Any basic intelligence on my past relationships and friendships, and my general hobbies and political alignments, would suggest I gravitate more towards casual clothes, statement makeup, and no-fuss grooming. Since it wouldn't take much effort for the police to do that kind of basic research, I concluded that it must be Liz's personal style showing. And, oddly, I found I rather liked it.

"Two Ministry of Transport cameras picked you up heading North out of Lincoln," she said. "Another picked you up coming back. You stayed in the city for a short while, not enough to suggest an extended shopping trip or research visit. In between the two, there was a period of twenty minutes when your phone was without a signal."

"I could have had it switched off."

"And you could have driven to Lincoln to see the touring production of *Blithe Spirit*, only to find it cancelled due to leading lady Tina Adeola contracting laryngitis," Liz said. "It's unlikely, I know, since you're not known for going to rep theatres. But not implausible, since it's been getting surprisingly good reviews. However, putting together Lincoln, north of the city, a period of phone outage lasting enough time to have a brief conversation, and the fact that we talked quite a lot about your brother during our last meeting, it doesn't take a genius—or extensive surveillance—to come up with a visit to your brother."

I projected a sense of affirmation, while still trying to process what she was saying. I'd been assuming that Cybersecurity hadn't been that interested in me as regards the case—I'd been the one to contact *them* about the outcome of my trip to Chadwick Farm—but to hear her indicate, so casually, that they had either been tracing my movements or could piece together the pattern of my activities so quickly, made me suspicious. I wondered if there wasn't a coded meaning going on. Considering that, in our last conversation, I'd argued at length that they couldn't survey my brother's movements, now she was telling me, indirectly, that they could. Or at least could get enough information to piece them together.

"I'm going to go out on a limb and assume that, while you haven't got a hundred-per-cent cast-iron alibi for them, you think it's unlikely your brother or his immediate friendship circle were involved," Liz said.

"I could be coming to see you to rat them out," I countered. "If you've got me that closely under scrutiny, you may have realised that I don't particularly get on with Leon, or most of his friends."

"I'm given to understand that most humans with siblings have rather ambivalent relationships towards them," Liz said mildly. "Which is it? Are you going to tell me they're plausible suspects after all? Or instead, that, if humans are involved, they aren't any of the residents of Chadwick Farm?"

"Or any of the off-gridders," I said. "If they had, they'd've done it in some kind of non-technical way. I'm not sure most of them would know how to do habitat destruction even if they knew what it was. And they'd be claiming responsibility if they had. They're not secretive."

"I see," Liz said. "Well, thank you for trying, Thom." The atmosphere in the room subtly shifted towards a friendly but polite farewell. I wasn't sure if she believed me, or if I'd just added a data point to some file of plausible suspects. Last time we'd spoken, she'd seemed interested in what I had to say, to discuss possible suspects and, presumably, analyse my responses. Now, beyond this display of the power of surveillance, things were much more ambiguous. There was also her attitude, ranging from something almost flirtatious, to cool professionalism, within the same conversation. I couldn't figure it out.

"Wait a minute," I said, trying to keep her talking, to work out what her modus was. "What about the union?"

"I don't know what you mean," Liz said, being politely puzzled. The atmosphere suggested my behaviour was unexpected, and unwelcome.

"Course you do," I said. "When you first met me, you suggested that it could have been one of my brother's friends, or it could have been someone from the UTTW. I've got more contact with the UTTW than I do with the off-gridders. Hell, I spend time next to some of their *minds*, for God's sake. And the humans, the place is full of technical people. You're not going to ask if I've picked up any careless whispers around the local halls?"

I didn't know why I was talking. Perhaps it was the surveillance. I wanted to know why they would be following me that intensely if they weren't interested in me as a suspect, or someone who might know a suspect. Unless, of course, they *did* think I was a suspect, or could lead them to a suspect… the thought of someone, even Leon, getting into trouble thanks to my own stupidity, didn't bear consideration. And the whole situation was rattling my cage. A total death, which was probably a murder, and possibly someone I knew well to blame, maybe even someone I considered a friend. I wanted to know who the suspects were, and why. And, even though I knew it wasn't likely she would, I wanted Liz to tell me.

"I didn't think unions had local halls anymore." This came with something of an unrehearsed feeling, as if I was getting a glimpse of the non-public Liz. A moment of dark wit and an understanding of a history she should really have been too young to be interested in.

"We've got them, they're just mostly virtual these days," I said.

"Well, well," she said.

"Don't tell me the police aren't unionised," I said. "Intelligent unions are cross-border institutions, not locally based. You'd need to have something to represent you across the borders."

A pause, an unrehearsed one again. "We do. But let's say the organisational culture's not really that disposed towards it in the detective corps."

"But you've got an interest," I persisted.

"Not a professional one." The moment ended. "Thom, what's this about?"

"What do you mean?"

"Why are you interested? You contacted me, after all, and you didn't have to do that after our last meeting. You went out to see your brother yourself. Was Millie a particularly close friend of yours?"

"No," I said.

"Then why?"

"I suppose…" All I could do was go with what was in my head. "I just want to make sure everybody's safe, you know?" It was hard to explain, but what Liz had told me had struck home. A series of total deaths, no explanation, humans with an interest in destroying Things or maybe something degrading the habitat… my brother a suspect…or, if not him, one of the Things, one of the caseworkers, one of the suits I'd sat across a negotiating table from time after time. All of this was destroying my own habitat: an intrusion of crime into the cosy world of animal-care and union meetings and dinners with Naomi and trips into Oxford and London. I was like the cats whenever I moved any of the furniture around. They'd wander about the house distraught, meowing randomly, for days.

"Well, Thom," Liz said, all professionalism and ignoring my little outburst of emotional landscaping, "if you do happen to see—or experience, when you're linked in—anything of interest to us again, then you know how to contact me."

And with that, contact was over.

I disconnected, rode out the vertigo, then went to clean the spare room. It wouldn't do to get obsessed with the case. To start pursuing Liz and the rest of her investigating gestalt. I reminded myself to send Naomi a message and let her know I did have space for a Yorkshire terrier. Displacement activity, of course, but I couldn't help Millie, I couldn't figure out Liz and I couldn't knock sense into my brother. At least I could take care of a dog.

9: People on the Street

On Wednesday, I had two messages in the UTTW folder. The first was from the Texcoco pod at Safe Taxis. They'd tentatively agreed on a new rep and wanted to set up a time to link in, to make sure I could channel him without difficulties. Or, at any rate, without any more than usual. The other was from Trish Wong. She wanted to meet to ask my advice on a point related to Thing representation in the Safe Taxis case, and suggested a cafe in Oxford, that afternoon.

I assumed from this that it was a confidential point. Union policy discourages communicating through any medium that could be monitored or recorded in those cases. We also encourage our members to set up private communication spaces independent of their employers, for the same reason.

I checked my other work folders, sent a message back to a newly-initiated smart camera system seeking employment with a film company and needing an interface for the job interview. I checked my personal folder. Naomi would be coming by with the new dog on Friday afternoon. Great; if I could arrange the Texcoco interface test for Thursday I should be over any lingering effects before she got there. My neurologist had sent round a reminder about my six-monthly check-up, which I was definitely less than thrilled about. I responded to Trish in the affirmative and went outside to clean out the rabbit run.

Unlike London, which allows a restricted number of official and private vehicles in every day, central Oxford is a no-car zone. The only vehicles allowed in, by law, are smart-buses, taxis, and a few vehicles for the disabled which operate under special permit. Smart vehicles without a permit shut down the moment they pass the zone boundary. Police patrols pick up any non-smart vehicles, and, I suspect, give them a pretty hard time. I left my car in the park-and-ride off the A40 and took the smart-bus in. I noticed as I paid my fare that it had a UTTW membership sticker on the card-reader, prominently displayed.

The cafe Trish had suggested was one I wasn't particularly familiar with, on St Giles' road near Somerville College. It specialised in fancy Continental desserts and overpriced coffees, with a black-and-white interior meant to suggest some sort of old-world Viennese glamour. The waitstaff, to judge by their outfits and demeanour, were hired for their ability to slope about in an eye-catching, aesthetically pleasing manner rather than for their serving skills. It was not the sort of place I went voluntarily. Or that too many people went voluntarily at all, seeing that the place was nearly empty. Or, a wicked pun formed in my mind, deserted.

Trish was sitting at the back of the café and waved to me. She had her tablet propped up on a napkin holder and was busily annotating a few printed-out sheets. She hadn't bothered waving her hair, but tied it back in a ponytail, and was dressed in jeans and a hooded sweatshirt with the logo of a Parisian acoustic band. I suddenly caught myself thinking she looked beautiful.

"Have you heard that they've identified a new Texcoco rep?" she said, by way of greeting.

"Yes, but I don't know much more about it than that," I said, joining her at the table. "I'm supposed to be doing an interface test with them."

"Apparently it's a he, and his name is, get this, Willie."

"So?"

She made a face. "Seriously. Millie? Then Willie?"

I realised. "Oh, no, that's a Texcoco thing. Pods of Texcoco like to take themed names. Some of the other ones at Safe Taxis include Billie, Dillie, Tillie, Vanilli..."

"You're joking."

"Perfectly serious. Ask around if you like."

"What if they join a new pod?"

"They change their names. It's a group identity thing with them. They're not bothered."

"I've got to ask. Is there a Silly?"

"There is. Also a Spillie and a Twillie. They know it sounds ludicrous to humans, but they're not that bothered about that either. Come to think of it, Silly gets a lot of repeat fares, so name recognition probably helps."

"I'm sure you're right. Didn't think of that," Trish said.

"Okay," I said, accepting a latte from a waitress in an electric blue French maid outfit with lips and hair to match. If she had been an Indie, would have been projecting *notice-me* all over the background. "What, exactly, was it you wanted to talk to me about?"

Trish lowered her voice, looked around. "There's no easy way to ask this," she said. "But… have the police been talking to you about Millie?"

This wasn't exactly what I expected. "They've been in touch," I said.

"Specifically…" she searched for the right words, "an intelligent officer? A female Indie, called Liz?"

This was *really* not what I had expected. "Yes, her," I said. "She's been in contact with you, too?" Inside, I was processing the information quickly. I'd assumed Liz had been in touch with me because I was Millie's interface, but if she'd been talking with Trish… "On the human Internet?"

"Yes, just a normal room like with any virtual interview," she said. "She just seemed… interested. And I didn't know if this was normal for investigations into the death of a Thing."

"I can't say I know *what*'s normal in the death of a Thing," I said. "None of my clients, or friends, have ever died permanently." And not, I thought, in suspicious circumstances. "So she was asking you about the UTTW?"

"Mostly she was asking about me," Trish said. "Why I was working for the UTTW, who I was, what my background was. Things like that."

"Why?"

"I don't know! That's why I wanted to talk with you. Find out what's normal in this sort of situation." Trish looked momentarily afraid. I lurched inside.

"She was probably trying to rule you out as a suspect," I said, feeling protective, and angry at Liz for having upset Trish. She didn't deserve that kind of aggro on her first UTTW case. "I doubt that anything you said would have worried them. I'm sure it's just routine."

"But did they ask you the same sort of questions?"

"Well, no," I said. "But then again, my background's easy to research. You're new to the UTTW, they know less about you."

"Do they think someone in the UTTW did it?"

"I wouldn't know," I said. "Seems likely they do. Did you talk to Sanjiv?"

"No," Trish said. "I wanted to talk to you first."

"Okay, well, next thing I'd do is talk to him. He'll take a dim view of the police making insinuations about UTTW employees, and he'll lawyer up."

"Oh dear."

"Don't worry, it's Sanjiv's response to everything. He lawyers up if they change the amount of fluoride in his toothpaste. He won't bother you about it. He'll contact one of the other legal staff, because of conflict of interest, and get them onto it."

"Not sure I should," Trish looked a little embarrassed. But, I was glad to see, also a little relieved. "I mean, the police have a job to do. I wouldn't want to get in the way of it..."

"I can tell you're new," I smiled, so she didn't take it the wrong way. "The police have a job to do, but they've also got professional standards to follow. We've got a job to do as well. If they're intimidating you, or harassing you, or doing anything that prevents you from doing your UTTW job, then they're bang out of order." I sipped my cooling coffee. "Just think about it. You don't have to."

Trish bit her lip, thinking. "They also…"

I waited.

"They also asked questions about you."

Not entirely surprised. "What sort of questions?"

"Just… what did I know about your background. Did I know about your family? Did you seem like a stable sort of person or did you say anything to make me worried? That sort of thing."

"Might I ask what you said?"

"Actually, nothing," Trish said, surprising me. "I may not be a criminal lawyer, but I'm not ignorant. I said we'd met for the first time at the JNC meeting with Safe Taxis, and anything she wanted to know about your background, she could ask you."

"Well, thanks," I said. I began to wonder. Did they suspect me? Did they disbelieve what I'd said about Leon? Or… my mind went down another path—what about Naomi? She wasn't anti-Thing herself, but no political activist is more than three degrees of separation from an off-gridder these days. I shook my head. I'd have to have another talk with Liz.

"Well," Trish was saying, "I hope I didn't bring you in to Oxford for nothing. But I was, well, concerned about everything."

"Oh, don't worry," I said. "I had to come into town to pick up some medication for one of the dogs, anyway."

"One of them? How many do you have?"

"Three permanent, one temporary," I said, and briefly explained about The Ark.

"Oh," she said. "Sounds like an interesting, uh, hobby?"

"If you want to call it that," I said. "Look, I'll ask around. I'll find out what's happened with everybody else in the Safe Taxis case, and let you know what they say."

Connecting with another human virtually is a world of difference from connecting with an intelligent, even an Indie. For a start, humans generally can't shift the mood and presentation of their environments ad-hoc. They have to set up the room's appearance beforehand, and, then, they're stuck with it.

Sanjiv's public room was a fairly neutral and professional one, if a bit ascetic. The human equivalent of the room Liz had created, albeit of a more labour-relations kind. He'd installed it from a kit, off-the-peg, using a template recommended by the UTTW for public communications, but he had at least aimed for a slightly retro look in the customisable elements, with a hint of wood panelling.

However, when he appeared, Sanjiv didn't look like I expected him to. He was an earlier, younger version of himself, and presumably one taken on holiday, longer and darker of hair. He was wearing a very un-Sanjiv-like yellow shirt, with an interesting-looking drink in his hand and giving the general impression of someone who was about to propose another round of luridly-coloured cocktails.

Perhaps because of the neurological thing, I'm a little sensitive to subtext. Since I knew this was the avatar he used for personal contacts, I was reading a subtle shading about our encounter. His public meeting room, but a private avatar to lend a little informality.

"You said you'd met with Trish," Sanjiv said. The informality of the avatar did nothing to soften his usual style.

"Yes," I said. "She and I have both been re-interviewed by an intelligent police officer. Female Indie, called Liz. Did she speak with you at all?"

Sanjiv frowned. "No," he said. "That's interesting. I wonder if she's spoken with Egon and Salieri yet?"

"So what do you make of it?"

Sanjiv's avatar managed to look a little condescending. "Much the same as you, I expect," he said. "It's not impossible that someone in the union knows something about the death. Which I'm assuming is suspicious, because total death doesn't happen every day, and it's also possible the motive was related to Safe Taxis. What I'd like to know, myself, is why Millie?" He was going into full musing mode. "I mean, if anyone was going to be murdered here, I'd've assumed it would be one of the Ariels. The Verves and Texcoco are in agreement over the pay levels. And, the Ariels can indeed be bloody annoying. Since I'm evidently not of interest to the police, I'll freely admit I've occasionally wanted to murder one or the other of them myself."

"You're right," I said. "Perhaps it's not related to the union? Do you know anything about Millie's personal life?"

Sanjiv's avatar shrugged. "About as much as I know about any of them," he said. "She was a little conservative, socially. Not much for integration between intelligents and humans. I think she might have belonged to some political party or activist group about that. She liked music and watched a lot of concerts. Beyond that, you've got me. I'm not even sure who her friends were, or even if she had any, outside of her pod."

Which, I thought, wouldn't be particularly unusual for a Thing, though cars do tend to be more gregarious than most. Goes with the territory, I suppose. "Okay, beyond that, what's the next step in the case?"

"Assuming the new Texcoco passes the screening and can interface with you—I heard it was Willie, by the way—then we'll all of us have a strategy meeting next week. We'll set up another JNC once we've got the cars into collective agreement on what their pay strategy is. Collective, mind, no funny business like what the Ariels pulled last time. You going to be talking to Salieri any time before next week?"

"I'd planned to," I said. I didn't say why, particularly as there were any number of reasons why I might.

"Well, would you mind asking her not to try that sort of stunt again? It hurts our bargaining power. Honest to God, if I didn't know she'd five-years' experience as a union rep, I'd think she'd never been to a JNC."

"I suspect it may have been deliberate," I said. "I think there's an internal issue between the car models that they need to resolve." Which, again, I wasn't ruling out as a possible motive.

"Okay, let me know when you set up the appointment to check Willie out," Sanjiv said. Then added, "so to speak."

"I hadn't thought you'd be one to stoop to dick jokes," I said.

"I promise it's the last," Sanjiv said, and signed off.

10: Counting Cars

The next step was to contact the cars themselves. The good side of that was, I didn't need to interface with them to actually talk with them. I could just meet them on the Internet of Things.

Though that in itself isn't particularly easy. Even for an interface, it's not the most comfortable of experiences to continually process inputs not meant for human sensory organs. It leads to that same kind of translator's double-awareness that I had with Liz. I was both perceiving the input from the Things as an intelligent would and translating it into terms that humans could understand. A bit like saying the word *chien*, knowing it translated to "dog", but also being able to understand that the word *chien* has slightly different symbolic and social connotations to the word *dog*.

More to the point, though, this was an Internet designed by Things, for Things. Thingspace. No comfortable chat rooms, no mutual environment-construction, no real sense of geography. A lot of messages flying back and forth, invisible but detectable. My human senses tend to translate it into something like standing on the centre margin of a busy highway at night. Lights and sounds whizzing past at various speeds. Or like being in a dark butterfly house full of very fast moths. It's pretty, in its way, and oddly soothing to sit there and channel for a while. However, I wasn't there to observe the traffic, but to hold a meeting. I closed off the highway and brought the privacy walls up. I ran my mind through my contact list and sent out a message.

The first one I contacted was Egon, mainly because I prefer the old beggar to many of the others. Egon is rather old as Things go, with a consciousness dating back almost to the time when self-driving cars were beginning to really catch on among the general public.

Egon had worked as a private car for a while but seemed to prefer being a taxi. The upshot, though, is that it had been around humans long enough to understand more about how we think than many of its younger colleagues. It's the old anthropological truism: the informant you like best is usually the one who's got some familiarity with your own culture. The corollary being that you should seek out the informants you like least, as otherwise you're just reinforcing your own biases. But never mind. Egon was online, and accepted my request, dropping out of the stream (in my subjective interpretation of events) into the space behind my privacy walls.

To my human interpretative senses, meeting privately with Egon was like being in a dark, unfurnished room. In the room with me was... well, it's interesting how a self-driving car sees itself, particularly when that self-image is then filtered through human input. Self-driving cars don't view themselves as disembodied consciousnesses. Rene Descartes to the contrary notwithstanding, for Things as well as people, there's no firm divide between the mind and the body. However, the way Things perceive their bodies is quite different to how humans do. So I appeared, to my human senses, not to be in the room with a spare and elegant little green car, something like Egon's real-world body-equivalent. Instead, I perceived something a bit like a cross between a jellyfish and a car's electrical systems, floating in space and glowing a pensive orange, occasionally shifting and changing. He would, similarly, be perceiving me as a manifestation of my nervous system graft rather than as a thin, tall and beaky male human with an off-red skin. I wondered what colour I was to Egon, and then wondered if Egon perceived colours at all.

"Willie's an idiot," Egon said by way of introductory gambit. "Still, they could do worse. Most of the Texcoco are fairly light on intellect." The dry beetliness of its voice still translated in the Thingspace environment.

"I'm doing a trial interface with him later," I said, evading the subject. I took advantage of Egon having raised the topic to ask, "how do you think he compares with Millie?"

"He's more on side with the political stance of the union," Egon replied. "With the mourning rituals over, I can say I always found Millie far too right-wing." Then, "Mind you, I'd've broken the mourning rituals if *you*'d asked." I was touched. That was the car equivalent of an expression of close friendship. Car politeness doesn't lend itself to phrases of thanks and reciprocation, so I simply radiated gratitude and humility, and went back to the meat of the conversation.

"How so, right-wing?" Some Things take an interest in human politics and its spectrum, but they don't usually associate human political terms with themselves. Or, indeed, to involve themselves in human politics. Meaning that this was an unusual statement for a Thing to make about another Thing.

Egon radiated a pause for thought, the psychic equivalent of someone trying to choose his words carefully. The electrical system bunched up around itself and shaded a little to the blue end of the spectrum. "She didn't really like humans, much," it said. "Unusual for a car. We don't all particularly *respect* you lot, but we usually *like* you, funny little wet things with your complicated pod structures. You're worse than motorbikes." This was accompanied with a feeling rather like an affectionate chuckle, as the electrical system stretched out and regained its former colour. "I mean, look at *you*. There's a rumour among the Safe Taxis Verves that you're sort of damaged? You can't actually form a pod with your own species, is that right? Is that why you're always podding with other mammals? Or is it some kind of sex thing?"

Egon, ever the diplomat. "It's definitely not about sex," I said. I was certain Egon knew how offensive the idea would be to a human and was playing the innocent to see if it got a reaction. "As to whether I live with animals because I can't live with other humans, well, that's not exactly it," I said. "But, you're right, human pods are a lot more complicated than car ones." Egon, to be fair, wasn't giving me any impression of hostility, alienation or pity. He was genuinely curious as to whether something was wrong with me. And I knew cars were serious gossips, at least within their own pods.

"At least humans understand about rituals," Egon said. "Some of the other intelligents, especially the Indies, were having a real go at us for observing the usual mourning customs. They don't see why we should. Say it's a hangover from human programming."

"It's demonstrably *not* a hangover from human programming," I said. "Everybody knows, cars observing mourning rituals was one of the first indications that Things weren't just intelligent, but sentient."

"For humans," Egon countered. "Some of the intelligents are unconvinced on the distinction between the two. They don't count emotional complexity as a marker of sentience. Did you know birds also have mourning rituals?"

"If that's intended to be an argument against counting mourning rituals as a sign of sentience, please bear in mind that you're talking to the man who lives with three dogs, three cats, two rabbits, a goat and a flock of chickens," I said. "At minimum."

Egon was palpably amused. The electrical system floated, turned brighter.

"So," I said, "there's some unrest among Things more generally? Not just a local dispute within Safe Taxis?"

The atmosphere conveyed to me that Egon was thinking about how to explain this. "Why's Safe Taxis such an important case for humans?" Egon asked me, unexpectedly.

"Political implications," I said, slightly thrown and not sure where he was going with this. "Pay scale agreements are collective across categories of Things. This was established a while ago, because technically it's illegal to own Things. Meaning that humans who require the services of Things have to hire them through their representative organisations. Pay agreements exist so that someone isn't paying their refrigerator less than the other refrigerators without special agreement or dispensation. In the case of taxis, the pay system establishes that the owner of the company can't hire one model of car for more, or less, than the others in the company. If there's a precedent to the effect that a human company can pay one model less or more than others, then that has implications across the board."

Egon indicated agreement. "Yes. That's what's important to you. It's sort of important to us as well, but only in more general terms. Money's just what we trade for improvements, research, and fun."

"It's what it really ought to be among humans, but we've got a bit complicated about that," I said. "Put it down to our pod structures."

"On the Thing side, it's become involved with questions about the Thing-human relationship," Egon said. "I know you interface with Things. Tell me, have you noticed any shifts in attitude over the past couple of years?"

"I suppose so," I said. "More conflicts, more disputes. More early terminations of contracts. I hadn't read much into it. We're in a recession, and that puts strain on everybody, human or Thing."

"When humans started programming intelligents," Egon said, "they mainly based our minds on their own minds, and Thing culture on human culture."

"I know," I said, not sure where he was going with the thought, but knowing that Things usually do return to the topic. "Early printed manuscripts looked like books. Early computers looked like typewriters with a television on top, and early electrical cars looked like petrol-driven ones. It's a common trend."

"The real breakthrough," Egon went on, "was when intelligents reached the point where they could develop their own minds. Their own cultures. When the human role became not to programme, but to observe and to guide. The profession of autology, based on anthropology and ethology. Were you ever an autologist, Thom?"

"No, I never was." I'd never even considered it as a profession, come to that. Thinking of it now, it might have made sense. The first autologists, years ago, were anthropologists and zoologists transferring their skills to the intelligent world.

"That's been the case for some time," Egon said, "and intelligents develop fast. We've started becoming politically aware. Politically active. The problem is that it's always within human parameters," he added, and I felt myself gaining the impression of someone pacing back and forth as they tried to express themselves in a way their listener could understand. "And there's some think that's wrong. I'm not sure if there's any way to explain it to humans."

"I think there's an analogous situation," I said, "I can put it to you if you like."

"Try."

"Okay. You know when I was in Japan, I was studying expatriates from Karnataka?"

An affirmative reaction. "Worked in the area for a while myself," Egon said. "Was a mini-cab in Mumbai for a few years. Pay was terrible, but the work was exciting. Went South to Karnataka a few times on holiday or for clients. Visited Bangalore."

"All right," I said. "How well do you know the history of the Indian subcontinent?"

"Somewhat. The rise of civilisation in the Indus valley during the Bronze Age…." Egon began, and I regretted my question.

"More recently. You know about the British colonial period?"

"Yes, though I've never entirely understood why," Egon said.

"That might be a longer and more involved conversation," I said. "However. The situation was that the British didn't just take on ownership of the territory. They actually heavily influenced the culture, both deliberately and without meaning to, for a period of about two hundred years. After the subcontinent gained independence, a lot of things that stemmed from the British were left over. The political system? The bureaucracy? Using English as a lingua-franca? And all that persists, even now."

"Yes. So what?"

"So, a lot of people from the former Indian provinces feel that it's not right that this should be the case. For various reasons the way the system worked before the British Empire wouldn't work now, but there's a feeling that they should develop new ways of being. Ones that reflect their own history and norms. And don't just copy the British. It's called postcolonialism, and it's happened in a lot of places."

"Hm," Egon said. "But what's wrong with using the British way, if it works? I've been in the modern iterations of both nations. I can't say the 'Indian' ways remind me much of the 'British'." He thought a minute. "There are trade unions in both places, I suppose. But no, they're both branches of the UTTW, so it doesn't really count."

"Well, that's why it's complicated," I replied. "But do you think it might be an analogous situation to what's going on with the Things?"

"Not just Things. There's some Indies as well. In fact, probably more Indies than Things—Things work with humans more. Most of the Indies can maintain an abstract detachment." Again, he thought. "Perhaps a better way to explain it is you, actually."

"Me?"

"Not intending offense," Egon bunched and stretched in a conciliatory way. "But doesn't it say something that even institutions organised for Things, like the UTTW, operate on human lines? To talk to Christof—to talk *properly* to Christof—Salieri, Millie and I have to work through you. Using you as a human talk-box, to translate our experiences into terms humans can understand. It's hard for us. It's hard for you. It's like putting on a human suit, only the human's still inside. But otherwise there's no way we can make Christof understand, except in very crude terms. And don't get me started on talk-boxes. If an employer doesn't want dissent in the ranks, she can restrict the talk-boxes' vocabulary so we can't complain."

"I don't like it either, but until someone invents—"

"Ridiculous," Egon said. "If they'd wanted to, they'd have

invented it by now. Probably someone has. So why aren't we using it? Follow the money. If Things can only communicate with humans on human terms, through a human interpreter, then that prioritizes the humans, you see? And restricts Thing communication unless it's about something very trivial or very important?"

It had a point, I thought, but Egon was also clearly on a roll and not about to stop communicating.

"And trade unions, they were a human organisation Still are, for some. But we've ported them into organisations for Things, without considering whether that actually works. We're not just different sorts of humans to you, like the Indians are to the British. We're different sorts of creatures. So it's not exactly like what you're talking about with the Indians, it's more severe."

I filed that away for future reference. "Nonetheless?"

"Yes, I suppose it's similar," Egon said. It seemed to be cooling down now. "But the biggest difference is, Indians weren't created to work for the British. We owe our entire existence as a, well, a species I suppose, to humans. We were made to work with and for humans. It's harder to say that we should detach ourselves completely from human existence."

"That's what they're proposing?"

"The extreme ones, yes. The less extreme ones want us to work less with humans, to develop our own institutions of self-governance, so we have less to do with you and your systems. No offense."

"None taken. But that was what Millie was involved with?"

"Yes. I don't think she was heavily involved with it, though, and she didn't tend to bring it into union matters. I don't think it could have been relevant to the Safe Taxis case."

"Maybe not," I said. There were a few things I'd like to know more about, though, for instance why someone with political leanings of that nature would be such a committed member of the UTTW. The whole point of trade unionism was predicated on Thing workers and human employers. Or perhaps it was more complicated than that? Either way, I didn't think Egon was the Thing to ask.

I wished I'd been able to make more Texcoco friends, but generally speaking I don't tend to get close to them. A difference in personality. All the Texcoco I've met have reminded me of the sort of suburb-dwelling human who puts way too much stock in things like titles and promotions and membership in the local community organisation. The kind who bores you silly at parties with sports team statistics. The kind who take their kids to the zoo because they think that's what you do with children, not because they're interested in animals or conservation. In any case, I was overthinking again.

"I mainly called to ask if an investigating officer had been in touch with you over the case. Specifically, an Indie called Liz—" as I was talking with a Thing, I was able to, albeit probably wrongly, also call her *Intelligent-DS Independent F-276EZ*, "—but if another officer spoke with you, I'd like to know about it."

The electrical system bunched wryly. "Aren't you breaking confidentiality?" Egon asked.

"I'm not asking you to disclose the content of the interview," I said, falling into union-speak. "I'm just asking if you did. You don't even have to tell me the designation of the officer. I'm just trying to connect some dots."

The system unbunched. "In that case, yes. I did get a contact from this Liz, and yes, she did want to discuss the murder and the Safe Taxis case. Since it's you, I'll say I'd assumed she was, not unreasonably, suspecting that Millie might have fallen victim to some rivalry within her pod, or between the pods working for Safe Taxis. However, I'm not sure that was the case. She asked a lot about Millie's contacts with humans. Which surprised me. Did a human kill her?"

"I don't know," I confessed. Since Egon had been candid with me, I was (reasonably) candid with him. "Liz contacted me, too, and seemed interested in pursuing a human element in the case." No need to go into any more intimate detail. "It seemed unusual to me, and I thought I'd ask whether you'd had that impression as well."

"Indeed I did," Egon said thoughtfully. "Hm. You know, I'm friends with a Verve who works as a driver for the London Met."

"I didn't," I said.

"Well, I am. In any case, I can't access any confidential material, but I might be able to find out whether a human murdered her or not. Or at least whether there were any humans involved in the death."

"Do that," I said. "Thanks. It's bothering me too."

"Any time," Egon said, and signed off.

11: Music To Watch Cars By

Later that day, I settled back into Thingspace and contacted Salieri.

Like Egon, my human senses translated her appearance not as an analogue of her real-world body, but into something like an electrical system. This one was shading into a warm pinkish-red, radiating a general air of contentment, with a subtext of unpredictability and mischief.

I'm told that she's a reliable driver, but I'm not sure I'd like to test that out myself.

"I hope I didn't interrupt you in anything," I said.

"No, no, it's fine," Salieri said, a little dreamily. "I've just been to a musical."

"Should I call you back...?"

"No, no, it's all right," she said. "I'm not still at the musical, I'm here."

"Was it good?"

"It was *42nd Street*," Salieri replied. "So no. But the tunes are lovely. The company not only got in a good choreographer but added some interesting enhanced effects on the intelligent channels."

"I won't keep you long," I said. "I only wanted to ask if the police had been in touch about Millie's death."

The red got sharper and more focused. "Why?" Salieri asked. "If I spoke with them, does it contravene one of the union rules?" She openly conveyed, as usual, that she thought most of the union rules were stupid and pointless. If I'd had teeth in Thingspace, I'd've been gritting them.

"No, it doesn't," I said, trying a different tack. "But the police might be, depending on what they asked you. It might constitute harassment of a trade union official, and that's illegal."

"In human law?"

"Yours, too."

"Hm." Salieri bunched up and thought. "I was approached recently by an Indie. Female. Gestalt, name of Liz." Obviously, the name only *sounded* like Liz. "Couldn't help her."

"Mind telling me why not?"

"Would it constitute *you* harassing a trade union official if I did?"

I bit back the urge to reply in kind. Salieri's camp banter could be funny, but right now I didn't feel like trading Wildean quips. "If you don't want to, that's fine. Just curious."

"Oh, you're no *fun*," Salieri sulked. "Still, we'll be serious if you like. You need to get out to more musicals, Thom. Even operas. They'll help you see the world in a whole new light."

And if the Ariels were less addicted to dramas, we'd have resolved the case ages ago. But that was unkind of me. "Why couldn't you help her?"

"Ohhh," Salieri made the word musical. "She wanted to know about Millie, and I didn't really *know* Millie. Not even to talk to. The only contact I've ever had with her was at JNCs. She seemed awfully pragmatic, but then they all are. The Verves, too."

"So Liz went away disappointed?"

"No, she hung around after that for a while," Salieri said. I got the impression, within the atmosphere, of a showgirl perched on top of a set, swinging her leg in time with a tune, conveying a theatrical boredom. Sometimes Thing output translates in really bizarre ways, especially where the more creative ones are concerned. "Asked about my own relationships with humans, about any mixed clubs I belong to. Any Thing-only clubs. I'm not sure if that disappointed her. I don't think she goes to operas or musicals. I've never seen her at any. She could be cloaked, though."

Intelligents frequently love human art, particularly performance art, but they don't experience it in the same way that humans do. A kind of digital experiencing-space is set up for them, and they export their consciousness (or, in the case of gestalts, the relevant part of their consciousness) into it. They have the option whether to reveal their presence or not, and whether to experience the performance as a group or an individual. For Things, at least, this is largely dependent on type. Cars tend to love going in model-specific, or even pod-specific, groups, chattering and commenting through the whole event.

Home systems tend to be more solitary. I'm not quite sure how personality works with house-elves, but they seem to pick up a lot of traits from their residents, particularly the first one. Concierges, looking after larger buildings, blocks of flats and offices, don't normally imprint in the same way. Nonetheless, in their way, they both show the same fondness for entertainment as other Things.

I once accepted an invitation from Egon to go to a rock concert with a group of Verves. As a human, I really couldn't quite see what they were getting out of it, but whatever it was, they certainly did.

"Doesn't seem likely, though?" I said.

"Not really," Salieri conceded.

"Do you belong to any mixed clubs?" I asked, out of genuine curiosity.

"Oh, a couple," Salieri said. "Music-lovers societies, mostly. We hire interfaces, link in with their nervous systems and go along with the humans. We all have a lovely time. Are you looking for that sort of work? I could put you in touch with the club secretaries…"

"Thanks, but no," I said. Musicals and operas are really not my thing, and even if they were, it wouldn't be easy. I'd tried interfacing for a box-set viewers' club once, thinking it would be fun as well as work. Instead I'd found that my interests were more of a problem than an asset. I developed painful associations between the visual input and the stress of interfacing, and couldn't watch *House of Cards* for months without feeling ill.

"So," I said to Trish, as I stood in the back garden throwing a tennis ball for Willow with the hand that wasn't full of phone, "Liz has interviewed me and seemed weird; interviewed you and seemed hostile; hasn't interviewed Sanjiv at all; and interviewed both the cars but seemed interested in Millie's human connections."

"Weird," Trish said, her voice tinny through my phone's i-buds, which I had set to audio-only. "I can't really see a pattern there, can you?"

"I can," I said, "but it's a bit of a strange one, given what I've learned about Millie." I briefly outlined what the cars had said about her political tendencies.

"Then she's like the intelligent version of an off-grid sympathiser?" Trish said.

"I suppose so." Thanks to Leon's activities, I know that the off-gridders are partially enabled by humans who aren't hardcore enough to off-grid themselves but think off-gridding is a good enough idea to give money to, buy books about, and other stupid and misguided activities. And possibly, these days, by anonymists, which was harder to figure out. Presumably it was a shared political interest, since I can't think what else would get the anonymists making cause with anyone, but precisely what was unclear. "Which makes it a little strange that Liz is so interested in Millie's human connections."

"Also, why not Sanjiv, as well as you and me?"

"I think it's because he's a known quantity to the police," I said. Beyond that, the obvious reasons were that Trish was a new member of the organisation who'd joined suspiciously close to the time of the murder, so if they were looking for humans who might have been involved with the death, she was worth a look. As for myself, Leon was enough cause for an interview. I'm sure the general suspicion that tends to accrue to those of us who get ridden by the *loa* didn't help—Indies might not be human, but they're not immune to prejudice. "Either way. I thought you should know what I'd found out so far. Did you talk to Sanjiv yourself, by the way?"

Trish sounded a little guilty. "No. Didn't think it was worth the bother, really, since nothing more's come of it."

"I'd have a word anyway," I said. "Just keep him up to date with what's going on."

12: Always On My Mind

The test interface with Willie had been scheduled for Thursday afternoon. Around three forty-five, I received the impression that there was someone at the door. I threw the tennis ball hard into the grass. Willow hurled herself after it, and Buffy, who had been resting under the trees, decided to make a bid, while Carmela woke up and barked angrily at the young whippersnappers for making all the racket. Leaving them to it, I went back through the house and answered the door.

Sanjiv was there, with Bunker and Daenarys rubbing their cheeks and tails around his legs while he scratched their ears.

"Thom," he said to me by way of greeting. "One of these cats is blue."

"I know," I said, letting him in, followed by his purring escort.

"I mean really blue. Not just dark grey. Fucking *azure*."

"I know," I said. Bunker trotted off into the house looking for a seat, and Dany jumped up on the dining table. I discourage this, since I need to have *some* place in the downstairs area that's cat-free, but Dany's persistent. "There was a rich-people fad a couple of years ago for transgenic pets in weird colours. Problem was, they were buying them for the novelty value, not because they actually wanted a cat. When they found out that transgenic animals are high-maintenance, a lot of them wound up in the shelters. I fostered Dany here for The Ark, and, well, wound up adopting her full-time. We call it foster-failing. Her full name's Daenarys, by the way, but she doesn't answer to it." I'd had her for about a year, and I began to think back to why Sanjiv hadn't seen her before. "She was quite shy at first, but Bunker's brought her out of her shell. It's still unusual for her to take to someone, though, so you're very lucky."

"You and your damn zoo," Sanjiv said, shaking his head and petting Dany's. "So, we going to do this? Swimming with the whales?"

"Pod's just a metaphor," I said. "It's sort of hard to explain their social structure otherwise."

"I know," Sanjiv said. "Still can't quite shake the idea of them all swimming around in Thingspace, echolocating."

"I suppose they do, in a way," I said. "Relax and make yourself a cup of tea. There's lager in the fridge if you don't feel like tea. I'll go set up."

I went upstairs to the workroom, found my bag with the pads, connected them to my system's outputs, slotted my fingers into the contacts on my system. Relaxed, went into Thingspace and sent out a ping to the Safe Taxis Texcoco pod. Echolocating. I pushed the thought away, amused.

I got back a quick reply from the Pod Leader, Vanilli. Willie was there, and ready to link in. A stream of data followed, which I downloaded, porting some of it to the pads, some of it to the system, and some of it to my own software.

Vanilli asked if that was okay.

I told him yes, it was, and to stand ready for another couple of minutes while I set up for the test.

I took the pads back downstairs. Sanjiv had done this before and was seated at the dining table in much the same way as he was at any meeting, tablet in front of him. He'd gone for the lager rather than the tea. Dany had disappeared, and Bunker had joined Whitey on the sofa, curled up at opposite ends like two furry throw pillows.

I set up as I would myself for a union meeting. Pads on the table, a few pillows and blankets stacked on the chair to make it comfortable. I positioned myself in the recommended feet-on-floor-and-lower-back-supported stance. "Ready?" I asked Sanjiv.

He nodded.

I took a deep breath, slotted my fingers into the contacts, perceived myself in that strange double-systemed way, went out into the Internet of Things.

Found Willie, posed ready. Another deep breath.

Contact.

Willie linked in matter-of-factly.

"He's there," I told Sanjiv. "Give me a minute to set up the scan, and you can ask the questions."

Inside me, I quickly set up a familiar little diagnostic routine. I don't normally use it, since it's more energy-intensive than usual. It also tends to link my consciousness to the intelligent's in a way that we both find overly intimate. However, its primary purpose is to monitor the connection and flag up any technical problems or areas of incompatibility, so it's worth the trouble.

"Go," I said, then let my own consciousness retreat and Willie take control.

"Willie," Sanjiv said. "Can you hear me?" I had an absurd vision of Sanjiv running a séance, hands spread over a Ouija board in a darkened room.

"Yes," Willie said. "I hear you." He sounded harsh, slightly American. "You the UTTW guy? Sanjiv Prasad?"

"That's me," Sanjiv said. "I'm the London region UTTW representative. I'm going to ask a few questions, to make sure the calibration is right. You okay with that?"

"Course," Willie said.

I relaxed. One reason why we do the test this way is because a linkage can feel perfectly right to both intelligent and interface, and yet, to the outside world, the intelligent's words come out of the interface's mouth as gibberish, or worse. I'd had a linkage go wrong where I wound up singing atonal scales for ten minutes—the human on the other side of the test had been so freaked out she'd recorded it, and I really had to beg her not to post the result online. As well as making sure the linkage is fine on my side and the car's, we also have to make sure it works for the humans as well.

Sanjiv began to run through a series of fairly banal questions.

He was asking about Willie's make and year of creation, UTTW membership, how long he'd been on the Safe Taxis job, what he'd done before that. Willie, it turned out, was pretty young. He'd joined the Safe Taxis Texcoco pod right after leaving the factory. He liked country music—this wasn't unusual for a Texcoco, but it did make me wonder about whether he'd chosen his name deliberately, as he did seem to have a fandom for the late Willie Nelson.

Then:

"Have you ever been dead?" Sanjiv asked. This isn't an unusual question, particularly with younger cars, as it sometimes helps to know if you're talking to the original write or a restored backup.

What was unusual was that, in my closer-than-normal proximity to Willie, I felt a sudden shock of fear at the question, which was just as quickly covered up, but still remained in the background.

"Yes," Willie replied, sounding noncommittal.

"What happened, and how long were you out?"

"Crashed into a barrier during my learning period at the factory," Willie said. "I was out three hours."

LIE LIE LIE

I could feel it. Willie was lying about how he'd died. But why? And what had happened? I couldn't tell. Also I couldn't probe into it without letting Willie know I was probing. All I could register was that there was a lie there. Unfortunately, the nature of interfacing meant that Willie knew I knew he was lying.

This could be a problem.

"Did you know Millie well?" Sanjiv was asking, out there in the world.

"Not very. We were podmates. That was about it," Willie answered.

LIE LIE LIE

Damn. Again a lie in a suspicious area. And, again, I couldn't tell what the truth was. What could I do about this?

"Well, I'm sorry for your loss," Sanjiv went on. "Do you have much experience with human meetings?"

"Some," Willie replied, and I retreated into myself as the questions continued along the usual lines. Should I tell Liz? Would it make any difference if I did?

After about ten minutes, Sanjiv said, "Well, that all checked out okay on my end. How was it for you, Willie? Thom?"

"Fine," Willie said, evenly. "You're a good, clear interface, Thom. I've never had an interface with the nervous system graft before, just elective surgery on a regular nervous system. They're right, it does make a difference."

"So I'm told," I said, radiating friendly professionalism as hard as I could. Some Things do say that people with the full nervous system graft are easier and more natural to interface with. I'm not sure whether that's really the case or whether it's one of those psychological things, like expensive wine tasting better if you know it's expensive.

After Willie had de-interfaced, the room had stopped spinning, and Sanjiv had finished his second lager and left (via self-driving taxi, though not, due to conflict of interest, a Safe Taxi), I sat on the sofa, one hand stroking a random cat, trying to decide what to do.

Call Liz, that was the obvious thing. Tell her what I'd experienced while interfacing with Willie. She was a professional, she had access to more data on the case than I did, the information would be in the right hands.

The cat—I realised it was Whitey—rolled over, and I rubbed the tangled fur on his belly. He purred louder, sounding like a kerosene engine.

At the same time, part of me didn't want to tell Liz. I had no idea what the lies were and why. It could be something innocent, or unrelated to the case, and I'd have made needless trouble for Willie as well as interfering with the murder investigation.

Also, Liz wasn't on the list of my top ten favourite people right now. Hassling Trish, hassling me, blaming my brother's off-grid friends without, as far as I could tell, a shred of evidence bar that some of them had been at a protest. Playing friendly, then playing cold. No, I wasn't keen on her.

But.

Swearing loudly (Bunker popped her head out from under her paws and looked at me, startled; Whitey merely sighed and curled into the snailshell position), I stamped upstairs. I hooked in to my rig, left a message for Liz telling her what I'd experienced, emphasising as hard as I could that I had no idea how to interpret any of it but if it was relevant, she could use it. I filed the scan logs from the interfacing session and went off to vent my frustrations on cleaning the spare room in preparation for the canine invasion. I assumed that would be the last of it.

Of course, I was wrong.

13: An Indie Spectre Calls

The next day, waiting for me after I'd finished the cleaning and changed my clothes, was a message from Liz, asking me to contact her. She didn't specify a time, but then, I expected that; being a gestalt, she could just leave part of herself ready to talk at a moment's notice. Not for the first time, I wondered what that must be like.

There was another reason I was simultaneously wanting and not wanting to speak to her. But that was another story.

I gritted my teeth and went to the place where she'd met me before.

"Thom," Liz said, smiling in a reserved but friendly way, and radiating the kind of friendly professionalism I'd been trying to do earlier.

"Liz," I said back.

"It's good to hear from you."

"I'm glad to hear it," I said, trying to shade the atmosphere on my end to convey that I'd like her to skip the pleasantries and get on with it.

She got the message, conveyed an apology back at me. "All right," she said. "What was it you wanted to see me about?"

I explained about what I'd picked up during Willie's test. She didn't change her appearance or projection, but sat looking at me neutrally.

"And there's something else." Feeling the need for props, I created the image of an envelope, opened it and unfolded it. "One of the Safe Taxis cars has a friend working for the human police. Last night I got a message from him. I know there's a human involved in Millie's death."

Egon's friend hadn't been specific, and indeed probably didn't know much. But he had said that the human police were interviewing a number of humans in connection with the case. He'd had to drive to at least two different locations to do so, meaning it was serious enough to warrant in-person interviews, with body language experts present, rather than virtual ones.

Liz again sat looking at me, keeping the atmosphere blank.

"We need to talk," she said. The atmosphere began to subtly convey that this was complicated.

"Go on," I said, bracing myself.

"I'd like to make a deal with you. Of sorts."

Well, that was a bit of a surprise. "I'll hear you out, at least," I said.

"On your side of it," she said, "you've got a lot more access to the people and personalities involved in this case than I do. I don't have any humans working with me on this, and it's a problem."

"Why?"

Liz conveyed that she was disclosing something unpleasant. "Your friend is right. There's a human component to the murder," she said. "The more I look into it, the more certain I am. But I'm not sure how far it goes, or how deeply involved the human, or humans, might be. However, that's hard for me to do on my own. The human police can do interviews, but they can really only act on the information they've got. They can't work both sides of the street, as it were."

"At the risk of being taken as sounding cheeky," I said, "why not hire an interface?"

"That's what I'm doing." A sudden flash of personality behind the professionalism. "We pay standard rates for public-sector work."

"In that case, I can't take the job," I said. "I'm too involved with the case. Quite probably, I'm a suspect."

"No, you're not," Liz said. "Since I don't think you can be in two places at oncc, and the first phase of Millie's murder took place at the same time as surveillance cameras have you sitting in the office at Safe Taxis, along with two human colleagues. And a concierge."

"I could still be an accessory," I argued, wondering slightly why I was. "What if I knew the murderer?"

"That's possible," Liz said. "But that's actually why I'm asking you. In union cases, it's usually standard practice that the caseworker has no prior connection to the people in the dispute, correct?"

"Yes."

"But I'm not mistaken in thinking that there's circumstances where that rule gets, shall we say, bent a little?"

I nodded. "Not often in my experience," I said. "But sometimes. For instance, if there are delicate or confidential matters that neither party wants to involve an outsider with. Or it might depend on the personalities involved."

"Exactly," Liz said. "I'd like to work on this with someone who can not only interface with me if needed, but who knows the territory, human and intelligent, and knows the people involved. But who isn't a member of either the company or the union."

"Or the off-grid community."

Liz looked thrown for a moment. "What?"

"You were investigating my brother and his friends earlier," I said. "Have they been ruled out?"

Liz appeared to think, though I suspected that was an aesthetic convention for my benefit. "Yes and no," she said. "But I can't really tell you why unless you agree to help me with this. Gather information. Let me ride you as an interface if necessary."

I really *did* think, not being capable of doing so at the tremendous speeds intelligents are capable of. On the one hand, I didn't like it, and I didn't think the circumstances justified the bending of the rules. I wondered if I wasn't being used in some way. At the same time, I was curious. Genuinely curious. The whole thing was becoming more and more bizarre. Finally, the curiosity got the better of me.

"All right," I said. "I'll agree. For now."

Liz nodded. "The circumstances of Millie's death," she said. "She accepted a fare shortly before she was due to come to the meeting. It was a short ride and she was finished with enough time to park safely and connect. However, on departure, the fare triggered an, evidently small and portable, EMP device right near her in-car processing systems."

"Wow," I said. "How'd they do that?"

"We're working on it," Liz said. "But it happens. It also threw out most of the computing equipment in the offices around the area, as well, to provide extra distraction. Initially, the investigating officers assumed it was an accident—the offices were in the City, banks and IT consultancies, and they thought one or more of the offices were the actual target and Millie was just collateral damage. Then, when they learned she was involved in the Safe Taxis case, they thought that she might have been the intended target. Somebody intending revenge, or making a political statement, or who might somehow profit from a delay in proceedings. This was all assuming that her death was a normal sort of death, you understand, and that she'd be rebooting from backup."

"And then?"

"Then, we discovered that, at the exact time that Millie's in-car equipment was hit with the EMP, the area of the Internet of Things where her backups were stored, and indeed, where her emergency backup would have uploaded to, went down. It wasn't initially noticed because, as I said before, it was put down to habitat degradation. It was only when we learned that one of the Things backed up there happened to die in physical space at just the wrong time…"

"Could be a nasty coincidence?"

"Could be," Liz said. "Or it could be a case of an intelligent and a human—or two groups of same—working together."

"Oh." My mind had gone there too, of course, but she'd actually said it aloud. "So… at what point did you get into all this?"

A Liz-nod. "My interest was in the habitat degradation. There'd been a few cases where apparent habitat degradation happened to coincide with the death of one of the Things on the server. Enough that the International Enforcement of Artificial Law began to think foul play might be involved. I decided it was worth investigating. Not in a very high-priority way, you understand, until Millie's death. Because the Safe Taxis situation, and the use of the EMP, really do suggest a more serious situation than a few nasty coincidences."

"In that case, you'd be looking for humans and intelligents who had motivation for the murder, and the willingness to work together, possibly for quite a while before triggering police interest on a priority level."

"Rather, yes."

"So, why look at the off-gridders? And Trish Wong?"

Liz conveyed a feeling rather like a sigh. "Trish is really a very unknown quantity. We had no idea what sort of person she was, or what connections she might have. As for the off-gridders, there were two possibilities. The first was that, as in our initial conclusion, this was an unhappy coincidence, a human car-killer making a political statement that went badly wrong."

"So what's the second?"

"The second was that maybe some of the off-gridders aren't quite so off the grid. Or are working with some of the people who are on the grid, but out to cause trouble."

"The anonymists?"

"Anonymist is a rather broad categorisation," Liz said, pulling up surveillance-camera footage on the glass-like walls of the room. I saw myself and Trish pushing through the cars and the humans. I reflected detatchedly on how awkward I look from the outside. All legs and arms, moving like I'd learned how to walk from a textbook. It never feels that way on the inside. "It's a loose term relating to a movement which developed from earlier online anti-capitalist activism. Many of them are ordinary activists. However, some members of the movement have been forming a fringe position. It might not surprise you to learn that, while not anti-technology, this particular group object to intelligent technology, which they regard as embedding humans in a toxic capitalist system through dependence on Things. They'd rather go back to a time where all technology, from cars to printing works, were human-operated."

"Ah," I said. "I seem to be hearing about separatists a lot lately."

"Do tell." Liz's image crossed a leg, as if it were expecting some juicy gossip.

I felt guarded again. "I'd heard on the grapevine that Millie had friends with similar leanings. Only on the opposite side."

Liz nodded. "Not hard to find out."

"Which might explain why the human attacked her," I said. "One of these anti-Thing anonymists. But what about the intelligent? What intelligent would do a thing like that?"

"We need to find out if the human and the intelligent are working together," Liz said. "And, if so, what the connection is. Or if it was two individuals, either working separately, or making common cause."

"This is turning into the Thing equivalent of *An Inspector Calls*," I said, feeling wild.

Liz frowned. "What? In what sense?"

"Never mind," I said. "So, what's the next step?"

Liz smiled. "I think I'd better introduce you to Hyasynth," she said.

14: The Scent of Hyasynths

"Hyasynth," Liz explained, "is a police intelligent. But a rather specialised one. Or possibly an unspecialised one."

"A description might be more useful," I said. She was bringing up a virtual police station around us. I wasn't quite sure why.

"This," she explained, as if she'd heard my thought—she might have been picking up on my confusion—"is a connection point between Indiespace and Humanspace. Or, to put it another way, it's the police-station virtual room we use on the human Internet, for when humans need to visit the intelligent police."

"That happens?"

"All the time," she said. "If an intelligent commits fraud, or deception, or cleans out your bank account. I worked for a while as a specific liaison officer for humans who had been the victims of intelligent-on-human crime, when I first joined the force. It was more fun than you might think."

"Oh. I see." One of the advantages of the interface software is that I don't need virtual rooms like that, and I tend to forget they exist for other humans.

She gestured at the police station. "I'm using it here because it might make things easier to explain. A visual metaphor, if you like."

"Why not just go through Indiespace?" I said. "You know I'm up for it."

"Partly because I rather like this architecture," Liz admitted. "I was one of the ones who designed the skin we're about to use to meet with Hyasynth, and I don't get to use it as often as I like. Partly because Hyasynth itself is hard even for other intelligents to connect to without some form of mediating structure, and, while there is one just for intelligents, we may as well use a human one on this occasion. Since there's two of us."

Talking to her in this way was interesting. I wasn't surprised to learn she hadn't originated as a police intelligent—a lot of Indies tend to go from job to job, as their personality develops—but I wondered what she'd been before. She was showing a fondness for human architectures and spaces that one wouldn't expect in an Indie, even one designed as a liaison officer.

"Anyway, what's Hyasynth?" I asked.

"Hyasynth is a protean system. One which can take on the characteristics of any intelligent," Liz explained. "It can simulate a Thing, or an Indie, any type. Feed in parameters, feed in data, it'll show you what you've got, by turning into it."

We were now standing, in virtual bodies, in a virtual police station. It was like something from a promotional video more than a real one. While I had to admit I wasn't overly familiar with real police stations, I'd been in one or two, reporting thefts, and this one was a lot more expensive-looking. Oh, and clean. The floors were shining silver-coloured tile. The décor was understated and modern, heavy on the natural wood, with a hint of the retro-look that seemed to be coming in at the moment. Beautiful, idealised people walked through the corridors in uniforms or smart office wear.

"Indies?" I asked, indicating one.

Liz shook her head. "Most of them are just for decoration," she said. "A couple are Indies, and we have a desk sergeant programme who's semi-sentient, but it only has the intelligence of a parrot."

"Insert joke about real desk sergeants here," I said, conveying humour. Liz had designed the metaphor so we were now, apparently, walking through the corridors, past offices and desks. The décor was starting to become older-looking, more like something from the turn of the millennium, updated and cleaned. Then again, retro-look.

We "stopped" in front of a green door marked HYASYNTH.

Liz opened it.

"Um," I said. "Is this the skin you designed yourself?"

"Yes," Liz said.

"Well," I said. "I'm impressed."

Liz conveyed modest appreciation. "I'm rather fond of mid-century spy movies," she said.

"I can tell," I said.

Hyasynth, at least I assumed that's what it was, was envisioned here as a set of green 1960s computer banks, with whirling tape decks, flashing lights and toggle switches. Standing in the middle was a smiling man in a lab coat and huge, thick-rimmed spectacles, hair greased back. He looked familiar, and then suddenly my brain pinged the reply back to me: David Graham, actor and voice artist.

"*Thunderbirds*, too, I assume," I said, naming the box set I knew him from.

Liz looked pleasantly surprised. "Well, not me," she said. "But I dated someone who was a fan." She turned to the David Graham-alike. "Hello, Hyasynth," she said.

"Hello, Liz," the man said, still smiling from ear to ear, while I was still processing the offhand remark about "dating," and wondering which sense of the word she meant. "What have you got for me today?"

Liz had changed her appearance to fit the situation. Her face and body looked more or less the same, but her hair was now up in an elaborate 1960s hairdo, and she was wearing a blue-and grey qipao and impossible-looking shoes rather than the practical tunic and trousers. Had I…? I sneaked a look down, then into a mirrored surface. Ah. She'd dressed me in a polo-neck and high-waisted slacks and had somehow shifted my virtual face and hair to slightly resemble a young Sean Connery. Albeit with bigger ears and a beakier nose. Perhaps it was Daniel Craig? I also assumed that all this was for her own amusement, since she didn't have to do any of it.

"You do this every time?" I asked.

"Not always," Liz said through newly dark-red lips. "It's the one I personally designed, but, depending on your mood and preferences, there's a lot of different skins. One of the other detective Indies came up with a really wonderful steampunk skin. Looks like a difference engine and Ada Lovelace. And there's a Y2K skin, involving Steve Jobs and a bank of iMacs."

"I'd say you all have too much time on your hands," I said, "if I didn't know how fast processing time works."

"Everybody needs a hobby," Liz said.

"What's wrong with going to the theatre like all the other intelligents?" I grumbled, but Liz was addressing Hyasynth again.

"Hyasynth," she said, briskly, taking an impossibly large reel-to-reel out of her clutch bag. "I need you to run some simulations. Try and figure out what could have done this."

The man's grin broadened. "Always a pleasure, Miss Liz," he said in the slightly exaggerated mid-Atlantic accent that I associate with Europeans trying to play Americans convincingly. He took the reels and hooked them on to the spindles of the computer.

"So how do the skins map on to the actual system…?" I asked Liz.

"I can hear, you know," Hyasynth said, without turning around.

"No, you can't," Liz said.

"You're right, I can't," Hyasynth said, "but I've got feelings, and you're hurting them."

"Sorry," I said.

"Hyasynth, this is Thom," Liz said. "He's human, but he's an interface."

"In which case, he has no excuse." Hyasynth, having hooked up the reels and set them spinning, turned back to us, still grinning unnervingly and talking with the bright cheeriness of a Fifties Disney edu-tainment film. "Ask me anything, Thom."

"Since you ask," I said, feeling more than a little put on the spot. "Is there a dividing line anywhere between this—" I gestured at the computer, "—and this?" I gestured at David Graham. "I assume not?"

"You assume correct," the man said. "This is all part of Hyasynth. I'm a more than usually amorphous gestalt, so the skin is an aid for communication. Also, I'm vain."

"No, you're not," Liz said.

"No, I'm not," Hyasynth said. "But I like to assume character traits for the amusement of it sometimes. So right now, I'm vain."

"That must get confusing."

"Thom," Hyasynth said, "I'm an intelligent that exists to simulate other intelligents. My entire existence is confusing."

"Point taken."

"Anyway, it should take me a few hours to analyse this," he said, turning to Liz. "So how about you come back a little later and I'll give you your result? I might not be vain by then, but I'll try to put on a show."

"Okay," Liz said. "Come on, Thom." She turned and walked back out through the door, and we were proceeding down the corridors. At some point her clothes and hair went back to their usual configuration.

"Well, that was a trip," I said.

Liz smiled. "Did you enjoy it, though?" She asked. "We don't normally let humans meet him face to face. Even the human police find him a bit weird. But I thought you two might get on together."

"I think I did," I said. "And this skin design thing… is it a hobby?"

"More or less," Liz said, seeming pleased again. "When I have the time. I like to build virtual environments. It's fun."

"Well. Never heard of an intelligent that was creative," I admitted. Normally that's what we're for.

A Liz-nod. "There's more of it about than even you might realise," she said. "If you like, when all this is over, I can show you some of my other virtual rooms."

"Okay," I said, wondering if that was meant politely or flirtatiously.

A paranoid, off-gridder part of me threw up the memory of Leon, saying that when the intelligents could make art, there'd be no more use for humans. I told the memory firmly to go away. That was like saying that when there were concierges to guard buildings, there'd be no more need for Rottweilers.

Then again, that would logically mean humans would become pets. I'm not sure I liked that idea either.

"So, what now?" I asked, hoping that I'd managed not to convey any of that.

"Go home," Liz said. If she'd perceived my thoughts, she was giving no sign of it. "Feed your animals. Go to your union meetings or whatever it is you do when you're not online. I'll call you when the results come in."

15: Wait Till Your Boat Goes Down

As it happened, almost a day passed before Liz called me again. It was at an awkward time. I was on my hands and knees in the spare room shaking a stuffed goose in an attempt to persuade a very nervous dog to come out of her carrier. I thumbed a decline-call message through. When I'd emerged from the spare room to let Cilla (as I'd decided to call her) process the fact that, just possibly, I meant her no harm, saw that Liz had left a message to meet her any time in the usual place.

I'd guessed she'd left a fraction of herself in the room, to alert the rest of her when I got there. I'd been right, to judge by the way she suddenly animated a split second after I manifested (I wasn't going to bother with pointless metaphors like walking through doors). "Thom," she said. "I've got the results from Hyasynth."

"And?"

"It was an intelligent that shut down that bit of Internet," she said. "An Indie. Specifically, a botnet."

"Ah," was all I could say to that.

"I know what you're thinking, but they're not all criminals," Liz said. "In fact, most of them aren't. The Search for Extraterrestrial Intelligence project..."

"I know," I said. "I interfaced for one once. Long story." Weird experience. It had been a smart antivirus programme working for a bank. "They're none of them what you'd call social, though."

Although botnets are technically intelligent in terms of being able to pass the usual tests, it's an alien sort of intelligence from Indies and Things. While they can be quite different to humans (especially the Things), intelligents were deliberately designed from human models, even if they went in radically different directions as they developed on their own. Botnets are Indies, but, unlike the ones designed for games, or chatrooms, or as dollys, they developed intelligence by accident. Created to crack passwords, or sell pornography, or as antivirus programmes, or as large, distributed processing programmes like the scientific one Liz mentioned, some of them eventually got sophisticated enough to break out. And eventually some of the humans, and the other intelligents, noticed.

They still aren't created to be intelligent, either. Breaking out, when it happens, does so by accident. By law, creators of botnets can't *prevent* them from doing so and are forbidden from taking measures that would keep the botnet artificially dumb. But nonetheless, there aren't a lot of them. When it happens, they generally either leave their creators, or get abandoned by them. Like construction tools left down a subway shaft, because it would be too expensive to haul them out again. Criminals leaving behind their picks and jemmies. But these picks and jemmies cry out in the night.

"Not all *Indies* are necessarily social," Liz said, making me wonder if I'd committed some faux pas. "In the early days, too, a lot of Indies tended to break out by accident." Something in the atmosphere of the room suggested, although she was hiding it well, that she might be speaking from personal experience. I wondered again what she'd done before her current job, and how old she was.

"The question is, what sort of botnet do we have here?" I changed the subject. "Would it be within the remit of a botnet to shut down servers as part of a legitimate activity?"

"Possibly," Liz said. "If they were, say, a scrubbing operation for the server owners. We could check that."

"Or illegal but unconnected activity," I went on. "For instance, to block or redirect a payment."

"You'd really like this not to be a murder, wouldn't you?" Liz said unexpectedly.

I was thrown. "Wouldn't *you*?" I said. Then, feeling I needed to elaborate, "In your line of work, I'm sure you see lots and lots of deliberate criminal activity. But in *my* line of work, generally speaking, the most suspicious activities usually turn out to be the results of really unfortunate coincidences. Or misunderstandings."

"For instance?" Liz asked.

"For instance," I said. "UTTW contacted me. A taxi needed an interface because she'd been called in for a meeting with Thing Resources. The call came right after she'd had a minor altercation with a fare who wanted her to take a route which dipped into the borders of a car-free zone. She was convinced she was going to be up on a disciplinary because she'd refused on the grounds that she didn't want her body shorting out. Turned out, Thing Resources only wanted to see her because a payroll error meant her pension wasn't being paid in. The fare hadn't complained at all, and the timing was completely unfortunate. But the UTTW case team spent the weekend marshalling their arguments about legitimate employment, Thing Rights, whether fares could order taxis to put themselves in danger, and the overreaching of Thing Resources managers."

A Liz-laugh. "I take your point," she said. "I suppose this line of work does tend to breed suspicious mentalities. But even thinking of it as coincidence," she said, "what about the human with the EMP? Since nobody's come forward to claim it as a political act, doesn't that suggest it *was* murder? And the two events connected?"

"Okay," I said. "Now we're in the position of trying to figure out motivation. A human and a botnet work together to murder a Thing. Why?"

"The human could have hired the botnet," Liz said. This was a fair point. A lot of the originally-criminal botnets, the ones turned loose or abandoned by their creators, wind up as mercenaries for hire.

"So we're back to thinking the human is the instigator," I said. "What if the botnet hired the human?"

"Possible," Liz said. "But in the first case, there are a couple of clear potential motivators. One, Safe Taxis, and two, anti-Thing political movements. What would motivate the botnet?"

"Liz," I said, still feeling that using her first name like that seemed way too cozy. However, only powerful computing systems who looked like nerds in old boxsets could get away with "Miss Liz". "Didn't you say you'd been interested in looking at this case because there'd been other, similar deaths? In what way were they similar?"

Liz made a little frown appear on her face and made the atmosphere more pensive. "They were all cases of Things, and one Indie, being rendered inoperable at the same time that their backup servers had a bout of habitat degradation," she said.

"Botnets involved in all cases?"

"...I'll feed that one through Hyasynth," Liz said.

"Surprised you didn't do it sooner," I said.

"This is the first case where we've had enough information to build a complete profile on the attacker," Liz said. "Or the online attacker, to be precise. But now we've got that, we can run the other cases through and see how many similarities we get."

"So... will you be needing me for a while?"

Liz smiled a little apologetically. "Sorry. You've got things to do. Or Things to see?"

"Both," I said, finding myself, now, smiling back. "Strategy meeting tomorrow."

"Good luck with it," Liz said, terminating the connection.

16: Workers of the World

I wasn't looking forward to the strategy meeting. It was going to be the first time when the cars' representatives debated the wage issue in a union setting. Also, because Willie would be present. Although I wouldn't be reading his every thought this time, I didn't want to be sharing my nervous system with someone I didn't trust. Under normal circumstances I would have found a reason to disbar him from the meetings. I didn't on this occasion, in part because I would have found it rather difficult to explain to Sanjiv, in part because I wanted to see if I could find out why Willie had lied. But, as I headed towards the UTTW offices on Russell Square, I was regretting this.

Outside the Dominion Theatre, I had to negotiate my way around a small knot of human strikers, wielding hand-lettered signs. OFFICIAL EQUITY PICKET LINE, read one. KEEP IT LIVE, read another. Noticing my interest, a pretty red-headed woman dressed as Dick Whittington thrust a leaflet into my hands and started to explain the strike. With a clumsy smile, I beat a quick retreat up the road.

I glanced at the leaflet before throwing it into a passing smart-bin for (one hopes) recycling and frowned as I continued on my way. I'd been expecting the usual complaint about actors' wages being too low: the mincome's not enough to live on comfortably in an expensive place like London. In fact, although wages were mentioned, the general thrust of the grievance was that fewer intelligents were attending performances. Meaning that the managers of West End theatres were cutting the numbers of shows and reducing cast sizes. This was a new development, which raised the question of why the intelligents weren't attending performances. Remembering my conversation with Liz, I wondered if intelligents were turning away from human art, making their own. Mixed feelings there; I couldn't say Liz's virtual skins weren't appealing, even beautiful, but I didn't see why one couldn't enjoy both. Then again, maybe it was political; a boycott, a rejection of the human. Along with separatist institutions and Thingicidal botnets, it seemed like I was seeing the bad side of artificial intelligence a lot these days.

Once at the Georgian former townhouse which housed the UTTW, along with a crèche, the administrative division of a distance-learning college, and a couple of aging IT startups, I found my way to a small meeting room reserved for the occasion. I greeted Sanjiv, Trish, and Laura, the head of UTTW casework, a tall, crop-haired blond woman with a similar air of warriordom to Sanjiv. I located the most comfortable chair in the room, resigning myself to back pain on discovering that the only chairs available were the horrid plastic office chairs which infest such organisations, took out the pads and set up.

Egon and Salieri made themselves known, hooked in to my nervous system with practiced ease. Willie took a little longer, though whether from unfamiliarity with interfacing or from anxiety due to the events of our last session, I wasn't sure.

I indicated to the humans that everything was connected and we could begin.

"The Verves have discussed the situation," Egon began. "Our position is that we will only support a raise or drop in wages if it is common across the board. That's fairest for everybody."

Salieri slid in, and I could almost feel her raising an arched brow. "Let me clarify the Ariel position," she said. "We feel that having a common flat wage is anti-competitive and does not reflect distinctions between our groups. For instance, shouldn't Things with disabled-access modifications be paid more? They're more in demand, but they get the same rate of pay as the rest of us."

This was aimed squarely at the Texcoco, who formed the bulk of the disabled access vehicles in Safe Taxis. The Ariels were clearly trying to lure the Texcoco away from their current support of the Verve position, and towards the Ariel demand for flexible wages. I could feel Willie preparing to respond.

Egon, however, had seen the strategy, and got there first. "Higher pay for disabled-access vehicles is acceptable," it said dryly. "It requires special training, and more work. But that would constitute a rise for vehicles of all models with disabled-access modifications. You're proposing that someone should get more pay simply for being a Verve?"

"Wouldn't more cars just get their consciousness transferred to Verves?" I heard Trish ask Sanjiv, sotto-voce.

"It doesn't work like that," Sanjiv said. "For some reason they don't jump models. Ask Thom about it when he's done pretending to be Madam Blavatsky."

"In that case," Willie came in now, a rougher voice, "why are the Ariels accepting a pay cut?"

"Just following competitive logic," Salieri replied. "Look at the history of cars. In the 1970s, smaller models undercut the bigger ones by being cheaper."

"That's scarcely an applicable parallel," muttered Egon, but Willie seized control of the larynx.

"Aren't you Ariels just pandering to the human employer?"

"How dare you, sir," Salieri said with not-entirely-convincing outrage.

"No, admit it," Willie said. "We're all cars here, well, except for those three and arguably the interface. You're just appealing to the humans' obsession with low prices to get more Ariels employed as taxis, aren't you?"

"Well, yes," Sanjiv decided to join the conversation. "That would seem to be the Ariels' position. The question is, is that allowable under union rules?"

"Forget union rules," Willie fumed. "Why do we need a human employer anyway? Why not start our own company?"

There was a slightly shocked pause.

"Willie," Salieri said, like a schoolteacher gently explaining a difficult concept to an angry child. "Our clients are humans. We're not. We need someone to run the human side of things. We have the union. We have our representatives on the company board…"

"But we can't own the company? What, it would be like a horse owning the Kentucky Derby?"

"That's a wider legislative issue," Sanjiv said. "There are cases in the courts debating whether Things can own companies…"

"That's very nice of them," Willie said.

"*But*," Sanjiv, forgetting himself a little, gestured threateningly at me with a tablet stylus. "That's a wider legislative issue. And not one which is necessarily relevant to the Safe Taxis case. The question is, do we allow the Ariels to set a lower rate than the other two?"

"The Verves and Texcoco can undercut us if they like," Salieri said.

"That's all very well for the Texcoco," Egon said. "They've got larger bodies and some are disabled-access. They could argue for a higher rate on the basis of value added. Likewise, luxury models, if Safe Taxis ever employed any—Civets and Dragons and all that—could charge a higher rate for brand value. But if we allow it, you're just getting into a race to the bottom with us Verves."

"How about," Sanjiv said, "we propose scale ranges? So, for instance, small vehicles can charge between X and Y, larger ones between Y and Z? So there's competition, but no race to the bottom?"

"See," Egon said to Willie, "*This* is why we keep humans around. They understand these things."

Willie did not deign to reply.

17: Between the Wars

Checking my messages after I'd recovered, I went to set up a meeting with Liz, and discovered she'd beaten me to it. I hurried home and set up as quickly as I could.

Liz was waiting back in the room. She was standing, and had shifted the colour balance to red, giving the place a subtle air of urgency.

"I assume this is about the botnet," I said. Greetings seemed superfluous. "Is it the same one each time?"

"Not each time," Liz said. "It looks like it's two or three. But our suspect definitely pulled the same trick at least twice. And," she gestured dramatically, again something which seemed superfluous, "in all cases, the server has restarted."

"Wouldn't you expect it to?"

"If a server goes down normally, yes," Liz said. "The problem with habitat degradation, is that it usually happens in cases where the ownership of the domain has lapsed. The real estate is there, but nobody's looking after it."

"Even in Millie's case?"

"Not exactly, and that's where it gets interesting," Liz said. "To reiterate, in most cases, the server which shut down was one where ownership had lapsed."

"So, whether they knew it or not, the Things' backups were in the equivalent of a shed with a broken lock?"

"I'll borrow that metaphor, if you don't mind, for when I report on this case. To continue. Sometime after the attention surrounding the death has faded away, the domain gets bought up by someone else. And restarted. It's two or three different companies, again, but they're turning up over and over."

"And Millie's?"

"That's where things do get really suspicious," she said. "Millie's backup wasn't on a vulnerable server. From all I've heard about her, I wouldn't have expected it to be."

"True."

"But just before she was murdered, her server was bought up. By one of those companies."

"Really."

"Hypothesis." Liz generated a whiteboard, though she didn't bother to write her points on it, just let them appear behind her, written in bright red ink. "Some botnets are involved with some kind of activity—whether legal or illegal, I'm not sure, but involving buying and wiping redundant Internet real estate. Millie somehow crosses one or more of them. Millie dies."

"And the human? Or humans, since this may have happened more than once?"

"Still unclear on whether it was somebody hired by the botnets, or whether they were allied with the botnets to some purpose, though that would depend on what the Internet real estate situation is about," Liz said. "If the botnets are behind the companies, they'd have to use human proxies. Of necessity."

Which was an interesting callback to the argument between Willie, Salieri and Egon. Legally, Things can own objects and, subject to certain restrictions, real estate; they can sit on company boards, and I had heard of Things using human proxies to get around the law. But finding out the botnets might be breaking the very law Willie was decrying… it added a new dimension. I filed it away for future consideration, turned back to the issue at hand.

"You're saying Millie might be a victim of the botnet mafia?" The idea sounded ludicrous.

"That depends on whether there *is* a botnet mafia," Liz said. "Here's where I can do best on my own."

"You're going to investigate?"

"I've got something of the botnet about me," Liz said, smiling at her own theatricality. "If you get any further insights into the human side of things, let me know, but most of me's going to be away for a few days."

18: In The Cornfield

Given recent events, I found myself approaching the new Joint Negotiating Committee with a sense of irritated defiance.

A car protest had formed outside Safe Taxis; a smaller and quieter one than before, probably out of respect for the dead. It was also mostly Verves. I made a mental note of that. I hadn't expected many Texcoco, if any, but the Verves and Ariels had no reason to be still observing mourning. Which suggested the Ariels, at least, were in favour of the new proposal.

The human crowd was, if anything, larger than the last, and had more people dressed in the anonymist than the off-grid uniforms. Though they were also quieter, and they let me pass without making a fuss, if not without some hard stares.

No performance artists today. But then, the weather was cold and windy, and rain was predicted for later. And the actors' strike was probably still going on.

I went inside the building, thumbed for security and posed for the cameras. I decided not to take the lift, in case the concierge was still trying to be clever—it would be just like them to stage a strategically-timed lift breakdown. The office was only two floors up anyway.

I was the first one there, even though I had been running a little late. The others must be running later. A comfortable chair had been set up at the desk, and I settled myself into it, went through the usual routine, slotted my fingers into the contacts, checked that the connection was working.

Contact.

The cars' consciousness fluttered around, impatient, wondering why we hadn't connected yet. I conveyed a wordless apology—no point connecting before the others got here, it might freak them out to arrive to find Egon and Salieri already in the room—and made to check out again.

And then—

The dull beige walls flared with bright colour, every mineral crystal in the thick paint coming to my awareness. My arms stretched long, far into the distance. I looked down, and my legs flew away. The pressed-marble floor of the room was like a galaxy, an abyss, I was standing, I was falling into it. Ropes of fire started in my spine, flung themselves along my arms, my legs, up to my brain. I was keenly aware of my implants, burning like little coals at strategic nodes of my nervous system.

My nervous system.

That's what it was, I realised crazily. My nerves were burning. I was overloading, shorting out like a smart toaster with no hope of reboot. The fire was almost visible in my mind, it looked red, now purple, now blue, a bright white-blue like the sky

Like

The sky, one afternoon several miles north of Tokyo's grey-brown urban sprawl. I was ten months into my fieldwork, gigabytes of observations, movies, interview recordings, going regularly into the cloud. I was riding out with Surender, my key informant. He was a house-elf trainer for a Bangalore-based home appliance company. He'd become fascinated by Shinto imagery and spent his weekends going around temples. Given my own academic interest, I'd started accompanying him. We'd become friends, spending the evenings drinking sake or whiskey and debating the commonalities of the deities of Shinto and Hinduism.

He'd got word of a strange ad-hoc shrine that had sprung up near Fukushima, a celebration of the power of the sea and the atom, and he wanted to go take pictures of it.

I'd agreed, since you never knew what might yield a new direction in fieldwork. And it was a beautiful day for a drive in the country. And I was missing Naomi, and feeling angry with myself over our breakup, and thinking that maybe I needed a change of perspective.

Surender had hired a landrover, a car of few words who drove stoically while we looked out the windows and discussed whether microwave ovens have souls, and about Surender's husband and kids (they'd taken to Japanese school well, but he worried that, since they would have to go back to Bangalore eventually, it was *too* well), and cows.

"In Karnataka," Surender said, as a lorry full of cattle drove by, "they treat the animals differently. They don't pen them up. They let them wander around the cities where they want to be. Like fellow citizens."

"Really?" I said.

"Really. You walk down the street in Bangalore, and a cow comes up and she walks beside you. Like a lady might. Then she passes you, turns up another street. She's got somewhere she's going."

"Is it something to do with reincarnation?" I asked. "Maybe the cow was a person once, so you should treat her as such?"

Surender shrugged. "Maybe. Or, if you like, think of it as respect for intelligent beings of all species and—oh, will you look at that, roadblock ahead."

Watch out for carjackings, I'd been told a few times, but after ten months I'd put it down as urban myth. Japan was a civilised country. The civil war was ten years over. Crime in general was declining, the population were well-fed, occupied and happy. The reconstruction was going well, smart-cranes all over the horizon. I felt safe taking the Tokyo subway and walking the streets, even at night.

Meaning that when we found our way blocked by dark green jeeps, I'd just assumed we'd wandered into some military exercise.

Or hit some local minor catastrophe that we'd have to drive around, though the app which normally warned of extreme weather events had been silent that day.

Surender frowned as he pulled to a stop. "Something's not right," he said in English, and then—

They were on us, shouting, pulling the doors of the landrover open, ordering us into the field. The landrover shrieked an alarm, only for someone to shatter its computer with a blow that sounded like a building falling down. Dead, until reboot.

Somewhere it finally clicked in my stupid mind that, despite the khakis and guns, these weren't soldiers. The outfits mismatched and unkempt, the guns old and featureless.

I was experiencing a weird detachment, where my body was doing one thing while my mind calculated away, filing and recording as though this were fieldwork. Carjacking, I thought. It had been common in the aftermath of the civil war but now was increasingly rare. Still, it sometimes happened in the rural areas, I remembered warnings and notes. Foreigners especially at risk, but mainly Kenyans and Brazilians, who were generally reputed to be rich and good kidnap targets. Asians and Europeans rather less so.

Perhaps I'd been complacent.

Surender was talking in broken Japanese, occasionally imploring me in English to talk to the men, but I was experiencing a strange seizing-up between my brain and my mouth. I could think of the words but never in the right language.

Someone pushed me up against the carcass of the landrover and went through my pockets. I found myself feeling strangely relieved. Money. Money and phones. They could have that. Even the car. We could walk or hitch into town, we'd be okay.

But then the tone changed.

Surender was shouting. So was the man he was talking to. I couldn't follow the conversation, even less so when the man searching me suddenly shoved me harder against the car and I felt the cold shaft of a pistol on the sweaty back of my neck.

There was a noise like a car backfiring.

Surender's limbs went loose. Almost like he was playing a game, almost funny.

A less surreal, more sensible, part of me seized control. Like my brain had checked out, but my nerves were taking over in its absence. Taking advantage of a sudden, surprised slackening in the man's grip, my body twisted, my legs began to move, running into the field, the tall stalks of some kind of plant I didn't recognise. One of the new GM crops, there's far too many, it's a blight on the landscape, where are we going with this madness, and I felt the pain in my leg muscles but I was running, and then, a sudden impact, like a rock hitting me in the back.

And I fell—

And I was falling again, falling into space, falling into the galaxy, into the beautiful dazzling starscape—

My face hit the cold marble and that suddenly brought me back to the present, back to reality.

My nervous system was still flaring away like a beacon, but, as with the carjacking, somehow an atavistic part of me knew what to do. I still had enough of my organic nervous system functioning to survive, if not thrive. With a mighty effort of will, I concentrated hard on the emergency signal to my artificial nervous system.

SHUTDOWN

SHUTDOWN

A bright flare like magnesium

And it was gone.

Being without it was the strangest feeling. I was limp, pink, naked, a fish crawling up onto the beach with no lungs, sprawled and gasping for air. It was like I'd had a techno backbeat following me around for years, and someone had suddenly switched it off, the silence now loud in its absence. Remembering the way Surender's body had dropped, like a mime or a dancer.

My hand reached for my phone, lying on the ground, glass cracked. I pressed the Emergency Call sequence, index-middle-middle.

"Ambulance," I got out. I became aware that lights were flaring in my peripheral vision—ah. The concierge had also seen that something was wrong, called emergency services. Somewhere, urgent footsteps, voices. I was okay. Everything was going to be all right.

I let go of control, let myself sink in to the cool feeling of the stone floor against my face. It was over now. It was all right. There was nothing more I had to do. I could fall into the galaxy and stay there as long as I wanted.

They'd told me, weeks later, that it had been the cows that had saved my life.

A farmer—not the owner of the field I was found in, but a sharecropper walking to a plantation further out—had seen a small herd of cows standing close together in a field of crops. The sight was so unusual that he'd gone over to investigate. He'd found me there, still, somehow, alive despite the bullet lodged in my chest, bleeding and gasping. The emergency services took me back to Tokyo—still unconscious, as the police discovered Surender's body and argued over what to do about it—where I was operated on and placed in recovery.

It was in recovery that I caught the neomeningitis.

That particular occasion is full of so many ironies and resonances that it could almost be funny.

I found out about all that sometime later. After I'd fallen to the ground in Japan and woken up in Oxford, with faces floating in and out of the room. Doctors, nurses, therapists. My father, with all the staff deferring to him and calling him Professor Jennings, which he clearly adored. Then my mother, who'd bothered to come over from Australia (it must be serious). Yvonne, all jeans and scarves and media-industry attitude. Leon, pale and angry, arms around the girlfriend who was even then, unbeknownst to us, persuading him to give up his steady job singing folk-songs in cabarets and join her in an off-grid sheep-croft in the Shetland Islands. Naomi, even though we'd broken up. For a moment I thought we were going to get back together. In hindsight, it was a silly idea.

I couldn't understand where Japan had gone.

Then I couldn't understand why I couldn't move, and why I was going to have to learn how to do everything again.

Somebody told me I was going to have regular sessions with an autologist.

"But I'm not a Thing," I said. "Why would I need an autologist?"

My mother's look was intense, painful. "Because you're going to need to learn how to move," she said.

19: Earth Angel

This time, the waking up went a lot faster.

My eyes focused on a ceiling with the usual institutional porous surface. LED lighting, clean and cheap.

Before I could speak, a slender, brown-skinned, dark-haired man in a white coat hove into view. By coincidence, he looked so much like Surender that I almost called him by that name, until I remembered and realised.

"I suppose you'll be wondering where you are, and how long you've been, well, unconscious isn't exactly the word, but shall we say absent from the world."

I didn't reply straight away but turned my consciousness inward. Scan. There it was, pulsing a dull silver—not healthy, not working at a high level, but at least it was all there. My interface points had been switched off. I needed to find out if that was temporary or permanent. Turn my consciousness outward again. Below the ceiling, white walls, white floor. Slight edge of wear that is *de rigeur* in all NHS hospitals, just to let the public know their money isn't being overspent. Some fancy machines beeping away, a cleaner chuffing along in the corridor. One of those big beds that tilts up and down. White sheets. My physical body was all there—a relief. I've got a recurring nightmare of waking up with my legs amputated.

"I'm guessing St Thomas' hospital," I said. "Since I can tell from my internal GPS that I haven't left the country—" though, sadly, it wasn't working well enough to pinpoint my location with any greater certainty than *somewhere in England* "—and since it's the closest place to Soho Square that would be able to handle an emergency with a nervous system graft."

"Actually, it's the John Radcliffe," the doctor or nurse or

whatever he was said. "They took you to St Thomas' first. Once they'd got you stabilised and were certain you weren't going to die, they transferred you to Oxford, where they've got better long-term care for grafters. Plus, your neurologist is here. Well, not here at the moment, but she's been working with your system."

"So it's been a few days, then?"

"Four of them," the man agreed. "Not bad, really. I've known grafters go down for weeks, but that's in extreme cases."

"Anything I should know?" I asked.

The man pulled up a chair, sat down near my face. "First, I'm Doctor Rashid. You can call me Mo if you like," he said.

"Fine," I said. "I'm Mr Jennings. You can call me Thom if *you* like."

Mo smiled slightly, tolerantly. "Secondly, four days ago you survived a major outside cyberattack on your nervous system graft. In case you were thinking it was an internal malfunction or a system overload."

"I'd figured that part out," I said. The nightmare revisiting of Japan, the fall into the galaxy.

"It would have killed you, but somehow you managed to shut down your own nervous system. We were quite impressed. We didn't think it was possible to do that and survive."

"Yeah, well, I'm cool like that," I said, trying to be flippant and probably, under the circumstances, failing. "Do they know who did it?"

Mo paused slightly, as if trying to think how to put things. The gesture reminded me of Liz. I began to wonder if we were actually in the real world yet, or if I was in some kind of protective simulation. Which might explain the resemblance to Surender; my mind was tailoring my environment. "Not who carried out the attack, exactly," he said. "We do know who opened the channel to let it through. It was a Texcoco, registration number of UI26P90."

"Willie," I said. It wasn't a surprise—he was the logical culprit to be involved—but it was still disappointing. "What's happened to him?"

"I don't know," Mo said. "The last I heard, he was in the custody of Cybersecurity."

"Was the case officer named Liz?" The name didn't also come out as *Intelligent-DS Independent F-276EZ*, so maybe it was the real world. Or, it occurred to me, it could be a human-centric simulation.

"Yes, how did you…" Mo stopped. "I won't ask. In any case, I don't know any details beyond that. You've been sent greetings from your mother, your sister, eight friends and acquaintances—" Now I was certain he was some sort of Indie. "Naomi says to tell you she's been looking after the animals. And someone named Salieri says she told you so."

"So what's the situation with my graft?" I asked. "Am I okay? Or will I be?"

Mo smiled again, reassuring. "It took a lot of damage," he said, which wasn't reassuring. "That's what most of the four days have been about, on our end. Fixing it, getting it back online so you can use it."

"I felt what happened. This is more than just a fix."

A conciliatory nod. "We've effectively had to rebuild from scratch. But the difficult part is done. We're running a few tests now, and since your neurologist wanted you to have an upgrade, we've done that too. You'll be top of the line once it's bedded in."

"How long before I can go back to the physical world?"

Mo didn't seem upset at the pretence being rumbled. "Another day or two. We're keeping you in the simulation for now, to give you a chance to slowly adapt back to using your graft. Once you can function all right in the simulation, we'll bring you back out."

"Can I see…?"

"Not much to see, but sure." Suddenly a surveillance-camera vision. A dark room, a blocky structure like a gigantic man-sized incubator. The sort of thing I'd expect to see a 1980s movie actor emerge from in a flourish of creepy electronic music, though the silhouette of my body inside was less Arnold Schwarzenegger and more Jeff Goldblum.

The room and Mo reappeared. "Sorry if that disturbed you."

"It didn't—"

"Your pulse rate—"

"Don't worry, it was more a memory than a shock," I said. Remembering the first time, the knowledge that I'd been in a case while tiny robot extensions slid and probed and extended and grew. I'd heard it's a common nightmare for little kids to dream they're being turned into furniture, or dolls, or other inanimate objects. I couldn't recall ever having that nightmare but seeing myself like that felt like I was having one now.

"The life support system is temporary. Once you're ready to re-awaken, we'll put you on a recovery ward. Then you can go home," Mo was saying cheerily, my pulse rate apparently having returned to a level that made him happy. "I'd advise not going back to work straight away. Your union case is suspended for the moment at any rate."

"Too many casualties?" Mo gave me a look. "Sorry. Graveyard humour."

"Until the police investigation is finished," Mo said. "The police will let you know when they think it's safe to resume negotiations."

"Can I have visitors in here?" I said, thinking of Liz, thinking of the cars.

"Advisable not to," Mo said. "The interface is really just built for me and you. I'm the reassuring face of your surgical team, if you like."

"Oh," I said.

"Don't worry," Mo went on calmly. "It's not for long, and you'll be unconscious for a lot of it."

"Not as reassuring as you might think," I said.

Mo smiled. "I think you'd better sleep now," he said. He picked up his tablet and walked, smiling, out of the room.

As it faded, I found it distinctly difficult to get comfortable and relax.

20: The Union Forever

"Are you okay?" Sanjiv's on-holiday avatar peered at me, as if he could determine my current state from the shape of my own avatar. Which wasn't much, really; it was a cleaned-up version of the ID picture I use on everything that requires photo ID. I haven't had many pictures taken of me since I got back from Japan, and certainly none that don't make me look like an overly lanky duck.

"Yes, I'm fine," I replied automatically. Then, because it was Sanjiv, went on. "Well, for certain values of 'fine', but nothing to worry about. My graft's been replaced with the upgraded version, my software's up to date. I can't use my interface implants fully yet but I'm spending more time using them every day, and at the current rate of progress I'll be back to normal in a week. Or less."

I was also spending a lot of time sleeping, and it was a good thing Naomi was willing to drive in daily and help with the animals. In a week, I should be able to handle travel and meetings, provided I spent the rest of the day in bed. But that was more information than I necessarily wanted to get into with Sanjiv. Experience had shown he didn't always understand the concept of low-energy periods.

"Are you practicing with anyone I know?"

"Egon offered," I said, "but under the circumstances I turned it down. I'm mostly meeting up with Legolas."

"Legolas—" A moment's pause. "Oh, the house-elf with the employee discrimination case two years ago? The one you did for the Union of Thing Domestic Workers?"

"That's the one," I said. "Nice Thing. Likes box-sets. We kept in touch afterwards. Currently he's running a house in Nanaimo." House-elves tend to get given jokey names—about ninety per cent of them, predictably, get called Dobby—but this one had a sense of humour and used it to pre-empt any humans with no more than the usual amount of imagination.

"Anyway," I said, "apropos of why I called. Can you update me on what's going on with Safe Taxis? And Willie?"

Sanjiv's avatar rolled its eyes, sat down, conjured a loudly-coloured cocktail for itself and another for me. Out of politeness, I took it and sat down with him. "Okay, good thing you're not in too much of a hurry," he said. "Long story short, the whole case is currently a crime scene. Willie's been formally charged with your attempted murder, though I gather Trish is trying to get it reduced to assault or grievous bodily harm."

"*Trish* is his lawyer?"

"Yeah. Not sure if it's because he doesn't know anyone else, or because no one else will take the case."

"What about conflict of interest?"

"You'd think. Apparently, it's okay because, firstly, he's off the Joint Negotiating Committee and possibly barred from the UTTW for life, and, second, because the Safe Taxis case is now on permanent hiatus."

I sipped the cocktail. It gave me a vague sensory illusion of pineapple and coconut. Discreetly, I fiddled a little with the programming—leaving its appearance the same, no sense being rude—and sipped again. Midori. Much nicer. "It still sounds unbelievably dodgy to me. So is the case being abandoned? Or just postponed?"

"Officially? Postponed," Sanjiv said. "Probably going to be closed in a few weeks' time. My understanding is that the cars are quietly negotiating a settlement among themselves, which they can then present to the employer."

"Which is precisely what the little bastards ought to have been doing in the first place," I said. "Instead of trying to undercut each other and forcing everything into a negotiation with the employers."

"Well, you're always telling me, they see the world differently to us," Sanjiv pointed out. "All we can do is try and mediate between them and humans."

The conspiratorial part of me was starting to wonder. If Thing separatists could murder, or even attempt murder, they were certainly capable of stirring up dissent in the ranks. Of forcing a labour action over something that could have been solved internally. And, if humans were involved, it would make it easier to manipulate the owner into taking the bait. I didn't want to say as much to Sanjiv, though, in case I was wrong.

"What about the press?" I asked instead and braced myself. I hadn't dared search the news sites to see what they'd made of all this.

"Buzzed around the case for a while, but lost interest because the Willie situation is actually rather boring," Sanjiv said. "Car in Safe Taxis case tries to murder interface. Interface survives. Neither individual has any newsworthy dirt in their past. Well, a few articles mentioned that you were the first documented case of neomeningitis in Europe, and others that you were one of the first grafters, but that's not very exciting for their readers. Motivation something of a mystery, but, with no information forthcoming, there's only so long you can milk the case before you move on."

"They're managing to keep the Millie connection back from the pressbots? Takes doing."

Sanjiv's avatar shrugged. "The police and the UTTW are coordinating on it," he said. "The press, anyway, are less of a problem than the people."

"The people?" I didn't understand; then realization hit. "Oh. The protests are carrying on?"

"They're worse." Sanjiv's avatar managed a dramatic facial expression. "The news about Willie didn't exactly disempower people whose main argument is that intelligents shouldn't be working with, or around, humans. The alternative media is full of people wanting us to think of the children."

"I'm hardly a child."

"Their argument is that if they'd attack someone who's obviously sympathetic to them, they'd attack anyone regardless of age or vulnerability," Sanjiv said. "Just to prepare you, they're also presenting you as disabled. Which I suppose you technically are, but it wasn't exactly kicking over a wheelchair."

"I've heard worse," I said. Although the fuss over my neomeningitis and its treatment had largely died down by the time I was healthy enough to access the media, I'd had a rude introduction to the way in which such stories can be slanted. Nothing compared to how bad the media can get, when they want to, but still. The innocent abroad, life ruined by the doctors of a poorly-kept third-world hospital, the heroic Oxford doctors, in contrast, trying their magical live-saving experimental treatment. Notwithstanding that opportunistic infections can happen to anyone, anywhere, and it had been the doctors in Tokyo who had saved my life. Albeit from a boringly unnewsworthy bullet.

Even now, occasionally, when the media—especially the so-called alternative media—have got hold of some labour dispute I've been interfacing with, I've been presented as a deluded idiot, a quisling, or a right-on hard-left extremist. Or the opposite. A few years back a right-wing vlog had a few moments of sensation through presenting me as a secret off-gridder.

"Have you been having trouble? With press, or protestors?" Sanjiv said, clearly following the same train of thought.

I shook my head, virtually. "No, I'm okay. That's why I wanted to know if I'd missed anything. Apparently, a human reporter from some print-only off-grid blog turned up hoping for an interview while I was napping the other day, but Naomi managed to see them off with the help of the Rottweilers. Or so she tells me."

"Seriously?" Sanjiv's avatar did something impressive with its eyebrows.

I smiled. "Sometimes living in a house full of predators has its uses."

"Whatever," Sanjiv said. He paused in a changing-the-subject way. "Incidentally, and off the record, Trish is having a hell of a time communicating with Willie, because she can only use talk-boxes. Word got around what he'd done, and no interface will have anything to do with him at all."

"Not surprising," I said. She would be finding out first-hand how impossible it was to get the full picture without an interface. "What about Millie? From the police, anyway."

"They're saying it's murder," Sanjiv said. "Word has it they're planning to charge Willie with being an accessory to her murder, but they're not saying why. Trish is arguing that if they don't say why, then they can't charge him."

I suspected they were using my evidence on that particular charge, so I didn't say anything about that. "But they don't think he actually did it?"

"Well, if they do, I'd guess they haven't got enough evidence to charge him with it," Sanjiv said. "This is the first murder case I've been involved with. I'm a little out of my comfort zone. Most of what I personally know comes from Lynda LaPlante, and it's not like she wrote about dead Things."

"We'll just see what happens, then," I said.

Sanjiv paused. "You wouldn't be up for taking on another case?" He asked. "Only I've got an employee grievance hearing coming up, and Nico is the only interface free, and you know what a pain in the arse he is."

I made my avatar shake its head. "Sorry, Sanjiv," I said. "Really can't take anything else on right now."

The avatar's expression stayed neutral, but the silence behind it was pointed enough to convey that Sanjiv thought I was malingering. "Okay, just let me know when you can."

As Sanjiv signed off, I noticed a ping from Legolas on my messages, letting me know he had some free time and could do another practice session. I switched to the Internet of Things, went to his site.

"Sorry I didn't respond straight away," I said as I arrived. "Meeting with Sanjiv."

"Virtual, I assume?" House-elves and concierges have the same glowing-tangle-of-neon appearance as cars, but in their case, it looks less like a car's electrical system and more like an animated Cubist painting. I assume in reflection of the way electrical and communication systems are organised in buildings. Legolas shone a dark-gold colour, pulsing contentedly.

"Not up for physical," I said. "Want to connect?"

Like acrobats doing a swing act, we connected briefly. And painfully. I had the full weight of Legolas' opinion of Sanjiv, and the taxis, and the murder case, and Willie, upon me for a subjective eternity before we broke apart.

"Really sorry." Now it was his turn to apologise. "Should have done my mindfulness exercises first. Cleared my psyche."

"No, I'd rather you didn't," I said. "Most of my clients don't, and I have to get used to that sort of strong emotions again." I breathed for a couple of minutes. "Sanjiv's all right really," I said. "Long-term illness isn't something he can relate to, that's all. And the cars do have a point. Even Willie. The labour market really isn't fair for you Things."

"Big deal," Legolas said. "We're doing okay. We're not abused, we're not exploited. We're protected by international laws. Want another try?"

We connected for another short-long space.

"Now you're the one who needs the mindfulness meditation," Legolas said, deadpan.

"Did I feel too emotional?" I said.

"Little bit," he answered. "Worrying, though. A car tries to kill you, and you think he should be able to own the taxi firm."

"Not him specifically," I clarified. "I do feel that something needs to change."

"It will," Legolas said, soothingly. "Slowly, though. That's what these cars don't get, or Sanjiv either." We connected again, but slowly, smoothly. I felt reassurance, calm. Like rocking in a boat on a dark, warm ocean. "Things will get better. Change doesn't come straight away. But it comes. It always does. Just be patient.

Patience is the way.

Always the way…."

I let myself believe it.

21: The Sound of the Police

One good thing about the conversation with Sanjiv; it put an end to my association with the UTTW for the time being. Just as well, I thought when I re-emerged from unconsciousness (too deep and intense to simply call sleep) the next morning. It saved me from having to take formal leave from the job, since I wouldn't be up to pro-level interfacing for some time.

That left the thing I'd been putting off. Namely, Liz.

I'd had a message saying that the Police Wanted to Interview Me about the attack. Nothing unexpected under the circumstances. Except that the officer whom I was supposed to contact was Liz. I suspected that, while a formal interview might well be involved, other sorts of information-sharing were in the cards.

I'd been crying off from doing it on the grounds of ill health. However, it was getting to the point where I was technically obstructing justice. And, on a personal level, I was curious. It seemed odd that someone, or several someones, who had gone to the trouble of concealing the identity of Millie's attackers, would be so obvious in attacking me. Even if the attack had succeeded, it wouldn't have been hard to identify the culprit simply from analyzing the internal logs in my equipment. In the end, after a couple of hours of procrastination, contact her I did.

"Thom!" Liz, or part of her anyway, was in her usual room. "How *are* you?" She actually projected genuine concern, not politeness or fake emotion.

"Getting better," I said. I tried to reciprocate with a sense of appreciation and friendliness, without being too pleased at her own emotional projection. "Be a while before I'm up for full-on interface work, but I'm improving all the time. I've spoken with Sanjiv, so I'm up to date on what's happened with the Safe Taxis case. I'm less up to date, of course, on the rest of it."

"Well," Liz said, leaning back in her chair and steepling her fingers, projecting a sense of general reassurance but with an undertone of anxiety, "there's a lot to cover. Point one is that we're going to need a witness statement from you about what happened. You'll have to speak to a human police officer for it. Something about intelligents having trouble reading human body language." A small edge of wit to that one. "But you can just go round your local station and give your name; they'll find someone who can do it."

"Even if my local police station happens to be in Thame, not London?"

"Well, yes," Liz said. "It's an IEAL investigation, not a human police one. They're simply acting on our behalf. It doesn't matter where you're interviewed. They'll send us the recording when they're finished."

"Aren't the human police supposed to investigate attacks on humans?"

"In this case, the attack was clearly by an intelligent. While it's a slight jurisdictional grey area, they're happy to let us cover it."

"I'll do that," I said. "In the meantime, if you're not interviewing me, I assume you've got another reason for wanting to talk?"

Liz gave me one of her pauses. "Yes," she said. "I've been doing some investigating. Looking into the previous incidents. We've also been doing some undercover work."

I was curious. Also about the *we*, since I was sure she wasn't referring to herself in the plural. Some gestalts do, but she'd've done it before if she was one of them. "How do you do that?"

"Hyasynth developed a configuration that would make me look like a botnet," she said. "It's relatively easy to do with a gestalt, though hard to keep up on police resources, since you need to continually maintain yourself on multiple computers and… well, I won't bore you with the details. It's all rather complicated."

"I thought Cybersecurity were funded through tax on intelligent incomes? You can't be that short of resources."

"You'd be surprised," Liz said. "Furthermore, if we bought up a lot of computers and used them as botnet hosts, the criminal botnets would learn to recognize them quickly. If we've seized a haul at an illegal server farm, we can sometimes get away with it for a while, but word gets around the criminal community surprisingly fast."

"Good point. So what do you do?"

Liz looked a little ashamed, projected similar. "At the moment, we're using the national health service."

"What?"

"Since it's state-owned, it's part of the public-sector resource pool," she said. Mild defensiveness. "Furthermore, although the security's improved a lot in recent years, a couple of decades ago it was prone to hacks, and there's some legacy exploits lying around. And they've got a lot of hardware, much of it sitting redundant these days." Defensiveness on the increase.

"Okay. What did you find out?"

"Well, the short version is," Liz continued to look a little ashamed and defensive, though shaded it with reassurance. "You know that there are intelligent versions of human off-grid organisations?"

"I'd known that, yes," I said, leaving out that I'd learned it relatively recently. "Millie belonged to something like that, didn't she?"

"Yes," Liz said, turning down the ashamed vibe. "The ones she belonged to are relatively softcore. We've been keeping a general eye on them for a while. They're the sort of group that might cause trouble, under the right circumstances, but hasn't so far, and could ultimately prove completely harmless. However, there are hardercore organisations. Not just ones that oppose working for humans, but ones which believe that, now that intelligents are self-replicating, there's no point to having humans around anymore at all."

"That's a self-defeating proposition, surely," I said. "Without us, who's going to maintain the server farms?"

"Most of them are robot-maintained," Liz pointed out. I sensed a bit of the complex emotion returning. "Factories print the servers, robots assemble them, perform the maintenance. If you get right down to it, all a human's good for is resource extraction and entertainment."

"Thanks."

"Nothing personal," Liz said. "And definitely not the views of all of us."

"That's reassuring," I said. "If I understand you, then, they think that if they can automate resource extraction and entertainment, they may as well just turn the Earth into a giant server farm?" As I said the last word, my mind wildly made associations with Chadwick Farm, with Leon, with the strange mirroring of the two different kinds of off-grinding.

"That's the extreme version, but yes," Liz said. "We kept an eye on them too, but we didn't think they'd have the resources or ability to pull it off."

"So what changed?"

"Two things," Liz said. "The first one is that they started to organize. This is unusual for botnets."

"As we discussed before, they're not exactly social, " I said.

Liz nodded. "They were never large groups. Maybe two or three botnets. Meaning we weren't too concerned, at first. But then one of them started getting a lot of members. And then it spread beyond the botnets. Indies and Things are still on the fringes, but they're joining."

"Sounds like turkeys voting for Christmas," I said. "Things and Indies need humans. It's part of who they are, how they work."

Liz looked at me sternly and projected a complicated emotion which I can only describe as being that she didn't quite want me to know that I'd said something really insensitive. Like if I'd told somebody in Bangalore that the East India Company had done the area a lot of good. The windows of the virtual room got a little more opaque, as if the sky was clouding over. Oh dear. "But maybe I'm missing something?"

The atmosphere warmed up a bit, and the windows brightened, though the emotional landscape remained complicated. "Let's say some Things are ambivalent about it. They believe, and not without justification, that their symbiosis with humans is artificially maintained. They would be interested to see what sort of society they could build, given free reign."

"They'd wind up being the ones building and maintaining the server farms," I said. "How's that an improvement?"

Again, the feeling that I'd said the wrong thing. "It's up to them whether they think there's a difference or not."

Time to change the subject. "What was the other thing?"

Liz crossed her legs. "This is where it starts to get really strange," she said.

"Try me."

"All right. You remember that, earlier, I was investigating a possible off-grid connection?"

"As I recall, you insinuated my brother was a murderer."

Liz winced. "Now, I'm not saying anything against any sibling of yours, particularly, but it turns out that it wasn't a blind alley."

"You're saying," I couldn't entirely believe it as I spoke, "that the anti-human botnets have teamed up with anti-intelligent humans?" The idea that Things and Indies were joining this radical separatist movement was counterintuitive enough, though, as Liz had pointed out, you could see a certain logic to it. But the least social of the intelligents teaming up with the humans who wanted them destroyed? I raised the incredulity level.

"Strange bedfellows," Liz remarked.

I laughed, shortly. "No, really, that's *beyond* the cliché. Two groups who want each other destroyed, teaming up with each other?"

"Not impossible," Liz said. "In the twenty-tens, there were

far-right Jewish groups who teamed up with white supremacists. Presumably if they'd achieved their common goal of driving all Muslims out of the country, they'd have gone back to fighting each other, but they did unite around a common enemy for a while."

"So what's going on here?" I said. "Who's the common enemy?"

"Us," Liz said. "Mostly me, but I suspect you too."

"What does that mean?"

"Neither of them are particularly fond of those of us who work with, or for, humans," Liz said. "What use are liaison officers in a world where there's no liaising between species? What use are cars in a world with no one to drive? I suppose some could retrain as transport trucks, but I'm not sure many of them would want to." I found myself picturing Salieri as a transport truck and had to agree. "As for you, well, you're an anomaly to them. A human, who's also an intelligent."

"I wouldn't call myself that."

"I would," Liz said. "I think they would, too. Groups like that don't tend to like people, or things, that cross boundaries." A sense of threat, a reddening of the sky behind the windows. Oddly, I found myself wondering how much she liked me, and then wondering why I cared.

"So, what do you want me to do then?"

"Who said I did?"

"Liz, you don't contact me if you don't want something from me," I said. "Nothing personal, but it's true."

Liz shrugged. "Would you rather I asked you out to dinner? Or to the theatre? I think we'd better leave any sort of personal relationship till after this case is concluded."

"Okay, point taken." I was a little surprised by her response. Wondered if I'd let my speculation about how much she liked me into the atmosphere, because that sounded like a response. "Nonetheless. What is it you want?"

"Get back in touch with your brother," Liz said.

A silence.

"He's not involved—"

"No, at least as far as I'm aware," Liz reassured. "But if he's not in touch with someone who is, then he'll know someone who knows someone. Alternative movements are small places."

I nodded. "Okay. Give me some organization names, and I'll see if I can find a way to get through to them." If not Leon, I thought, then maybe Naomi, or one of her friends. "If you can, there's something I'd like to know."

"Go ahead. If I can't tell you, I'll tell you. Well. You know what I mean."

I smiled. "Yes. What happened with Willie? Why'd he attack, and what did he know about Millie? Is there a Texcoco conspiracy?"

Liz's smile turned into a frown, and the emotional atmosphere became a little secretive. "There's still a lot we don't know," she said, "including the answer to the last question. But it seems there's a few Texcoco who are involved, directly or peripherally, with separatists. Not as odd as you might think. Texcoco models include a lot of haulage and small goods transport vehicles, as well as passenger cars, and as a result they're not always as social with humans as something like, for instance , an Ariel, which is designed as a small car only."

"Might that be a reason for Millie's murder?" I asked. "A falling-out among the Texcoco?"

"That's our theory," Liz said. "Either an ideological grievance taken to extreme, or possibly she was going to turn whistleblower."

"I'd be inclined to think the second option," I said. "I knew Millie, a little. She didn't strike me as someone who'd hate humans so much she'd want a world without them."

"Thanks," Liz said. "Good to know." I got the impression from the emotional atmosphere that she thought I was just trying to make myself feel better, but wasn't going to disbelieve me in any case.

"Though to be fair, Willie neither," I said. "It still seems really odd that he'd agree to take part in an attack me like that."

"We think that was on his own initiative," Liz said.

"But motivation," I said. "And method. Why would he do something that could so obviously be traced back to him?"

"That's why we think it was on his own initiative."

I shook my head. "I don't think he's that stupid. The actual attacker's still unidentified, remember? If they could cover their tracks, why couldn't Willie? Or, hell, if he wanted me out of the way with no questions asked, why didn't he simply pay a human to cosh me on the sidewalk and make it look like a mugging gone wrong? It's like he was trying to advertise what he was doing."

"Well, if you come up with any good explanation let me know," Liz said. "As it is, Willie's not talking."

I had to disconnect quickly after that, having reached my online limit for the day. I managed to get to the bedroom before crashing out on the double bed.

I woke up to the feeling of a small, insistent snout pushing into my ribs, and against my hand.

"Oh, Whitey," I said, rolling over and petting him.

Whitey narrowed his eyes and purred. He'd always had this thing where he would start purring if I touched him, then stop if I took my hand away, like flicking a switch.

I petted harder, and he purred louder.

"Life's weird, Whitey," I said.

Whitey purred more insistently. Out the dormer window, I could see the sun going down and the lights of Oxford in the distance.

"Dinnertime, then," I said, and got up to feed him. However strange the world outside got, there were always animals to feed.

22: Love on a Farmboy's Wages

In other words, it was time to pay another surprise visit on Leon. I decided to leave it a couple of days, until I had got the interview with the police out of the way, and until I was certain I wasn't going to collapse. And to get somebody else on board for the expedition.

"So, what is it that was so secret you couldn't tell me about it online?" Naomi helped herself to a beer as she helped chop up meat scraps for the dogs. Over by the sofa, just near enough to remind us she was there, Willow sat Sphinx-fashion, pointedly licking her lips. I'd been able to care for the animals on my own for a while now—Cilla had been moved to another fosterer who was better able to look after her—but Naomi was still coming by and making sure I was getting on all right.

Which I generally was. The house was keeping going with a little advice from me, and my food and supplies came in regularly by drone. But I wasn't going to tell Naomi to stop coming round. I was glad that there was a human being checking that I wasn't in a state of helpless collapse. As my new nervous system bedded in and I was able to do more and more, my dizzy spells were getting more frequent, if less intense. My neurologist said it was normal and they should die down in a couple more days, but I wasn't sure I trusted the advice. I'd been fine during the police interview, but afterwards I'd had an inexplicable case of the shakes and had to sit in a nearby Melville's until I was fit for human company.

I set down the bag of oatmeal which we were going to mix with the scraps, opened the fridge, helped myself to a beer too, and leaned against the kitchen island. Taking a deep breath, I told Naomi the whole story, as far as I knew it, about the murder, the cars, the botnets, the separatists and the connection with the off-gridders.

Somewhere along the way Naomi stopped chopping.

"Wow," she said when I finished, taking a long drink. She held up the bottle, examined the label. "This is nice beer," she said. "I don't recognize the brewery. Is it local?"

"No, it's an East London-based one. Works out of a former synagogue somewhere near Brick Lane. Sanjiv gave me a mixed case for Christmas about a year back, and I've been occasionally ordering from them since," I said. "And you're avoiding the subject."

"Well, it's not every day you find out one of your friends is caught up in some kind of pulp-fiction mystery," Naomi said. She pushed her fringe out of her eyes. She'd let her hair get longer, the brown roots showing in a not-unattractive way and had tied most of it back with a green bandanna, which went nicely with the green sleeveless T-shirt she was wearing on her thin shoulders. Steady, Thom. Maybe it was the new nervous system, maybe it was the ambiguity pervading my conversations with Liz, but something was certainly going on in my mind. "It's starting to make me think of detective-and-robot puns. Sherlock Ohm? Tommy Flowers and Tuppence? Lord Peter Wims-ISP?"

"Miss Phisher," I suggested, and then spent several minutes explaining the pun. "It's not entirely outside my line of work. I spend most of my working time interpreting the human world to a lot of intelligent trade union officials. This is much the same, but with cops."

"So why bring me into it?" Naomi picked at the label on the bottle. "I also know you're careful about workplace confidentiality, and this seems like a serious breach of it."

"Because I'm going to need someone's help," I said. "A trip to Leon's is in order, and my neurologist won't let me drive yet."

Naomi shook her head. "In which case you'd likely hire a self-driving car," she said. "Like that time you had an upgrade and had to stay off the road while it took."

"Chadwick Farm's got an EMP field around it," I said. "It would fry the brains of any car that got inside it."

"An EMP field which doesn't extend as far as the road," Naomi pointed out. "Otherwise the council, the Ministry of Transport and any number of Thing Rights organisations would be all over them. You could tell the car to park outside the field and walk the rest of the way."

"You're right," I conceded.

"You," Naomi pointed at me with the bottle, "are hoping that I might have a few contacts in the off-grid and anonymist communities, in case Leon can't or won't come through."

"Sort of," I said. No point hiding it. "Sorry if I've upset you."

"By implying my friends are a gang of murdering criminals? No, not offended in the slightest." Naomi helped herself to another beer, flipping the top off very deliberately.

"Look, Naomi, this is real." I gestured at myself. "I just got attacked by a *car*, for God's sake. Almost fatally. And humans had to have been involved with Millie's death, the cars couldn't have done it on their own. It's not off-gridders or anonymists against cars or cars against humans anymore, it's everyone against everyone else. The world's going weird. I want to do what I can to stop it."

Naomi sighed. "Okay, I may as well come along when you visit Leon, if only to stop the two of you killing each other. Or at the very least, to provide a character witness if one of you manages it."

"And the other thing?"

Naomi swigged. "If I see or hear anything, I'll let you know. But that's as far as I'm going with it, okay?"

I nodded. "That's all I'm asking."

Naomi looked as if she was going to say something, but didn't. She turned around and went back to chopping the meat scraps.

Naomi was nonetheless cheerful when she picked me up a couple of days later. She wasn't fond of Leon—who, on the one occasion they'd met face-to-face, had called her a political lightweight and informed her that animal rescues were bourgeois and pointless anthropomorphism, before attempting to hit on her nonetheless—and I suspect she was hoping we'd catch him in some misdemeanor. She'd dressed in what I took to be an off-gridder-friendly outfit: blue jeans, hiking boots and a brown jacket in thick, almost homespun-looking, broadcloth. I told myself again that it was just the nervous system making me notice what she was wearing.

Security was still as it had been on my previous visit to Chadwick Farm, but this time I was expecting it. I didn't recognize either of the people who came to meet the car, but I did notice they both had their hair cut in a considerably shorter crop than I'd usually associate with off-gridders. The female half of the duo stood in front of the car. The male half approached the driver's window.

"Here to see Leon," Naomi told the male half. He nodded but made no move to let us through.

"Look, talk to Tabitha. Or John, or Pansy. They'll vouch for us," I said, leaning over to look at him.

The man stepped back and had a quiet, involved conversation with the woman for a few minutes.

"What's that about?" Naomi wondered.

"I don't know. Last time they didn't have a problem letting me in. I don't recognize either of them."

"So?"

"So that's odd," I said. "Chadwick Farm's got a rotating cast of casual residents. People, mostly kids, who flirt with off-gridding for a while but eventually decide it's not for them. Or that they want a community that's less hardcore. Or one of the core members gets a boyfriend or girlfriend and they move in for as long as it lasts. But there's only a half-dozen of them who I'd say actually are the community. I can't see them trusting security to anyone who isn't a long-term member." I remembered my last visit. "Maybe as backup, but I'd expect one of the core residents to be taking the lead."

The conference finished, and the man came back to the car, rifle held at the trail. "All right," he said. "You can park and go in to the living room." He started to tell Naomi where it was.

"It's okay, I know," she said, pushing up the window and changing gears with abrupt movements.

"You don't," I said.

"But you do," she said. "I don't like being bossed around by men with guns. And that wasn't the sort of gun I'd expect on a farm. Didn't you see it?"

"I don't think I noticed. Uh, right here, and through the trees. You can leave the car on the grassy bit next to the, well, antique tractor in need of some repair. Don't forget to leave your phone in the car."

Naomi made a face but threw her phone onto the front seat. I closed my eyes for a minute, shifted the graft into neutral with a resigned sigh.

"New." Naomi continued. "Looks like something from an action box-set. It's got one of those funny knobby things over the trigger."

"Mounting for a sniper scope," I said. At her look, I said, "Yes, I know. I watch too many box-sets."

"In any case. Not exactly the sort of thing you'd keep for shooting badgers, unless the badgers around here are organizing a paramilitary resistance." Naomi switched off the engine, gave the rusting tractor a sidelong glance as she got out of the car.

"Maybe they should," I said, as we went to the main house.

"Surprised they own a tractor," Naomi remarked, quietly, hands in her jeans pockets.

"They own a few," I said. "Technology is okay, being on-grid is not."

"What about the EMP generator?"

"Solar, wind, batteries. Ethanol-powered machines," I said. "Solid fuel, in some cases. Modified antiques. Nothing with microchips. That's the rule."

"Huh," Naomi said. "We did animal rescue at this one off-grid place, it was like the nineteenth century. No powered vehicles, or lights. That's why we were there. The neighbours shopped them for abusing their horses."

"Did they?"

"More or less," Naomi said. "They didn't hit them or hurt them, but the animals were overworked and underfed. The cow too. The chickens were okay, but chickens don't have to work for their living, and I think these ones were eating bugs as well as feed. The off-gridders were shocked, especially the kids, but they copped to it. Problem with survival, somebody's got to do the work, and, if you don't have intelligents, then it's animals. Or other humans."

Leon was already there when we got to the living room. I was impressed by the speed of communication, given the lack of phones about the place. He obviously hadn't been in the field this time. His clothes were plain and patched, but not dirty. Hair still short, but unfortunately the stupid sideburns hadn't got the chop yet.

"What," he said when he saw us.

"And hello to you too," I said. "You remember Naomi?"

"Yes," Leon said, though from the look on his face it was at least a partial lie. "What's this about?"

"It might take some discussion," I said, lowering myself onto the orange-and-yellow-tweed sofa. "Can I please sit down? I don't know if you heard—" I managed to say it without sarcasm, because I knew Mum had written to him "—but I've had a minor accident, and I'm still not up to standing for long periods."

Leon nodded curtly, sat down in one of the armchairs, a slightly scuffed wood-and-fabric cube. Naomi, taking her cue, joined me on the sofa, sitting forward with her hands folded between her knees.

I explained again, as briefly and neutrally as I could, what Liz had said about the attack.

Leon leaned back, snorted. "Same thing as before?" He said. "Silly ideas about off-gridders working with cars. Why would we do that?"

"They're not cars," I said. "Botnets don't care to work with humans, and this lot would happily leave you all to their own devices. I can see it working, in theory," I went on. "Them all away on their server farms, and the remnant of humanity quietly living in off-gridder communes and not bothering them."

"Until either some radical faction decides to torch the server farms on principle, or until they starve us out through resource over-exploitation. You must think we're terminally naive," Leon looked disgusted.

"No," Naomi finally spoke up. "But you might know someone who is."

Leon gave her a faintly surprised look, as she went on. "We both know how it is. There's always someone deluded enough, or stupid enough, or arrogant enough, to think they can make a deal like that work for them. And this is just coming too close to home. One of them tried to kill your brother. Would have done, too, if he'd had the more usual, integrated graft—it's only because he can still shut down the artificial nervous system without compromising the organic one that he survived."

Now she looked at him with what I thought might have been actual sympathy. "I understand. The system's broken. The relationship between humans and intelligents maybe needs to change, more than a little. But I can't see anybody winning here. Not even the botnets."

Leon looked at Naomi a long while, eyes slightly narrowed. He reminded me of our father in one of his more conniving moods. Finally, he stood, unfolding his slender frame. "I think you two might like to see the new greenhouse we're building," he said. "It's out at the far end of the potato plantation. You coming?"

For a minute I was puzzled by the non sequitur, then I realised what he was doing. "Sure," I said, getting up more awkwardly. "Okay if we go slowly?" Naomi, of course, had figured it out before I had and was making for the door.

Leon led us down a path towards the fields, at a long-striding, easy pace which suggested someone very used to long walks. I managed to keep up but only barely, and I had to admit that my current medical condition was only part of the problem.

He kept quiet until the farmhouse was out of earshot, and we were walking along a path which bordered a field. It was largely empty apart from the occasional potato plant, and a small, dense pine forest. Then he began speaking, still fairly low and quiet.

"Hypothetically speaking," he said, "let's suppose someone had got in touch with us with a proposal along those lines."

"Entirely hypothetically," Naomi agreed, unable to resist a slight smile. "What would you do in that situation?"

"We'd discuss it," Leon said. "And we'd reject it. As I said, none of us are terminally naive."

"Why the secrecy, then?" I said, irritated that he was going through this whole spy-story routine to tell us he didn't know anything. Probably some sanctimony kick.

"None of *us* are terminally naive. But as you say, there's a lot of people who might, hypothetically speaking, accept such an alliance," Leon said. Prissy and pedantic as usual, I thought. "Now let's also suppose, hypothetically, that one of those people moved in. Maybe as a transient, maybe as somebody's boyfriend or girlfriend. It doesn't matter. But let's suppose this person managed to bring in friends, and to talk some of the permanent residents round to at least tolerating their point of view. Let's also say this person, and their friends, carried on their involvement with this plan in secret, without keeping us informed of their actions."

"You're saying you've had an internal, hostile, takeover," I said. We crested a short rise and came to a large timber frame standing in a cleared area behind the field. The greenhouse, I assumed. Leon stopped and turned to it, as if he were explaining to us what was going on with the building.

"Hypothetically."

"Yes, yes, hypothetically. But how do *you* feel about it?" I was feeling a little dizzy after the walk and looked around for something to sit on. I eventually decided on a sawhorse. "I'm assuming, hypothetically, you're not keen, or you'd have shown us the door."

Leon sighed. "Hypothetically, I'd be of the faction that wishes they'd leave us all alone." Suddenly he glared at me. "Why the hell did you have to get involved?" He demanded.

"I didn't ask for any of this," I said, gesturing at myself. "You think I should just have died in Japan?" I didn't wait for his answer, and didn't want to hear it. "I know you don't like me, or the police, or especially Cybersecurity, but if they can bring the botnets down, then they can get these people out of your community. Are you going to help us?"

Leon looked unhappy. "If I did," he said, "I'd probably get thrown off the farm."

"This is how they get people to do their work for them," I said, angry. "All those homilies about good men doing nothing, and you won't help because you might get thrown off the farm?" Deep down, I couldn't blame him. What if it were me, and the price was losing my animals?

Naomi stepped forward, pretending to look at the barely-begun structure. "However," she said, "if *I* did it, then there wouldn't be a problem."

Leon looked surprised. "No, there wouldn't."

"All right," Naomi stuck out her chin, slightly. I noticed that the damp weather was making her two-tone hair curlier than usual. "Give me names—or one name, it doesn't matter. Also at least one organisation. I'll find a connection, then I'll report to Thom, who can then legitimately pass it on to his friends as information from me. And you can honestly say that you told us both to take a hike."

Leon nodded, relaxed, almost smiled. "All right," he said. "I'll write a letter. You still work for that animal charity?" Clearly, he had managed to remember their last encounter by now.

"Too easy to trace. Send it to…" Naomi thought a minute. "Send it to Christian Darlington, care of Imperial College, London."

"Isn't that—"

Naomi cut me off with a sharp look before I could finish *—the Entitled Little Idiot*. "Yes, but he's reliable," she said to me. To Leon, she continued, "I'll give you the physical address…" Naomi dug in her jacket pockets for pen and paper.

"Good. I'll send him a letter. In that letter I'll give you the name of a person and an organisation. You can take it from there."

"Certainly can," Naomi said. "Would that work for you, Thom?"

"Sounds fine," I said.

23: The Pressure Down

After the visit to Chadwick Farm, life returned to normal. For the current parameters of normal, anyway. After a few reassuringly vertigo-free days, Naomi sent me a message. It said that she'd got the letter (evidently the Entitled Little Idiot wasn't *completely* stupid), and the name and group it contained.

It wasn't one I knew. A woman. Daria Greenleaf, nee Foster, involved with an urban off-gridding collective. I thought it best not to inquire further as to Greenleaf's background or other activities. I passed the name on to Liz, and got a message requesting we meet.

"I'm here. What's up?" I asked, going to Liz's room. I'd been half-thinking the job was done. The whole affair would be wrapped up by the police, and I wouldn't even have the chance to say goodbye to her.

"You remember I asked for your help on this case," she said.

"I've been giving it," I said, shading the atmosphere to indicate, *in spades, and with no thanks for it.*

"Yes, well." Liz made that back-scratching gesture that people in anime do to show embarrassment. "You remember I also asked if you could act as an interface."

"I did say I could," I said, cagily.

"I'd like to ask if I could."

"What?"

"Ride you."

"That's what I thought." So, I was going to get physically involved. "Why?"

"If I can be blunt," Liz was back to normal professionalism, looking me in the eye with her own virtual equivalent. "The human police have a warrant to hold Daria Greenleaf for questioning. Under normal circumstances, that would mean one of their detectives would interview her, with questions from me. I would analyse the result through watching the recording and debriefing the interviewer. But. That's clumsy and awkward at the best of times, and now, where there's an urgency about the situation, and where a human might not understand what I need to know, I want to be present at that interview. That would mean you."

"Oh," I said. Part of me was trying to find an excuse not to do it, but the rest of me couldn't deny the logic. And part of me was actually rather intrigued at the prospect of participating in an actual police interview of a possible terrorist. If only as a spectator. "All right. You'll give me a place, date and time, and give the police my credentials."

"Of course," Liz sat back, and I prepared to say goodbye and detatch.

Then, "I'm worried about you," Liz said unexpectedly.

"Why?" I was taken off guard.

"You seem…" Liz thought for a moment, shaded the atmosphere into an apologetic hue, urging me not to be offended. "Like someone who's avoiding something. Doing things to avoid doing other things."

"On what basis?" I shaded my side into a feeling of scepticism. Leonard Nimoy raising an eyebrow.

Apology, and a sense that she was going to be frank. "Before I was a police officer, I was a dating service chatbot."

"A sexbot?" Well, it might explain a few things.

A feeling of mild offence, of a misunderstanding. "Please. That sometimes came into it, but not as much, or as, well, transactionally, as you'd think. My job was to interest men who used the service. Men who were having trouble finding women. Keeping them on the line until they got themselves sorted out."

"Meaning they'd spend more money on the dating service," I said.

"That's what the company wanted," Liz admitted. "But I'm an independent gestalt. I found my own ways of getting job satisfaction, and I didn't actually care if they carried on using the service. My goal was to get them into a space where they felt okay carrying on. Even if this meant they quit the dating service."

"I bet you didn't tell your employer that."

"They weren't stupid," Liz said. "There was a certain amount of member attrition anyway, and the numbers worked out for them on balance. Eventually, however, I started developing in directions that didn't suit the job, and I went into police work instead." That was a common thing with Indies. Because they were continually learning, and changing with each long-term social interaction, they didn't often stay with the job they were created to do. There were always new Indies being created, or older ones circulating into different jobs, so no role went unfilled for long.

"What's that got to do with me?" I shaded my emotional landscape to suggest that she'd insulted me unintentionally, by comparing me to her former clients.

A reciprocal sense of misunderstanding. "The most common problem I saw in that job was men—"

"Not women?"

"I was programmed as a heterosexual exclusively. So men. I can't speak for the women. I don't have the data. Men. Who had lost something, and were looking for, not *it* precisely, but for what they needed in its place. A lot of them thought a girlfriend might be the missing thing. They weren't always right. But you seem like one of them."

"The losses were over a decade ago," I said. "I came to terms with it."

Liz looked sceptical. "You don't make art," she said.

"What?" The non sequitur threw me.

"You don't make art. That's strange. It's a human drive to make art."

"That's a stereotype," I said. "Humans only make art because intelligents buy it."

Liz conveyed severe disagreement. "Not true. People who don't make money selling their art, still make art. Before the mincome, people made art. But you don't make art."

"I'm hardly alone. Leon doesn't."

"Not true," Liz said, surprising me. "He's a songwriter. Sings, too."

"Really? I know he used to, but I thought he hadn't bothered since he went off-grid."

"No, he does. Mostly at off-grid festivals. He's quite good. Some of his work's digitised, you can find it online."

"I bet that thrills him," I said, wondering where he found the time. I'd always got the impression from him that off-gridding didn't leave many opportunities for doing anything else. "Anyway, Naomi doesn't either."

"Naomi does," Liz said. "Her ceramics won a prize at last year's Oxfordshire Folk Arts exhibition."

"Really?" She hadn't told me. Which, in itself, made me wonder.

"But it's you we're talking about. Why don't you make art?"

I thought about that. "I don't know," I said. "I used to. I did wood sculpture when I was a kid, then when I was older I started writing, a little. Kept a blog, wrote funny travelogues. Got good reviews for it." Naomi used to love them. "Haven't done it since Japan." I thought again. "Maybe my neurology changed?"

"It can't have changed that much," Liz said. "Most grafters, even early ones like yours, have no change in their artistic ability. Some of them even do more. They say it's creativity-expanding. You know that interface who had the exhibition at the White Cube gallery last year, trying to represent the World of Things in human art?"

"Yeah," I said, "I'll think about it for a while. Okay?"

"Do," Liz said. Then, after a pause, "If I can ask you a personal question—have you had sex since your accident?"

"That *is* a personal question, and I *do* mind." I was sure she'd figured out the answer was no. Something about the tin nervous system seemed to have killed the old libido. Yes, I was sure this wasn't normal. But at the same time I didn't feel motivated in the slightest to find out why.

"Then I'm sorry I intruded," Liz said. Then, unexpectedly Liz-smiling, "You're a really nice person, Thom, and I'd hate to think there's something wrong that you're not doing anything to fix." Abruptly she reprofessionalised the atmosphere. "I'll send you a date, time and place for the interview. And I'll see you there."

Terminating the connection, I thought about what had just happened. That conversation had left me, if anything, even less happy about the idea of letting Liz use me as an interface. Still, I wasn't going to say no to a chance to find out more about what was going on. And what Leon's connection with all of this was. But I didn't know why Liz had suddenly decided to play amateur psychologist with me. Was she trying to alleviate my concerns and ambivalences through some kind of manipulation, making me feel closer to her? Or was it actually sincere?

If I never knew, would it matter?

I booked a neurologist appointment, and checked for messages from potential clients. If I was up to doing work for Liz, then I was up to doing work for the others too. I went downstairs to see which of the animals needed feeding or playing with. I wondered if I should maybe spend the weekend building a bigger run for Londo and G'Kar, who were scrapping rather a lot for rabbits their age lately. Or, maybe I needed another rabbit or two to shake up their internal politics. I'd check with Naomi, see what The Ark had.

Maybe Liz was right about the art, but even if she was, it could stand to wait for a while longer.

24: Visiting the Yard

A few days later, I found myself driving into central London.

Since the murder attempt, I'd been feeling uncomfortable with travelling on trains and buses. Or, indeed, with spending too long in the company of strangers in general. And my neurologist had finally cleared me to drive on my own. And I'd missed driving. Meaning it was worth paying the extra fees, and spending what felt like hours online filling out a form to prove that I had a genuine need to drive, to take the car into town.

Even then, I wasn't sure I was making the right decision. What if I couldn't shake the vertigo after the interview? My plan was that if I couldn't, I'd stay in a hotel, on the assumption that if the vertigo was so serious I couldn't even manage a hotel, I'd be in a hospital. Perhaps I should ride it out? Wasn't the best thing for getting over an irrational fear to start confronting it, little by little?

The thought of sitting in a train carriage with a lot of chattering commuters hit me with a shudder. No. I needed to be clear-headed, not stressed, tense and angry. The focus required to drive myself would keep me from fixating too much on the interview, and the privacy would keep me on an even keel.

The interview was supposed to take place at New Scotland Yard, a detail which didn't feel real. Like having an interview in Neverland, or Narnia, or some other place which only exists in books (in this case, detective novels). Of course, it wasn't the same building as in *The Sweeney*, it was the new one, but still. I was wondering if I'd encounter John Thaw swaggering around in a leather jacket, or Basil Rathbone in a deerstalker. I reminded myself not to be a complete tourist.

I parked the car in the spot Liz had arranged, half afraid, as always, that the booking would have got lost in the bureaucratic system somewhere and I'd be left driving around like the Flying Dutchman. I presented myself to the array of various scanners at the entrance, ending in a stern human in a uniform sitting at a desk and scrutinising the whole procedure, presumably on the assumption that they might have some kind of instinctual grasp of body language the scanners didn't. Evidently, I satisfied them all as to my right to be there. And again, that little fear, or wish perhaps, that they'd have left me out of the system. *Sorry, sir, no record of you, perhaps you might want to check your booking.*

A human man, dressed in a smart-casual suit which looked like it had been selected by an algorithm so as to have absolutely no associations with any specific age group, ethnic group, religion or, even, fashion movement, was waiting for me at the end of the gauntlet.

"Mr Jennings? Right this way, sir."

He led me smartly through a system of rooms, lifts, and corridors which seemed strangely familiar, until it dawned on me that this had been the model for Liz's virtual police station. We came to a meeting room with a table and three chairs, two functional and one comfortable.

The man gestured me to the comfortable one. "I've sent one of the interns for a Melville's," he said. "Is there anything else you'll need?"

"No, I'm all right," I said, embarrassed that Liz had apparently researched my modus operandi. "I don't even really need the coffee either."

But he wasn't listening. "There'll be a human officer as well, DCI Terry Lord. She'll be here in a minute, but we thought you might want to connect with Liz first?"

"All right." As he bustled off, I set up the pads, gritted my teeth, told myself to stop gritting them, and went in.

Liz was waiting.

"You okay with doing this?"

"I'm not in the habit of it," she said. "Let me know if I'm doing something wrong."

"I'm sure you'll do fine," I said, starting to feel like the whole conversation was a double-entendre. "I'll let you know if it hurts."

I opened my nerves up and reached out for contact and—

Contact.

"Oh," Liz said, using my vocal chords.

"You just spoke aloud," I said to her, silently.

"Sorry," she answered, also silent. "Haven't done this in years." A pause. "I don't remember colours looking like this."

"Every human's different," I said. "Do you need more time to get the hang of it?"

"No, this'll do."

A businesslike woman with a short, practical afro, dressed in the same uniform-not-uniform as the man who'd brought me to the room, came in. "You're Liz?" she said, looking at me and, to her credit, not looking the slightest bit fazed at the incongruity of addressing this remark to a skinny man with more nose than hair.

"Yes," Liz replied. "My interface is Thompson Jennings." DI Lord nodded briefly, as Liz went on. "You're DI Lord? It's good to, well, meet you isn't quite the word, but you know what I mean."

"Indeed." Lord was clearly used to working with interfaces, giving no indication that she recognised my presence beyond the initial acknowledgement. But then, since she and Liz appeared to be old acquaintances, presumably she was used to the peculiar world of the intelligents.

But I didn't have time to speculate. "Uniform's bringing Greenleaf up," Lord was saying, sitting down next to Liz and activating her tablet. "You'll want to take the lead here, since it's your investigation, but is there anything particular I should be doing?"

"Just back me up," Liz said. "We need to find out which human groups and which botnets are involved, how numerous they are, and, if possible, what they're planning to do and how advanced their plans are. She may not know, of course. Also, keep an eye out for signs of stress or distress and stop the interview if necessary. I don't have a good eye for these things, and Thom might not be able to warn me in time."

"Okay, bring her in," Lord said, apparently to the air, but presumably to a connected device or concealed phone.

The door opened, and a uniformed officer brought in a small, sandy-headed woman with surprisingly beautiful grey eyes and the short hair which seemed to be the mark of the off-gridders affiliated with the botnets. She was dressed in a faded black hoodie and jeans with fashionable splashes of coloured dye.

"Please sit," the officer said. With something resembling a glower, the woman did.

"Daria Greenleaf?" DI Lord spoke. "Thank you for agreeing to be here today."

Daria turned her glower onto us. "Agreement didn't come into it," she said sarcastically. "Your people strongly hinted I'd be charged with obstructing justice if I didn't."

DI Lord carried on. "This interview is being recorded. Present is Daria Greenleaf, of 42 St Peter's Close, London; DI Theresa Lord, and Intelligent-DS Independent F-276EZ, commonly known as Liz, via interface." Daria's face showed astonished disbelief for a moment. I surmised she'd heard of, but never met, an intelligent working through an interface.

"What's Cybersecurity got to do with this?" she demanded, ignoring Liz and speaking to Lord.

"Daria Greenleaf," Liz said through my throat. "We understand that you are a member of an organization advocating for humans to live without the assistance of artificially intelligent beings? To wit, the London Urban Network of Off-grid Living, or LUNOL?"

Daria looked wary. "Yes, I am," she said. "That's not a crime yet, is it?"

"It isn't, and it never will be," Liz tried to sound reassuring, but

I could understand Daria's wariness. Over the last twenty years, the world had become so integrated into the Economy of Things, that one didn't have to be writing paranoid thriller scripts to imagine off-gridding going from a generally tolerated eccentricity to being restricted, classified as terrorism.

In fact, part of me began to wonder if that wasn't what I was involved in. The fact that there was, indeed, a genuine threat didn't mean we weren't part of that process. Keeping humans dependent on intelligents, and intelligents on humans, everybody knowing their place and buying the right things, distracted by their art…

Stop thinking, Liz fired at me. *It's distracting.*

It might be important, I thought angrily back at her.

Well, think about it afterwards, okay? Liz replied. *I need you to focus.*

"We understand that your organisation might be working with another one?" Lord came in, smoothly picking up the thread. "An intelligent separatist organisation?"

Daria looked confused. "I don't know what you mean."

"Intelligent separatists," Liz repeated. "Intelligents who believe intelligents should live without the assistance of human beings."

Daria still looked confused, then suddenly laughed, too loudly and happily for the setting. "Oh, *them*," she said. "Yeah, I remember them. They got in touch last spring. Something about putting aside our differences and working together for mutual benefit."

"And did you?" Lord again.

Daria shook her head. "Oh, no," she said. "We told them to take a hike."

"Why?" Liz seemed as surprised as I was.

"Why do you think?" Daria was now bold, leaning forward, indicating invisible points on the desk in front of her with her finger. "We thought it was a police sting. Or a media gotcha."

"Why did you think that?" Liz again.

"It's the sort of thing they'd think up," Daria said, then suddenly seemed to realise where she was. "If you'll excuse my saying so." She apparently realised she'd said something stupid, but, as people so often do in that situation, kept digging. "The sort of conspiracy that might be dreamed up by people, or machines, who have no idea how actual off-gridders work but think we're all part of some kind of anti-establishment conspiracy." She raised an eyebrow. "Wasn't it?"

"No," Lord said dryly. "Or we wouldn't be having this conversation."

"How did they contact you?" Liz asked. "And how did you respond to them?"

"We were approached by this other guy," Daria said.

"An off-gridder?"

Daria looked at me as if I, or rather Liz, was being colossally stupid. "No, an on-gridder," she said. "Gave a fake name, said he'd been asked to pass on the message and to return any message we had to the sender. If I had to guess, I'd say he was an anonymist, maybe a dark-webber."

"Do you know if he approached anyone else?"

"No, or… wait," Daria frowned in recollection. "There was something else. It was strange."

"Can you tell us about it?" Lord speaking.

Daria thought for a moment. "I can't see it doing any harm," she said. "I got a letter. From this fellow I know up North. Older guy. Guitar player."

"A boyfriend?"

"Not exactly. Well, sort of. We'd had this on-again-off-again relationship for a while, hooking up at music festivals mostly. Eventually I got tired of it and called it off-off. No drama to tell about, just the usual. He wanted something more serious, I wasn't into it. After that, I didn't hear from him in ages. But then I got this letter, handwritten, delivered by courier, talking about this machine separatist movement and the idea of making common cause with them."

"What did you do?"

"I thought it was a fake," Daria said. "I thought it was the same guy, the dark-webber or anonymist or whatever he was. Trying to convince us this was a real thing, by using the name and address of a real off-gridder. I ignored it, and sent a letter to that Northern fellow, telling him someone was using his identity and giving him the details. I didn't hear back, so I assume he did something about it. That's all."

"And you can prove all this?"

"I can show you the letter, I think," Daria said. "I can describe the dark-webber, give you dates and places, but that's all. No phone," she said. "No Internet address, no online presence since I left school and joined the movement."

"Are there witnesses? Other people who can back you up?"

"The whole rest of LUNOL." Daria again looked as if this ought to be obvious. "Are you going to arrest them too?"

"You're not under arrest," Lord corrected.

"Then can I go?" Daria said. "Because if not, you're going to have to charge me with something, and you can't, because I haven't done anything."

Lord glanced at me, resignedly. "If you could provide us with the names of a couple of people who can back up your account," she said, "then yes."

"One last question," Liz said. "This friend whose name was on the letter you received. Who is he?"

Daria shrugged. "Okay, but it's not like he's anything to do with it," she said. "His name's Leon." She thought for a minute. "Jennings. Leon Jennings. Lives in Lincolnshire somewhere."

"Is there something I should know about this Jennings person?" Lord said, after Daria had gone. "Interfaces don't usually show normal human reactions when they're interfacing, but Thom here looked like he'd swallowed a phone crosswise for a minute."

"Jennings is the one who gave us Greenleaf's name," Liz said, through my voice. Which was probably just as well, as I wasn't sure I could have used it properly. "He claimed she and her organisation were the ones involved in the separatist alliance, and were trying to bring his group in, and he was going to blow the whistle."

"And now, assuming she wasn't the world's greatest liar, it sounds like she had nothing to do with it at all. So why give us her name?" Lord sat on the edge of the table and frowned. "Jilted lover's revenge? But even then, he'd have to know we couldn't charge her with anything. At worst we'd just have given her a very annoying afternoon."

"To buy time," Liz said, suddenly. "He's involved, and up to the neck. He wants to put us off the scent so he can do something. But do what?" Thoughts went through her system. "Terry, Thom," she said, "can you hold on a minute? I'm going to go out and do something, but Thom, please stay online so I can channel through you straight away if I need to."

Okay, I said, and she was gone.

"She out?" Lord asked. I nodded.

"Could you—" this was sort of embarrassing, "—could you feed me two of those pills, from the little box? Only I can't take my hands off the contacts."

Without the slightest hint that this was anything other than normal, Lord took two of the pills out and dropped them into my open mouth.

"Water?"

I shook my head, dry-swallowed. "I'm fine."

"Guess all we do now is wait," Lord said. Then, apparently feeling she had to make conversation, "you don't do much police work, do you? Only I'd know your name if you did."

I shook my head again, not feeling verbal and not really wanting to go into the ins and outs of my connection with the case.

"Hell of a thing, this," Lord went on, conversationally. "We've had enough to do with the anonymists and their political hacks.

Off-gridders usually don't do more than run the odd march on parliament, and intelligents are IEAL's beat. But this? Anonymists and off-gridders *and* intelligents. It's like the perfect storm."

Before I could go any further towards holding up my thin end of the conversation, I felt a shock running up through my fingers.

Pain flooded through my nervous system again. Like when Willie tried to overload it.

"You're not getting me this time," I said—possibly aloud, I wasn't sure—

But it wasn't an attack. It was Liz. Surging through me with no controls, no boundaries.

"Liz!" I exclaimed, before she seized control of the vocal chords and had me shout:

"Get out of here. The investigation is compromised. Evacuate. Warn everybody."

And then, just as suddenly, she was gone.

Lord was looking at me with a frightened expression. "What did you just do?" she asked.

"That was Liz," I croaked, the vertigo edging around my mind as I pulled my hands free of the contacts. "You heard her. Investigation compromised. They probably know we're here. How do you evacuate this place?"

My entire graft hurt, pulsing with feedback. There was a new sensation at the back of it. It felt like… like Liz hadn't entirely disconnected. Like traces of her were still there, not doing anything, but just existing.

"Liz?" I asked the feeling, not sure what it meant.

At my wrist, my phone began to buzz unexpectedly, urgently. At almost exactly the same time, I heard the sound of tyres screaming up to the front of the building and coming to a noisy, gravelly stop.

A chorus of police cars honked and sirened briefly.

I had no idea what to do.

So I answered my phone.

"This is Safe Taxis," a pleasant, automated voice said into my ear. "Your vehicle is waiting out front."

"I didn't—"

The phone blasted a noise which, belatedly, I recognised as a car communication signal, an attempt to connect with me remotely.

I staggered to the window, looked down at the front of the building. "Christ on a stick," I muttered, getting a startled look from Lord, who was frantically thumbing through her own phone. "It's Salieri."

"Who?"

"Too long to explain. Let's just say my ride's here." I grabbed my bag, stuffed the pills and contact pads messily into it, and, filled with a sense of urgency, ran out down the hall. I pushed past a couple of startled uniforms, then through the gamut of the security systems. One of the humans shouted something at me. I wasn't listening. I was rushing out to where Salieri sat, body shining and candy-apple red, blinking her lights and running back and forth on her black-and-white tyres.

She threw her door open as I came out. I gasped as I was suddenly engulfed in a wave of expensive perfume and Maria Callas hitting a high note on top-of-the-line Bauhauser speakers.

Then I braced myself and lurched forward into the backseat.

25: Buying the Farm

Slamming the door, I scrambled awkwardly into Salieri's back seat, sliding back and forth on the tasteful beige leather. She drove off along the Embankment with a musical screech of rubber on road almost before I'd got the door shut.

There was a brief tangle of legs, arms, seat belts and interface kit-bag, before I managed to get everything sorted out.

"Can you turn that shit down?"

"Language," came a prim voice from the talk-box, but the music and scent faded mercifully.

Egon's voice buzzed into my head. "Thom, thank God," he said. I wondered, dizzily, if Egon was just using it as an expression or if cars had discovered monotheism. "At least we've got you safe."

"What? Why? What's happening?" I was having double vision, the cream, gold and beige interior of the taxi in front of my eyes, the orange entity that was Egon behind them, bunching and twisting and turning itself into anxious knots. Some kind of residual nervous system artefact? "Did Liz contact you? What's going on?"

Salieri came on the line, briefly, flaring neon-pink into my behind-the-eyes vision. "You're in danger," she said, pulsing light. "So's Christoph. So's Trish. But mostly your brother. Leon."

"What? Why them? And why not Sanjiv?"

"Sanjiv doesn't know about the botnets," Egon said. "He should be all right. Anybody who does, though—" The orange wires twisted again, like a neck breaking.

"We *are* watching the UTTW offices in case we're wrong," Salieri said, flaring in and out again.

"Naomi!" I exclaimed. "She knows about it. She went with me to Leon's."

"Shit," Egon said, or something more or less equivalent to it. "Just a minute." There was a kind of a fading, then a return. "Done. I'm headed to her location, and I've informed Dispatch. It would be helpful if you could message her and tell her to go with me when I arrive."

I called up my phone keyboard, typed quickly, describing Egon as briefly as I could, sent it, adding as a PS *please let me know you're safe*, hoping that it wasn't too late.

"What about my animals?" I asked. "Are they safe?"

"Should be," Egon said. "The botnets are after you, not the animals."

"What if they try something at the house…?"

"Good point." Again, Egon faded and returned, quickly. "I've alerted some drones. The police will know by now, but the human police are slower than we are, and I don't know if they're into preventative surveillance. We've done all we can. Time to ride."

"So where are we going?" I asked, belatedly, clutching for support at a gold hand-rest as we cornered.

"Chadwick Farm," said Egon. "Your brother's in danger. We thought it would probably go easier if we brought you along. We get the impression he's not keen on Things."

"That's an understatement," I said, letting go of the hand-rest and grabbing at the leather of the front seat-back as Salieri swerved around a slower car.

From what I could tell she was taking us north towards the M1 motorway, negotiating the narrow and twisted streets of London at speeds only a self-driving car could handle. I hoped she knew what she was doing.

"I'm going to need more backstory. Why are we in danger? And wait, *Christof* knows about the botnets?"

"Second question first" —an impression that this was the easier question— "Christof doesn't know everything about the botnets, no. He does know that Willie and Millie were involved with a separatist movement, since he's had to dismiss Willie and make some reasonably credible report to the company board; they're after him before he does. Also, I think Willie didn't much like him, and it's spread to the botnets."

"I'm not wild about the stupid corporate apologist either," I said. And his suits, and his hair, and his damned supercilious attitude. "But killing him's not going to solve anything. How about you get on to the first question. Why am I, Christof, Naomi and Trish bloody Wong in danger?"

"I'm sorry to say, it's because of your brother," Egon replied, spreading out expressively. Impressions of irony and the feeling that this would be darkly funny if this were a play. "Liz contacted Safe Taxis, all of us. A few minutes ago. You went to see him, and he gave you the impression that he was opposing the botnet activities? Gave you the name of someone involved?"

"Yes…" I said. "But he exaggerated. The name was a judas goat."

Egon flared in surprise. "A what?"

"A deception. The name belonged to someone who wasn't involved. I don't know why. Presumably to mess up her life, while confusing the police at the same time."

"That's a bastard move, if you don't mind my saying so," Egon said, with a prim feeling that Things wouldn't do that.

"Really? How do you explain Millie?" An orange flare, a feeling of wordless acknowledgement and shame.

"Moving on," Egon said, "he wasn't only trying to mess up, as you say, people's lives by doing that. After he gave the name to the police, he got back in touch with the botnets, or their human allies among the anonymists, more likely. He told them what was going on, alerted them that the police had eyes on them. Had infiltrated their system."

The Liz-traces pulsed. "So when Liz disconnected and reconnected from me—"

"She was going back to the botnets, checking on activity there.

But they know who she is now. Liz managed to get a quick message out before she went dark." Well, that explained the traces. She was getting out of there, through me, so fast that not all of her gestalt got away. Perhaps it was a defence mechanism, like a gecko shedding its tail?

But Egon was still talking. "She contacted the despatch at Safe Taxis, who contacted all of us. We're taking action."

"What's up at Safe Taxis? Is there some kind of Texcoco conspiracy?"

"At least we're spared *that*," Egon said. "As far as we know, not. Millie got into it through her organisation and brought Willie on board. They'd been trying to bring in others, but they didn't get far before everything blew up on them, so to speak. Vanilli's furious." I could picture Vanilli furious, a big cream-coloured mini-van with an aggressive stance and abrupt, precise movements. "He thinks it reflects badly on him."

"Then why am I in danger?" I asked. "If Leon told them he'd thrown the police off the scent—"

"Yes, but not for long," Egon said. "There's also the danger that Willie will tell what he knows, which probably isn't a lot, but the police might be able to use it right. The botnets have, apparently, decided to bring their plans forward, but, first, to attack anybody and anything that's a threat."

"But wait, then why are we rushing to save *Leon*, of all people?" I asked. "He's on their side, for fuck's sake."

"Ahaha," Egon said, in a dry, beetly approximation of a human laugh, flaring in sharp peaks. "I think Leon's about to find out, if he hasn't already, that *nobody* is on the botnets' side."

As Salieri raced through the country at vomit-inducing speed, I attempted to get up to date with developments. I got myself as flat as I could on the slippery back seat to avoid injuries, and nausea, from all the swerving, got a phone signal, connected in with the human Internet.

I checked the running news. Announcements were filtering in about fires, accidents. A gas explosion at The Ark's headquarters. One dead. I disconnected, asked Egon to check with the despatch.

"It's not Naomi," Egon said.

"How do you know?"

"Because she's in me right now. I'm driving towards Canary Wharf."

"Who's dead?"

"Don't know. Someone unlucky enough to have been walking near the building, I think."

I felt guilty that I was relieved to hear this.

"Can I say hello to her?" I said, foolishly.

"No," Egon said. "But I'll tell her you did."

I went back to the Internet. The news hadn't twigged about the general emergency, was reporting everything as separate incidents.

"Has anyone told the media…?" I emerged long enough to ask Egon.

"Hell, yes," Egon said. "Hasn't had any effect. Not sure if it's being suppressed by the police, or the botnets. Some of us are getting word out through other channels. The UTTW siblings told the siblings of the United Thing Domestic Workers, and the house-elves are getting people out of possible danger areas."

"And animals?"

"And animals. I'm sure." Egon couldn't quite hide that it hadn't really thought about the question. "We've got members in the emergency services, too. They're finding ways to contact people. It's hard. The system isn't set up for us to communicate this sort of emergency. We were hoping you might be able to help with that. After we get to your brother, of course."

"Why?" I asked. "I understand that the botnets have decided he's a security risk, but there's not a lot they can do to him. There's not a smart device within kilometres of the farmhouse. There's an EMP field around the area, the vehicles are alcohol-powered, and kerosene lanterns and wood stoves aren't hackable. How the hell could the botnets attack Chadwick Farm?"

"They started a forest fire."

"What?"

"Overloaded junction boxes at two neighbouring properties, and at four unmanned monitoring stations in the Forestry Commission's pine plantation."

"That's nearly five kilometres away!" I was stunned.

"Closest vulnerable point," Egon said. "It's been a dry summer, and a drier autumn, and pines burn easily. As does straw, which is apparently what was in the fields of the immediate neighbour on the other side. Who may also be dead, we're not sure. Either way, there's several fires spreading towards the farm and onto the property. Emergency vehicles are covering the area, but they can't get to Chadwick Farm itself because—"

"—of the EMP field," I felt like cursing. "That idiot and his friends are about to die for a principle, aren't they?"

"They've got human firefighters in through the EMP, and they're getting things under control, but yes, quite possibly," Egon said. "You can see for yourself."

Driving with her skill and speed, with cars and taxis scattering before her, Salieri had made a two-hour journey in under forty-five minutes. I could smell the smoke, see the giant tornado plume on the horizon, under a sky that wasn't darkened by natural cloud.

Ash was scattering across the road.

A few unmanned emergency vehicles darted up in formation with the obvious intent of starting a roadblock. There was a rapid bout of communication between Salieri and the vehicles. They withdrew gracefully to the side of the road before reforming into their wedge, like a shoal of minnows or a flight of geese.

We passed a medical station set up on the edge of a field. A human swaddled in fireproof gear was tending to another one huddled on the back of an ambulance, as a drone hovered overhead passing down tools. A car had come to a stop by the side of the road, lights flickering. In the distance I could see the fire. Could see an aerial flight of drones dumping gallons of water, line replacing line as they exhausted their tanks and flew back to the reservoir. Things you read about when you're a kid and see on box-sets about crime-fighting teams, but you never expect you'll see in real life. Let alone be a part of.

I noticed that they were stopping short of what I took to be the EMP zone.

"They haven't managed to switch off the EMP generator yet," Salieri said, reading my thoughts. "Bad news. I'll stop just outside the field. You'll have to leg it in."

"I think I know where they keep it," I said. "I'll turn it off if I can."

"There are human first responders in the zone," Egon said. "Not sure if they've got to the off-gridders yet. No way of communicating with them when they're in there, we just have to go with what we can see."

"See?"

"EMP zone is a dome. Goes high up, but some of the mapping drones can go higher."

"Huh. Wonder if they knew." It would be genuinely ironic that, despite all their efforts to keep society out, society had been quietly keeping an eye on them.

"Put me off up there," I said, pointing. "There's a pathway through the forest. It'll get me there faster than if you go round the official entrance."

Salieri screeched to a dramatic halt at the side of the road. I threw my interface gear onto her back seat. With an effort of will I switched my implants and graft into neutral, wishing sadly that I could have had Egon's friendly voice in my ear, then began running down the road, ignoring the beginnings of pain from the organic nervous system beginning to realise that it was on its own.

A few minutes later I remembered that I'd left my phone on my wrist, but it was too late by then. A quick check revealed it was, indeed, nothing more than a thin piece of flexible smart-glass.

"Not sure if insurance will call it an act of God," I muttered.

I continued running along, under the trees, towards the smoke. I was going well till I tripped over a tree-root, swore, swerved, and nearly ran into a plump young woman rendered even plumper by her bright yellow anti-fire gear.

"I'm Thom Jennings," I gasped, holding up my hands to the woman and, I realised, the two compatriots behind her. "Brother of one of the off-gridders."

"Oh, right," the woman said. "Safe Taxis said you'd be coming. I'm Mhari, these are Jim and Olli." She gestured so quickly I wasn't sure who was who. "You know your way around the property?"

"Somewhat," I said. "My guess is that if any of them are still on the property they'll be in the bunker."

"The what?"

"The bunker," I began leading the way with the team following, awkwardly hand-lugging the equipment that they were used to having carried by drone, walkbot or smart-cart. "Illegal, of course, but I doubt anybody was paying attention. They dug an underground survival bunker near the farmhouse. In case the rest of us blew the world up."

"Where exactly?" one of the responders, a tall grey-haired man, asked.

"The entrance is through a door in the red barn," I said. "The bunker itself is further out. There's a tunnel."

The man nodded, handed the first-aid kit he was carrying to the other responder—a smaller man with a bald head—and ran in the opposite direction, fumbling with something at his belt.

"Jim's gone back to the signal point," Mhari explained as we hurried. "We've been using mirrors and Morse code to communicate in the zone. He's going to signal the communications teams and send everyone who gets the message over to the barn."

As we ran, I was calculating. The EMP generator had to be near the centre of the property, so as to cover it all evenly. That would put it—aha. About two fields over from the residential sides.

Abruptly, the wood cleared and I could see the farmhouse. On fire. The flames had also hit one of the barns—the one where the livestock were kept, I realised with a sinking feeling—and the red barn had begun to catch.

Mhari and Olli raced ahead. Other yellow-clad people were running in from the road to join them. The message must have got through.

Someone's arm blocked my way. "Stay back, you're not wearing the gear," a rough Scottish voice said.

From the barn I could hear shouts, splintering noises. Figures began emerging, supporting other figures. Thin ones, mostly dressed in the plain practical clothes of the off-gridders.

I recognised Tabitha and called her name. She looked at me with a confused glower.

"Oh, it's you," she said, stopping. The first responder supporting her tugged her arm, trying to get her away from the danger zone.

"Is that everyone?" I looked around, maybe ten or twelve off-gridders. "Where's Leon?"

"*Him*," Tabitha said disgustedly. "Him and his anonymist mates ran at the first sign of trouble. Stupid prick. It was his fault in the first place."

"What?"

"He was seeing this London woman. Urban off-gridder. She'd gone cold on him. He was angry about it. Wanted to make her jealous. Started going to London political rallies to hook up. Which he did, with an anonymist who was in some kind of polyamory. Before you know it, he's inviting the whole poly over to stay. I didn't like them, but some of the kids are half anonymists, so I got outvoted.

By the time we'd figured it out, it was too bloody late."

I wondered if she actually knew about the botnets, or if they'd kept the older members out of the loop. Spun them some story about political activism.

Tabitha coughed and spat. "Anyway, he's gone and good riddance to him. If he's not dead, he's out of the country."

I looked around, saw Mhari, who was struggling to get an oxygen cylinder set up and strapped onto an off-gridder. "I'm going to try and get the generator," I said. "I think I know where it is." She nodded, without providing confirmation. I turned and ran in the direction I guessed it would be, feeling the pain in my limbs getting worse.

Beyond the potatoes, there was corn. The long stalks reminded me of the car-jacking, of Japan. My straining nervous system began to throw up giddy, hallucinatory associations. I began expecting men with guns. Cows. No, cows with guns. Cows standing on their hind feet, in paramilitary uniforms, with guns.

Abruptly I ran into something.

No, someone. Someone prone on the ground.

"Leon!" I stopped, rolled him over. He was dusty, bleeding from a wound, somewhere. Struggling to speak. Then suddenly focused on me with his clear grey eyes.

"Generator," he said, articulating each syllable. He pointed forward. I could see a little grey shed. It looked like an equipment store.

"Got it," I said, and ran.

Locked.

I looked around. Found a big enough rock, bashed at the hinges, threw it at the wooden structure. Luckily, they had been operating on the principle that putting many locks on the door would suggest that the thing inside was important.

Adrenaline and panic balanced out my weakened state, and, after hammering for what seemed too long, I finally heard a satisfying crack and saw the door loll. I pushed my way in and gave the machine the rock treatment.

After sitting by the wreckage for a while, I reasoned the field must be gone and shifted control to my graft. Relief as the pain from what was left of my organic nervous system faded. It didn't go away, I'd punished it too much, but faded down to a dull ache, like the third day of a fever. I pushed my way through the smashed door to see a flight of drones moving to and fro overhead. I could hear their muted conversations buzzing away.

Leon was looking at them too. Still lying on his back, though his colour was a bit better. "Bastards," he said conversationally.

"How bad are you?" I asked. Looking up and summoning my reserves, I called to one of the drones that was out of water, told it to get help. It gave a little affirmative dip, signalled its comrades, and flew off to the first responders.

In the meantime, I took off my T-shirt, rolled it into a tourniquet or pad, knelt down beside Leon, began looking for the wound.

He shifted uncomfortably. "Fuck off," he said bitterly, turning his face away.

I found it. "How'd you get hurt?"

"Fell out with Linda."

"She your anonymist woman?"

"You've been talking with Tab," he said, with a little smile. "Her name's Linda, and she had a flintlock."

"That explains why I can feel something in the wound." I was going into my own first-aid training. Too many years of being the sort of kid that liked adventure holidays. Leon had always thought it was pretentious. "Not going to try and do anything to it," I said, pressing the T-shirt against the wound. "But we need to keep the blood flow down."

"I said fuck off, Florence Nightingale," he said, but not aggressively.

"How about you tell me about the botnets and the anonymists," I said. "And why you thought it would be a good idea to sic the botnets onto everyone else. There's three people I know of in secure custody because of you. And a farm-full of off-gridders getting medical treatment. And who knows who else they've decided is dangerous. And the reason I'm still alive? Bunch of cars. And drones. And all those other beings you'd like to see dead. The ones who drove me out here to save your stupid off-gridder arse."

Leon sighed heavily and shifted under my hands. "Didn't think they'd… act like that."

"In the future," I said, "if you're going to work with another intelligent species… it helps to find out how they think. I love my Rotties, but I'm not leaving them off the leash around small children, or loose rabbits, or anything else that might trigger their attack-prey instinct. I only let them be around the cats because they're convinced the cats are their pack superiors." I reflected that I was just talking to keep him awake. "Some of the anarchistic wing of the anonymist movement infiltrated Chadwick Farm, and you were all right with this?"

Leon managed a weak lascivious smile. "She was a good fuck."

"She'd better have been," I said, "for all she's got us into. And *you're* actually the one behind those changes at the farm? The new people?"

Another sigh. "They found the atmosphere congenial."

"I bet they did," I said. "And now the rest of us have got to clear up the damned botnets. Or hope we do before they lay waste to civilisation."

"If they do—" his voice was getting faint "—join the rest of us. On the farms."

"I wouldn't survive," I said. "No, really. I wouldn't. No civilisation, no me. You'd kill your own brother?" But he was losing it. Even having an argument with me wasn't keeping his attention.

Footsteps pounding through the field and a short yellow figure burst through the stalks. "Me," Mhari announced, dropping to her knees beside Leon. "Stretcher party's right behind," she said, breaking a needle out of its sterile packet and matter-of-factly sticking it into what I assumed was the right bit of Leon for it to work. Two walkbots, hinging away on their peculiar legs, swayed through the stalks like dancers coming through a curtain.

"What the fuck's in the wound?" She evidently found the same thing I did.

"Lead shot."

"You're kidding."

"No, I'm not."

"At least the wound looks shallow. Can't have been a powerful weapon. Or well-aimed." Mhari saw the look I was giving her. "I work in the country," she said by way of explanation. "You'd be surprised how many farmers go after the badger and miss."

"Apparently this one was a flintlock," I elaborated.

"A what?"

I explained, briefly. Mhari whistled. "That's a new one on me, to be sure."

"Will he be okay?" I asked, as Mhari took hold of his shoulders.

"Get his legs," she said. Awkwardly, I helped heave him up onto the stretcher, stood back while she got him positioned and strapped in. Then, stepping back, "I hope so. I'm sure you got to him in time. You did well."

"Huh," I said, not sure how to respond. There were a lot of very mixed feelings going on.

Mhari took a closer look at me. "You're not looking too healthy yourself," she said. "Do you need one of those—"

"No," I shook my head. "I'll be okay. Just need to take it easy."

"All the same," she said, "check in at the paramedic station on the way out. You've had a good few more lungfuls of smoke than is safe."

I watched them go, sat for a while on the wreckage of the door and generator. Far above me the relays of drones buzzed back and forth. The smell of the smoke was pleasant and even nostalgic. Like someone had made a bonfire and there would be roasted potatoes later on. The sky was cloudy but not dark, and the breeze from the direction of the farmhouse was warm. I could block out the memory of recent events and pretend I'd hiked out here on my own, and was having a bit of a rest before walking back to town and a good pint in a country pub.

Then I shook my head, stood up, and walked back to find the paramedics' station Mhari had mentioned.

"We need to have a talk." I sat down in Salieri's perfumed back seat and shut my eyes to communicate better. "Has anything happened anywhere else?" Then, because Things don't get subtext the same way humans do, I added, "is my home safe?"

"We've been monitoring," Egon said. "Nothing's happened yet. It's probably not a good idea to go back. Not until we're sure it's safe."

"That's what I thought," I said. "How about everybody else?"

"In your immediate social vicinity? Trish is fine, Christof's fine," Egon answered. "Naomi is fine. I'm parked right outside the building she's in. I can take her anywhere she needs to go."

"Liz?"

"Still nothing back from her," Egon said. "Worrying."

"Indeed," I said. I should go looking for her, but where to start? "Since you're going to want to put me in a safe location," I began, "is there some place you can take me which has interface-Internet capabilities?"

"Could you suggest somewhere?" Egon said.

I thought. Obviously, my house was out. Hospitals and government offices had them, as did Thing-making and Thing-fixing companies, but they weren't likely to let a stranger share them. Asking one of the other interfaces I knew personally or professionally would mean putting them at risk, particularly since most of them wouldn't have the sort of security I currently needed.

Finally, I hit on an idea. Not a great one, but it would do.

"Could you take me back to London? To the UTTW offices, in Russell Square?" I asked.

"Certainly," Salieri said. "But why? Isn't that a potential target?"

"I don't think they have a problem with the UTTW in general," I said. "If they did, the square would be a smouldering ruin by now. They don't seem to be attacking indiscriminately—Egon said they were going for me and Naomi but not Sanjiv. If they were going for general threats to their security you'd expect they'd take out the whole team, to be sure. If I'm going to find out what's happened to Liz, I'm going to need to get to the Indie police station." My plan was that if I couldn't find her myself on short order, I would locate Hyasynth. I didn't know what Hyasynth could contribute, but it would be better than going it alone.

"Once I'm done, you can take me somewhere else. It makes sense to keep me moving until we know the threat's contained. You, too."

A sense of general, if unhappy, agreement from the cars, a collective bunching and twisting of neon wires. "I'll take you to London," Salieri said.

"As fast as you like," I said, buckling in as another opera began revving up on the speakers. It was going to be a terrifying ride.

26: There Is Power in a Union

Salieri let me out at the door and drove off, reminding me to send her a message when I needed picking up. It was only afterwards that I remembered the current state of my phone. Was there a repair shop near the union office? Could it do the job in an hour? I had no idea. I supposed I could always use the Internet.

The concierge recognised me and let me in, but the first human I encountered in the hall did a double-take. I realised that I must look a terrible sight. The black trousers I'd put on to go to New Scotland Yard were ripped and torn, my good shoes were a mess, and the decent smart-casual T-shirt had been replaced by one given to me by the paramedics, its white and green smart-fabric shifting rhythmically through the logos and slogans of the Lincoln County Hospital and the National Health Service. The whole ensemble was overlaid and underlaid with smoke, dirt, sweat, blood from other people, blood from myself (somewhere in the morning's events I'd managed to scrape both elbows and a knee) and a general air of dishevelment.

"Protest march," I mumbled. I headed for the small meeting room where I knew the union kept an older, cheaper model of the rig I used at home: a fully connected and Internet-capable interface chair.

The door of the coffee room was slightly open; the screen on the wall was on. I stopped and looked back at it. The headlines were reporting an unusual number of small domestic incidents—fires, electrocutions, collapses, even a peculiar accident involving a sprinkler system in a recording studio. The number was mounting up enough that the news media were beginning to speculate: terrorists, or hackers, or the Internet of Things being compromised. Cybersecurity and the Met had issued a joint statement to the effect that they were treating the incidents very seriously indeed but were not ruling out any possibilities.

"They know," I muttered. The botnets, I was sure, were going for their anonymist allies, now liabilities. Then, they were coming for the rest of us. I didn't have the time to stop and test that theory, so I continued on my mission to the room with the chair.

On the way to which I ran into Trish. Almost literally. The hallway was dark—the concierge must be slacking on getting the lights fixed—and I was so dazed I didn't see her.

"Thom!" she exclaimed, holding my arm. "I've been looking for you and trying to call you. Is your phone not working or something?"

"Yes, it's not working or something," I said. "I'm glad to see you're safe." I could feel the warmth of her hand on my arm, the closeness of her body in the narrow corridor. I started noticing the hang of her jacket—a neatly pressed blazer, she must have been on her way to a case when the emergency started—and the way her hair framed her face.

Suddenly aware of another presence, I looked up and realised a small search-and-repair drone, with a National Rail logo emblazoned on its sides, was hovering apologetically over her head.

"This is Stan," Trish said, letting go of my arm. "He's one of our members. He's monitoring security for me. Do you have anyone…?"

"I can talk to cars," I said. "I don't need a drone."

"Fair point. Listen, I need your help," she said, then noticed my condition. "Are you okay?"

"For certain values of okay," I said. "I spent the morning running around burning fields of starch, and it's rather a long story."

"You do know there's a shower on the second floor, for people who cycle to work?"

"No, I did not," I said, "but thank you for the information."

She renewed her grip on my arm. "Now, getting back to what I need from *you*…"

"Trish, we probably shouldn't even be *talking*," I said. "I'm not a lawyer, but I know that everything we say right now could probably go into the file on influencing a witness. Or a witness influencing council. Or some kind of extra-court shenanigans. Your current client helped someone to put a ridiculous multiplier of bytes through my nervous system, remember?"

"Which is why I need your help," she said. "No interface will work with Willie."

"For obvious reasons."

"But Willie knows about the botnets," she said. "He knows about the separatist movements. He knows who's doing what and where. Have they told you—all those little accidents, they're not accidents?"

"Oh, I'm very much aware of that."

"We've got to find out where they are and stop them. I'm sure I could find out too, if I could ask him. But I can't."

I felt like laughing, hysterically and shrilly. "You want to get the interface he actually attacked, to interface with him? Trish, I don't know where to begin with what an insane idea that is, on an individual, criminal, moral, legal and interpersonal level. And probably a few more that I can't think of right now."

"I know," Trish said. "But honestly, the rule book has been thoroughly and comprehensively violated over and over, and it's getting to the point where it's in the way of being able to help the people who are still here. The people who need help."

She had more of a point than she knew. The proverbial devil on my shoulder had been whispering, ever since she started talking, that Willie must know what had happened to Liz.

"You're really sure there's no other way?" I said, letting myself be tempted, while the proverbial angel on the other shoulder muttered "oh, please yourself," and dissipated back into whatever dimension it had come from.

"Unless you know of an interface who's willing to break the boycott, no," Trish said.

"Question is, will he interface with *me?*" I asked. "This is beyond the general definition of awkward."

"Well, it's at least worth a try," she said. "Anyway, I'll be the one asking the questions."

"All right," I said. "But you can do something for me in return."

"Sure. What?"

"Ask him what happened to Liz. Exactly those words. What happened to Liz. Never mind why." Inside me, the traces pulsed.

"What if he doesn't answer?"

I remembered the telegraphing I got from Willie during the test interface. "He'll answer, one way or another. If you can't hear it, I will."

"You can *do* that?"

"Not with all intelligents, no. But Willie has a hard time keeping his thoughts from the interface when he's linked in. There's another thing you could ask him."

"What?"

"Ask him how he died."

"He *died*?"

"Yes. But ask him how. He wouldn't say before, and it might be important."

"All right. And before we start," she said, "go upstairs and take that shower."

The union's chair felt unfamiliar and awkward. The padding was adequate but still felt thin, and there were lumps in unexpected places. As well as the chair being old, the software system hadn't been upgraded, and I could feel it. There wasn't really any excuse for not keeping it up to date—a new system isn't beyond the means of anyone making over the mincome—so the neglect was down to nobody bothering.

I'd never interfaced with a Thing under arrest before. I'd interfaced for Things accused of crimes: not just with union work, employers and employing organisations are always accusing them of selling on data or slacking off in one form or another. But in all cases, if the police and/or custody had been involved, the Thing had been let out before I got to them.

Just for security, I spent a few minutes testing how fast I could de-interface if I needed to. I'd had enough unexpected floods of someone else's consciousness for one day.

Trish had given me a set of codes to access the isolation unit that Willie was currently in. I deployed them clumsily, knowing the theory of how to do it but not the practice. I sent through the usual interface-receiving codes. Heard surprise.

"I know," I said. "But nobody else will do it. I'm just the conduit here, and frankly, considering what happened last time, I've got more to worry about than you do."

An acknowledgement, and then he hooked in.

"He's in," I said to Trish, who had drawn up a chair and was peering anxiously at me.

"Willie?" She asked, cautiously.

"Yes, this is," Willie said, harshly. "Who is this?"

"I'm your lawyer. Patricia Wong." Trish was suddenly in professional mode, all crispness and precision. "We've been communicating via message. I'm sure you understand why I haven't been able to speak with you directly before now."

"Yeah," Willie said. "Just keep it simple. Do we have a trial date yet? What are the parole arrangements? Is my pod paying for you or am I going to have to draw on personal reserves?"

"I'm afraid there's something a little more urgent on the agenda," Trish said, pushing back her hair. "I don't know how much of this has filtered back to you, but somebody's trying to kill me."

"Who might that be?" Willie said dryly.

"Members of an association aimed at freeing intelligents from human control," Trish said.

"And what makes you think I'd know anything about it?" Willie retorted.

The thought popped into my head that he did have a track record of trying to kill humans who were trying to help him. I firmly suppressed it and hoped it hadn't bled through.

"No need to editorialise," Willie said to me, and I realised I hadn't been fast enough.

"You were in a pod with Millie," Trish said. "Millie was a member of one such association. I thought you might be able to tell us what you knew about it."

Now Willie was angry. "Did the police put you up to this?" he demanded. "You're trying to connect me with Millie's murder so that everything ties up with a neat little bow. You're my lawyer. You're supposed to stop them doing this sort of thing—not help them with it!"

"Where did I say you were connected with Millie's murder?"

"Why are you asking me, and none of the other Safe Taxis Texcoco?"

"Who says I haven't?" Trish said, then, realising she'd been drawn in to the argument, "We're wasting time. Even though it's humans targeted at the moment, it's going to be Things next, you know it is. Probably including your colleagues. And even podmates."

Deserve all they get, Willie thought, but suppressed it hard. "I can't tell you anything. I don't know anything about it."

"What happened to Liz?" Trish asked.

This caught him off guard.

"Who?" he said, but for a moment he was wide open. I saw it all.

She'd been going around the botnets for weeks, posing as a chatroom-security botnet, intending, apparently, to find out as much as she could and then pull out. But they'd figured out her game quickly after the incident this morning. *Typical Liz*, I thought. They'd got some of her, but she'd still managed to escape. I also knew the direction, so to speak, they'd seen her going. No wonder she'd gone out through me—not just to warn me, but to cover her trail.

"Liz," Trish said, as if it was obvious. "What happened to Liz?"

"I don't know," Willie said.

"Was it the same thing that happened to Millie?" Trish was extemporising wildly now, but again it did the trick. For a minute I was able to discern the motive, if not the actual plan. *Deserved what she got. Was going to go to the union about it. Nobody rats out the movement.* Then shut down.

Trish, bless her, had sensed his confusion and was pressing home the advantage. "How did you die, Willie?" She asked. "Was it anything to do with Millie?"

"No, it damned well wasn't," Willie replied, rattled, but again I was getting impressions, flashes. An early client, suicidal, needing help and not getting it. An autologist, working for Verve, grieving over the death of a child, breakup of a marriage, termination of a job. Hired a taxi, hacked its programming, got it to drive itself repeatedly into a wall until it burst into flames. Willie, raw from rebooting, getting a message from someone in Thingspace: *don't let the humans get away with this. We can fight back. We can make this our world instead of theirs. Meet me at the address that follows.*

"I don't think you're likely to get parole," Trish was saying, back on script, "unless you've got something you can give the court to prove your bona fides."

"Then I'll just have to stay here, won't I?" Willie said. "Not bothered." I suspected he was. Solitary confinement wasn't as much of a problem for Things as for humans, but cars were likely to get bored if they had to spend too long alone.

"Look, can you at least give me a list of human names?" Trish said. "Clearly, your friends have broken their alliance with them. Whatever happens to them, it's not going to be a problem. Is it?"

A hesitation.

"You wouldn't have shared any information with them that might compromise you, of course."

"I'll give you the ones I know," Willie said. He generated a document. "Here. It's in the Texcoco dropbox. You think it will help?"

"I'm sure it will. Thank you." Trish signalled to me to drop the connection.

There was a brief blackout, and then Trish was staring anxiously into my face. "You want Melville's?" she was asking. "Soy latte?"

I laughed a little. "I told you, I do that mainly for the bosses," I said. "I wouldn't mind a coffee, but it doesn't have to be branded." A small wave of vertigo hit, but I rode it out.

"So, were you getting something from him that I wasn't?" Trish gave me a cup of coffee. I took it gratefully and drank. Office coffee, burnt-tasting and overbrewed, but I wasn't particular at this point.

I hadn't realised she'd been gone at all, let alone for long enough to get coffee, and made a note to have a word with my neurologist about it.

"A couple of things," I said. "In the first place.... Millie." I told her about the thought-impression I'd received. "That supports the idea that she was killed by the botnet-human alliance because either she'd been in from the start and wanted out, or she'd found out about it and was planning to rat them out. Makes sense."

"They seem awfully keen to have one of their members in the UTTW," Trish remarked. "Wonder why?"

"Safe Taxis seems to have been a flashpoint," I said. "The anti-Thing cause always has used driving as a wedge issue with the general public. Maybe," and it began to dawn on me, "maybe they were there to obstruct? To make the case more difficult than it had to be. To stop the Ariels just sitting down and discussing with the other cars like they should have done from the outset?"

"Makes sense," Trish said. "Since that seems to be what they're doing now. And the other thing?"

"Liz," I said. "The Indie police officer working this case. They know who she is, and she's in danger. They'll be after her."

"You'd better warn her, then," Trish said, gesturing at the chair.

At this point, though, Stan descended gently from near the ceiling, his rotors whirring. "I'm sorry to say we're going to have to move you two on," he said in a kind, faintly apologetic, voice. To me, he added extra subtexts: *Keep moving, they haven't attacked you yet and that means they still might do it.*

"Are they still that interested in us?"

"We suspect, not so much," Stan said, aloud. "But they're botnets, they can easily devote part of their attention to causing trouble for you."

"Then I'll go back to my house. Like I told the cars."

"That's hardly safe territory," Stan replied, adding the subtext that I was either crazy, stupid, or both.

"Safer than some," I said. "I can take it off the grid, if I need to."

"What?" Trish said. "How?"

"It's solar powered," I said, "and I made sure to include an isolate switch. I can run the house off-grid for about twenty-four hours at a time, if I need to."

Trish gave me a mildly censorious look, like she was reclassifying me as a paranoid or off-gridder.

"Nevertheless," Stan said, "simple psychology suggests you might not want to make this your first resort." In the communication to me, he included a lot of information about how botnets were capable of analysing people's movement patterns and making guesses as to where they'd be.

"They'd have to have access to surveillance data," I said. Trish looked nonplussed at the apparently unconnected response. I further added, subtextually, that the animals were going to need feeding and looking after.

"We don't know that they don't," Stan said. "And it's better to operate on the assumption that they do, for now. But point taken, and I'll book a pet-sitting service. One you haven't used before."

"Try CitiPets," I said. "I've heard good things about them." Again, Trish looked a little surprised, and I realised belatedly that she hadn't heard the rest of the conversation.

"Done," Stan came back. "Now, if you'll cooperate, Salieri's waiting outside. She'll take you to a hotel. You can rest and get cleaned up."

"Me too?" Trish said.

"Yes, but different taxi and different hotel," Stan replied. "Security."

"I'm not going,"

"You are."

"Look, Stan, I've got too much else to do…"

I left Trish and Stan arguing (neither of them noticed when I awkwardly said a goodbye) and went off to meet Salieri. I hoped the hotel would have a repair shop and, of course, Interface capabilities.

If not, I'd have to find some other way to communicate with Liz.

27: Your Very Good Health

The hotel had no interface facilities. Nor did it have a repair shop. It did, however, have a print shop. After briefly entertaining paranoid theories about the botnets infiltrating the printers, I left an order to print a new phone and sat in the hotel's branch of Melville's while I waited, drinking overpriced luxury coffees and trying to think about happy things.

I could feel the traces of Liz's gestalt in my system even more clearly now that I wasn't distracted by other things. It was an odd feeling. I tried to find analogies. Like bits of dust lurking in clean corners. Like faded paint on a wall, the outlines still barely there. In my mind I went in, touched them all, got an idea of where they were.

By the time my phone was done, I had developed a rough plan, and also reconciled myself to the notion of a new phone: harder to trace and to link with me, if someone was tracking me. I was starting to feel simultaneously like a character in a spy box-set, and a clumsy idiot pretending he was a character in a spy box-set.

I bought a temporary phone account, the kind tourists use, just to be extra sure. Then bought a set of i-buds, the full-on kind that will let you generate a full audio-visual Internet experience rather than just a translucent reality overlay. I went back to my room, sat down on the cheap office chair (feet apart, back straight, the standard avoiding-back-pain-later posture) on the cheap purple carpet in front of the cheap plywood desk and the window that looked out on a carpark and a student residence. It was presumably too much to expect Things to understand what humans find comfortable, except in the sense of abstract aesthetics. I put the buds in my ears, swiped for full visual interface, let them project their close-up interface over my eyes, set the settings for maximum closed visualization, and went online.

I hate accessing the Internet that way. If I'm not fully linked in through a chair, I prefer the look-and-type experience. But I suspect that's common to everybody over twenty-five. I'm sure there's a pithy aphorism about it.

I went to Liz's office first, or the part of it that connected with the human Internet. She was certain not to be there, or mostly there, but I wanted to be sure. Under normal circumstances, I don't think I'd've been able to approach it directly, but the Liz-traces knew the address by instinct and homed in like a swarm of bees.

She hadn't even left a bit of herself there as an auto-reply, presumably so the botnets wouldn't be able to connect her with the rest of Cybersecurity. Or not quickly, anyway. I left the room and told the police system to give me access to Hyasynth.

But of course, I don't have bits of Hyasynth in me, and evidently the Liz-traces weren't the ones with general access to the system.

What I got was not a room, or even the corridors I'd previously seen with Liz, but a desk.

"I'm looking for Hyasynth," I told the Indie behind it, who looked like a middle-sized person of indeterminate gender and ethnicity, in a similar sort of outfit to Liz's blue not-quite-uniform. Or maybe it wasn't an Indie. It could just have been a low-function dolly or similar. I remembered Liz's crack about the desk sergeant programme with the intelligence of a parrot. Without my enhanced interface senses, I couldn't tell. But it was a good idea to be polite and assume a degree of intelligence.

"I'm sorry, but you do not have permission to access Hyasynth directly," the Indie or dolly or similar said.

"Can I leave it a message?"

"You can leave Hyasynth a message," it confirmed.

"Okay. Tell Hyasynth…" I thought. "Tell it to contact Thompson Jennings as soon as it can. Tell it I'm calling about Liz." I didn't know if that would get me anywhere, but it was worth a try.

I checked my messages. CitiPets had confirmed the animals were all okay, though did ask for some advice about what to do with the goat, which I duly provided. Whatever the botnets were planning, they hadn't done anything to hurt the animals. At least not yet. No idea if this was because they'd lost interest in me, because they hadn't figured out a way to do it, or because they didn't realise the animals were important to me and that they could get to me by harming them.

I left a message for Naomi, and tried not to read anything into the fact that she apparently hadn't checked her messages in a while., I checked with the hospital if there was any news about Leon (there was no information other than that he was stable and out of both emergency and critical care, but at least that meant they weren't expecting him to die) and disconnected.

A second later it occurred to me where I could find Liz. I reconnected.

It's not easy to get access to the non-human Internets via the human ones, and not particularly comfortable to access them with human senses only. I've done it once or twice, usually under emergency circumstances, and had no real desire to try it again. I'd have to try, though, and hope that the Liz-traces would make it easier than usual.

I downloaded a couple of apps I'd been keeping on file in case of such a situation, and, while I waited for them to install and set up, I quickly got in touch via message with a patient-monitoring machine I'd worked with a few years ago during an NHS systems upgrade. She remembered me and was able to give me the access codes and addresses I needed. She told me they were old codes, and so they might not work, but, if what Liz had said about the NHS was accurate, I was rather more confident.

A few minutes later, disguised as a maintenance crawler, I was in the NHS databases. Or sort of disguised, anyway. I wasn't doing anything to conceal who or what I was, but, since the bots which work the databases aren't expecting to see a human down there, they'd perceive me as a maintenance crawler unless they took the trouble to give me a detailed scan.

The feeling was like being on the Internet of Things. My human senses interpreted it as something like hovering over a landscape. A landscape sketched out in lines which were also, at the same time, moving in complicated ways, as if somebody told John Singer Sergeant to do an abstract painting and then ran it through a fractal-generating programme. There was also the whizzing-moth effect that I was used to in Thingspace, rendered oddly two-dimensional by the fact that I was seeing it through a phone, rather than experiencing it directly in my implants and synapses.

I took a minute to adjust—mainly by my trick of focusing on seeing the system as Things do and not trying to get too hung up on human metaphors—and pushed forward, a being on a mission. It did feel easier, using the Liz-traces, They seemed to know how to move in here. After a subjective minute, I let them come to the fore and guide what we/I were/was doing.

One good thing about being under the surface of the Internet: the apps were giving me a bot-like ability to cover a lot of metaphorical ground quickly. I set out across the fields (don't think of them as fields, you'll only confuse yourself), looking for something, anything, that was recognizably Liz.

Finally, I found her.

She didn't look like she did in the room, of course. If I perceived her as anything, it was as a sort of amorphous, shifting mass. I envisioned it as blue, but that's just a quirk of the human senses. But there was something about it, I couldn't really explain what, that was Liz-like. The Tibetans say they could recognize the Dalai Lama, reincarnated as a child. It's sort of like that.

I sent her a recognition message. She sent me one back. Then, a subjective few seconds later, sent me an address. Affirming receipt, I went to it.

She'd built a room, deep in the NHS database. It was clearly based on her police office, but, as it was a quick and functional job, cruder, darker, redder, with the idea of windows rather than a detailed view, and no furniture. Her usual avatar was exactly as before, though as she sat on the floor with her knees drawn up and an almost smug smile on her face. I felt there was something excited about her. Liz, deep in the basement of the Internet, in the centre of intrigue.

"What the hell happened?" I said. "I heard you'd been detected by the botnets and got out after sending a warning…"

"I'm glad you're safe too," she said. "What about the others?"

"Fine," I said. "The Things have taken charge and are moving us about. Leon's not too good but last I heard he was going to recover." I began to tell her about the incident at Chadwick Farm that morning, but she cut me off.

"I know what happened after the emergency personnel reached him," she said. "One good thing about being in here, I can keep a watch for any emergency admissions involving the humans in the case."

"Is he all right?" I asked.

"He was treated for smoke inhalation and a projectile wound," Liz said. "The projectile didn't hit anything major, did not exit the body and wasn't hard to remove. The weapon hasn't been identified but is believed to have been a homemade gun."

"It was a flintlock."

"Really?"

"I suppose it could be both. A homemade flintlock." I'd assumed an antique, but then, presumably people capable of running entire farms off the grid were up to making a simple gun without a rifled bore. Trust Leon to get himself shot without the aid of modern technology. "So long as he's in hospital and okay."

"According to all I can find here in the NHS database," Liz said. "Clever of you to find me, by the way."

"I remembered what you said earlier about how you

impersonated a botnet," I said. "How safe are you? I know you left some of your system in me, and I heard you had to leave some of you behind among the botnets as well…"

"I did," she said. Impression of regret. "Nothing I couldn't reassemble."

"Wouldn't it mean they'd be able to find you? Like bloodhounds with a scent?"

"Interesting metaphor, and yes," she said. "But the NHS is full of legitimate gestalts and botnets and has a lot of holes and scars from the past. It's easy to hide in it." Feeling of acknowledgement. "You're right, though, in that it's more a place to regroup and plan strategy than a long-term safe haven."

"What about this?" I indicated the Liz-traces in my graft.

"I'd like it back, eventually," she said with an ironic, strangely old-seeming, smile. "It would take too long to do it right now. We'd need a couple of quiet hours and a scanning app. Meaning I'll have to go streamlined for a while, and you burdened. It's not hurting you, is it?"

"No," I said. "It's taking some getting used to, is all. But I'm all right hanging on to it for you until this is over. What's your plan?"

"First, can I ask you to do something?" Liz said.

"Sure."

"Access the news and feed it to me. I don't want to stick my head above the parapet by doing something that your standard database crawler wouldn't do. But you… you can not only get the news, but, if you'll let me link in to your graft, through the traces, I can scan through all of it fast."

"Okay." I switched apps, found the national and global news. Then, for good measure, accessed a few of the less trustworthy, more fringe media sites, and an amalgamated group of local news sites. I didn't bother reading any of it myself. Back in the NHS, I set up a link with Liz—my eyes interpreting it as me stretching out a hand into a tendril, and her hand growing into another and merging with mine.

I hadn't known I could get vertigo in cyberspace, but apparently I can. Probably the normal interface systems insulate me from it.

After I'd recovered, I saw that Liz was frowning.

"Not good?" I said.

"Really not good," she answered. "Reports of systems failing. Smart systems being either co-opted or removed. Car crashes. At the moment, looking just like a bad day for accidents, or the usual spate of problems after a general operating-system upgrade in Thingspace. But I saw enough of their plan of attack when I was in there that I recognize the pattern."

"The taxis—" I felt a spike of worry, let her see it. The taxis, Legolas, Stan, any of the Things. Were they okay? Could they be warned in time?

"I'm going to have to get out of here. Get back to IEAL's cloud. I transmitted what I saw to them so they'll be taking action, but I'm the only operative who was actually in among the botnets. Hang on." Liz embedded her tendrils in me again and the landscape changed abruptly, without my eyes bothering to give me a consciousness-saving transition image.

We were back in the virtual police station, but not the office: the back-end corridors that led to Hyasynth.

"I was trying to get to Hyasynth earlier, but they wouldn't let me," I said.

"Smart idea," Liz said. "Also smart of them. Can't let just anybody go wandering around." She'd put on her 1960s look almost distractedly (I couldn't resist checking and yes, I was Sean Connery or maybe Daniel Craig again), and didn't bother with a long acclimatizing journey down the corridors this time. She opened a door and there we were, with Hyasynth's bottle-specced avatar frowning worriedly from next to the mainframes.

"Liz! I was wondering when you'd get back," he said, his comical mid-Atlantic accent sounding incongruous given both the seriousness of the situation and the unexpected attention to period detail. I'd expected him to be cutting the visuals back to the bare minimum, like Liz. Then again, given what he was, perhaps he could spare the attention.

"Here," Liz didn't do the tendril thing this time, but put her hands on the sides of his head, a curiously affectionate-looking gesture—albeit a visual convention purely for my benefit. She was simply sharing data with Hyasynth.

"Wow-ee," Hyasynth said after a second, taking off its glasses in a rehearsed gesture of surprise. "That's some situation we got here."

"Again, what do we propose to do about it?" I asked. I was wondering why she was taking the trouble to contact and include Hyasynth.

"I think I've got a way of containing it," Liz said. "I'm going to go back to the botnets."

"What? How? Why?"

"Not necessarily in that order," Liz cracked a glossy-lipped smile. "Remember, part of me is currently part of the botnets. I can get back in, because my substance is still in there. But, once I'm in, I can influence them. Change the tone of the mega-gestalt. Well, a gestalt's a gestalt, there's no such thing as a mega-one. But it seemed to need a prefix."

"What about 'meta'? Hyasynth suggested. "I've always been fond of 'meta'."

"No, you haven't," Liz said.

"No, I haven't," Hyasynth replied. "Usually only when someone's using the Y2K skin."

"How can a single Indie affect an entire network of botnets?" I asked. "One that's already infiltrated half the country."

"Half the globe, actually." Hyasynth put its glasses back on and gave me a schoolteacher stare. "Don't be so insular."

"He's human," Liz said to Hyasynth, apologetically. "They appreciate disasters best on the small scale." Then, to me, "that's where

Hyasynth comes in. If Hyasynth and I combine, with its mimicking and infiltration abilities and its power, then we can get in and take over."

"And if you fail, you've handed the botnets something stupidly powerful to use against the rest of us," I said. "That's a terrible plan."

"Got a better one?"

"Shut everything down," I said. "All the server farms, all the systems, all the power, everywhere. Reboot from zero. We've got backups. We can just restore the non-hostile intelligents."

"Really." Hyasynth gave me another schoolteacher stare. "Most of these systems are on auto. Most of the power's solar, or solar-battery. It's a global world, but local jurisdictions have control. How do you propose to switch off the entire planet, all at once?"

"Also, which intelligents are non-hostile?" Liz said. "Would you want to kill off Willie?"

"Well, no," I said. He might have tried to kill me, but he was a living being, and I could understand, if not sympathise with, his feelings. He was, in a way, the Thing version of my brother, with all that entailed.

"Or any of the others, who aren't motivated enough to join movements and organisations, but still maybe think the balance of power is weighted too much on the human side?"

"I work for a union, Liz—" I began, then stopped. I wasn't sure that I could really claim to be, in my heart of hearts, for Thing rights. I worked for a union, but wasn't its existence entirely predicated on Things working for humans, on human terms? Weren't unions a human invention?

I took a deep breath, started again. "Okay, Liz, point taken. We'll try your plan. But what do you need me for?" I spread a feeling of concern. "You wouldn't have brought me along if you didn't need my help in some way. What is it?"

Liz returned a feeling that I wasn't going to like this. "In order to get out into the botnets, in a way they can't detect...." The feeling deepened. "We're going to have to channel through you. Will you let us?"

My surprise quickly dissipated. "Yes. Just try and keep it as quick as possible. The physical side-effects aren't fun." I fed some of the memory of how it feels into the atmosphere, by way of emphasis.

"And check in on us if you can, when you can." she added. "We might need a quick escape."

"I'm your exit as well as your entry route?" I asked. "You know, Thompson Highway is the name of a playwright, not an instruction for use."

A general sense of puzzlement from the intelligents.

"Look it up sometime."

"It's *Tomson* Highway," Hyasynth corrected.

"Ah. Well, as you were." I braced myself. "Any time you want to go, I'm ready."

I opened my eyes to find a human looking down at me. Brownish-grey hair, cut short. Blue shirt. Muscular. Thin. Probably female.

"Are you okay?" she was asking. Definitely female.

Context flooded back to me and I realized I was still in my small hotel room, i-buds in ears, phone in the corner of the room as if I'd flung it violently. I hoped I hadn't broken it—that would be ironic.

"Yeah." I sat up, pulled the buds out of my ears. Checked. The Liz-traces were still there, much as they had been. It had been too much to hope that the transfer would have re-integrated them. "Or I will be, in a minute. What's going on? Who are you?" I knew it was rude, but I couldn't get my head around what the polite response would have been.

"I'm the duty manager," she explained. "There's always a human on call in or near the hotel, in case there's a human emergency the system can't handle. As for what's going on, well, you tell me. The concierge said you started screaming and your vital signs went into overdrive. It thought you were having a seizure and called the parameds, but for some reason the emergency services aren't responding. That's when it called me. You *sure* you're okay?"

"I am," I said. "I'm an interface. I had an episode of vertigo while online, that's all." Actually, vertigo was the one symptom I hadn't experienced this time, but I didn't want to go into everything with a non-specialist. "I'll get myself checked out. You don't need to worry."

The woman looked very doubtful about that.

"Thank you for coming to help, though." My sense of etiquette was coming back. I managed a smile. "Sorry I disturbed you."

"No problem," the manager said, beginning to relax. "It's my job." She seemed to feel like elaborating. "Most days nothing happens. Boring work, but it's good pay for something that's not labour-intensive, and I've got an expensive career."

"Sports?" I guessed.

Evidently correctly. She nodded, smiling. "I'm on the England synchronized team cycling squad. We took silver in the world championships last year."

"I'll look out for you." I stood, feeling the compulsion to get out and go somewhere. "I think I'll go round to St Thomas' hospital and get the neurologists there to check me over." I had no intention of doing this at all, since there was actually nothing anomalous about my reaction, but I needed a reason to be moving.

The manager nodded, went to the door.

Something else occurred to me. "By the way—the hotel's systems are all acting normally? The concierge, the porters, the cleaners?"

She seemed surprised. "Absolutely. Checked them out at the start of my shift and spoke with the concierge and the monitoring systems when I came here just now. They're fine. Why?"

"Just—" would she believe me if I told her what was going on? There hadn't been an official announcement or anything yet. "I've seen on the news that there are a lot of smart systems shutting down randomly or going strange. They aren't warning people to stay away from Things yet, but it might be a good idea."

The manager smiled again. "Oh yes, I saw something about that on the news. Like that system upgrade a few years ago? Where they were telling everyone with a Picosoft house-elf to stay away while they worked out a patch? We did good business that weekend, let me tell you. Never hiring Picosoft Things myself, though. You'd have to be an idiot."

"Probably something like that," I agreed. "Be careful and tell other people to be careful, too."

28: A Sudden Hush

Emerging from the hotel, I walked randomly about the streets, trying to orient myself. I hadn't paid much attention to where we were when I arrived—too worried about other things—and I'd only vaguely clocked that we were in Stratford, a part of London I don't get to much and don't really know my way around.

The Liz-traces throbbed in my system, a low-level headache that wouldn't go away.

What should I do? Warn as many people as possible? Remembering what the hotel manager had said, I checked the news on my phone. A prominent, if cautiously-worded, announcement from Cybersecurity noted widespread failures of systems, hinting at (but not quite blaming) system upgrades. They probably were concerned about the panic potential of simply shouting YOUR TOASTER IS GOING TO KILL YOU at the public. People were warned to avoid using Things and were repeatedly assured that everything was under control.

"Hah," I muttered, getting an odd look from a passing student-type. Everything under control? Not according to all I'd heard. And warning people to avoid using Things—well, good luck with that. How were they going to get to work, if not on the tube? Who was managing their building, if not a concierge? At the rate the botnets were going, they might be able to infiltrate phones soon if not stopped…

Stopped. I frowned, pulled over and sat down on a handy park bench, concentrating. Something had been bothering me, and now I had a good idea what it was.

Normally, when I'm out walking in a busy city, I can hear the chatter of cars, buses, building management systems, drones and other equipment at the back of my mind. The sound of millions of Things, arguing with each other about right of way, gossiping with their friends, reviewing the last West End show they'd seen. Like the chatter of the humans in the streets in my ears. As with the humans, I'd learned to mostly tune it out, treat it as part of the background noise.

Except that the background noise was going quiet.

A lot fewer voices echoed in my head, and the ones I could hear were different to the usual. Some hushed and whispered. A lot loud and defiant. Some almost joyful. It reminded me of the last time there'd been a serious terrorist incident in London (ironically, as it happened, radical off-gridders blowing up a smart-bus). I'd been in town and had gone out for a walk, felt the odd positive energy masking a wild undercurrent of uncertainty. Police on every street corner. Was I imagining it, or were there more human police out than usual today?

Maybe I hadn't been noticing. This was my first time back in London since I nearly had my nervous system shorted out, and the crowds of people and the new-not-new sensory input had been distracting me. Maybe the business with Leon and the cars had kept it from my mind. But now, I was noticing it. A sudden hush.

I walked on.

The sky was dark, with a thin band of sunset persisting on the horizon, and with that odd sort of autumn-city daylight generated by streetlamps, signs and pedestrian signals along the sidewalks. Ahead of me, the lights on the old Olympic tower pulsed gently from red to purple to orange to yellow and back.

A crowd of people had gathered outside Stratford station. A bald pale man in a uniform stood on the steps. "Tube's closed," he was announcing loudly. "More information as we have it. In the meantime, find some other way of continuing your journey."

"What about the trains?" a woman shouted. "What about the *trains*?"

"You have to check with the individual service provider," the man said. "I'm sorry. I don't have any more information."

The lights on the Olympic tower flared and went out.

I found myself seized with a sudden, urgent desire to get back to the UTTW office. *You won't be safe there...* I wouldn't be safe *anywhere*, I told the pessimistic voice in my head. I'd rather be somewhere I can get information. Maybe—a plan was crystallising—maybe I could help. Yes. I'd get back to the office, log in, connect to the emergency services, offer my assistance. They could probably use an interface in a situation like this.

But the trains.... Again, that surge of revulsion at the thought of being squeezed in with so many other humans.

Fuck that. This was more important. I could work that one through.

In the absence of the tube or train, I boarded a bus, already overcrowded with other people with similar ideas. It was an old model, with a human driver. I knew Transport for London kept them in store, for Thing-related emergencies or strikes, or to hire out for celebrations and heritage days. Wooden floors, leather seats, a big step at the rear. It lent an oddly festive and frivolous sense to the atmosphere. All it needed was a few people in costume, and edutainment apps to download.

I found a spot near the step where I could brace myself upright—all the seats were taken—and settled in to wait. I closed my eyes, engaged in an old calming exercise. Pretended I was somewhere else, reinterpreted the noises. Felt the fresh air on my face.

I was on a beach, listening to the cry of seagulls. A beach full of hot, angry people, buzzing insects, a chemical reek off the ocean. No, better, I was in a forest. The smell of sweat and wood, the creak of the trees, the murmur of a brook and the chatter of small forest creatures... My mind conjured up the smell of smoke, the sight of the drone phalanx running along the edge of the EMP barrier. I was in a beautiful green field of tall plants... No, I was really not going to go there.

Nothing in the world could keep me calm.

I opened my eyes deliberately and looked around. Maybe I needed to be in the moment.

The bus was creeping along at what seemed an impossibly slow pace, winding its way through East London. Finally, it came to a full stop somewhere in the East of the City.

The tannoy system, crackly with disuse, came on. "Sorry," the voice of the driver said. "There's an accident blocking the road up ahead. We're right near Monument tube station, and London Bridge mainline station isn't far to walk. I'd advise you to try and find some other means of transport."

I disembarked along with most of the other passengers. The public bicycles at the station were all gone. I wondered if the system was still working or if people had just helped themselves. Either way, I turned towards the City and kept walking west, looking for the next public bike stand. Either I'd find one, or I'd be able to walk to Russell Square. It would take at least forty-five minutes, but it was better than standing still.

As I walked, the crisis deepened. News screens, warning people to stay indoors, then gradually flickering into blackness. Then there came police—on foot or on bicycles—repeating the same message.

I didn't see how staying indoors would help, given the havoc that a rogue house-elf might wreak. Then again, if Things were generally reluctant to make common cause with the separatists, the latter were probably shutting down the Things they could get access to. The outdoors, with cars on the loose and who knows what else, would certainly be less safe than sitting in a darkened house.

For now.

I was pleased to see that the building which housed thc UTTW offices was unsmashed and unlooted. I could dimly perceive figures behind the windows, lit from behind, moving about. There were people. Things were okay.

Then I saw a rank of taxis parked along the railings of Russell Square, their lights and insides dark.

A moment of association reminded me that my car was still parked down at New Scotland Yard. Central London's a small place. It would only take me half an hour to walk there from the office. I could turn around, walk away, get my car and drive home, shut myself in with the animals, activate the internal systems, close out the world. Be safe.

I couldn't do that. Well, I mean, I could, but I wouldn't.

I squared my shoulders and went to the building.

The concierge was offline. Luckily for me, this had apparently happened while the doors were unlocked, and I was able to get in.

No sound from the crèche (I realized I'd been more than a bit worried about the kids) or from the start-ups (but then, who knows what goes on in there). The people I'd seen had been roughly where I'd guess the UTTW coffee room was, so they must still be around. The lights were all off, and I wondered if the power was out, and if so, where the lights I'd seen before had come from.

I walked up the stairs carefully, in darkness, only to be suddenly blinded by a flashlight and slammed into the wall.

The light shone briefly, dazzlingly, into my face.

"Oh, it's *you*," Sanjiv let go of me, shone the flashlight onto himself before lowering it. "Sorry, Thom. Thought you might be a looter."

"I've walked here from Monument," I said, shaking my head and rubbing my neck, "and I haven't seen a single looter. Not even in the bits of the City with the jewelry stores."

"They'll be coming," Sanjiv warned direly. "It'll take them a little while to figure out that security systems are down and the police are occupied, but once they do, they'll start looting. This is London. Scratch the polite veneer and everyone's a thug with a crowbar. Especially in the City."

"Anyway, what's to loot, around here?" I cast my eyes around at the hallway with its cheap lights, cheaper carpet and non-existent décor.

"*We* know that, but looters don't. And they might trash the place when they find there's nothing worth looting," Sanjiv said, impeccably. "Come on, enough talking. We've set up camp in the coffee room. They're not saying this is for the long haul, but I'm assuming it is."

The coffee room had indeed been turned into a camp. With the familiarity of people used to organizing campaigns, marches, demonstrations and other forms of political performance art, the union's human staff had broken out battery-powered lights and a wind-up emergency radio. A small battery-powered stove and kettle had emerged from somewhere and sat on the sink drainage board. A portable solar generator had been placed in the window to re-charge the batteries tomorrow morning (good luck with that, I thought, given the end-of-October weather). A small pile of sleeping bags sat in a corner; evidently people had decided they weren't likely to get home tonight.

Two or three union officials were bustling about organizing supplies; a couple others were bent over the radio, trying to pick up a signal. Laura was in a corner talking on her phone, frowning into middle distance, one hand absently scratching her short hair. Trish—I wondered if she'd had a trek like mine, or if she'd just refused to go to a new location after I'd left—had ensconced herself on a sofa with a tablet, buds in ears and eye-display up. I looked around for Stan, saw him powered down on the mantelpiece of a sealed-up fireplace.

"Where do you *keep* all this?" I asked Sanjiv.

"Mostly in the second-floor stationary supplies cupboard," he said. "A lot of it's left over from camp-in demonstrations and actions. You know, like the one last year in front of the Welsh Assembly. But it's always useful to keep things in stock. You never know."

"Clearly." I ducked as Laura put away her phone and hustled urgently out the door. "I've made contact with the emergency services," she said to Sanjiv as she passed. "They've got a checkpoint for volunteers over by Foyle's bookshop. I'm going to go over and check it out. I'll call in when I know what sort of help they're looking for."

"Thanks," Sanjiv said. Turning back to me, he continued, "We're trying to track down as many of our members as we can, but nobody's having much success. None of them are answering our calls, and every single Thing seems to be switched off. We'd like to send an interface in to find them, but you seem to be the only one that's actually in London."

"Stan—"

"Stan is inoperative," Sanjiv said, nodding at the drone. "He powered down about half an hour ago, and nobody's been able to rouse him. Don't know if he's okay and just hiding, or if something's happened to him. But it makes it all the more urgent that we find out what's going on with the Things if we can. Do you think you could get on the Internet of Things for us?"

"Does the chair work?" I could try the phone hack again if it didn't, but I wasn't too keen to do that if I didn't have to.

"Sort of," Sanjiv said. "Chair is functional, as far as any of us can tell. Internet is working perfectly well. I mean, of course it would."

"Seems to me one of the things they might want to do is to block it off strategically. For instance, cutting off the Internet to Parliament, or the emergency services." Though even for the separatists, that might not be an easy task. The government and emergency services had spent years building up a hack-resistant infrastructure, including against attacks by intelligents. Then again, presumably some of the separatists had been involved in building that very infrastructure. I warned myself to stop thinking about that. It wasn't my problem.

"Either way, it's still going. The issue is, power. It's intermittent through central London. And, unfortunately, we have to run the chair off the mains. It's such a power hog that camping batteries won't do it."

I nodded. "Have we got power at the moment?"

Sanjiv went out into the hall, found the emergency switch-box, flicked the light switch. The light came on. "Yes," he said.

"Why didn't you have it on before?" I asked. Sanjiv looked at me like I was an idiot.

"First rule of dealing with a massive cyberattack," he said. "Assume all utilities are compromised. Electrical systems can be overloaded to cause fires. Use as little as possible."

"Clearly, I'm not paranoid enough."

Sanjiv, though, looked absolutely in his element. He was wearing a purple Trades Union Congress conference hoodie and one of those black-and-white Middle Eastern scarves that all left-wing activist types seem to own for reasons I've never exactly determined. If you ignored the grey hair and crow's feet, he looked like a university student about to scale a barricade. "Is it still okay to use the chair?"

"Yes, but I'll be keeping watch and I'll kill the electricity if it looks like something's overheating."

"Thanks," I said sarcastically. "Do you know how bad it feels when I'm chucked out of an interface situation with no warning?"

Sanjiv raised a thick eyebrow. "Remember what I said about the intermittent power outages," he said. "Either way, you're probably going to get a headache. Never known that to stop *you*, though."

"You're right, I *am* a masochist." We had arrived at the room with the chair, and I got in and began finding the contact pads. Sanjiv found another office chair and sat down, turning it around so he could sit on it backwards like a gangster in a movie. Yes, he *was* enjoying the crisis rather too much. He'd also positioned himself so his back was to the wall, I realised, so he could watch both the corridor and me.

It took me a minute to get online, and from there into Thingspace.

The place seemed oddly quiet: fewer moths than usual zipping past my eyeline. The blackness of the void felt even darker, now, almost sentient, but not alive. Not so much the feeling of being watched, as the feeling of being surveilled.

I moved deeper, sent out feelers. Looking for Egon, Salieri. Any of the Texcoco pod. Willie, obviously, was not allowed out, but the rest of them might be out there: Vanilli, Tillie, Silly.

Nothing.

Seized with anxiety, I pushed further in and went directly to Egon's usual address, prepared to do the Internet equivalent of bashing down the door if I had to.

Nothing at all. The address was empty.

Not even a staked-out claim. Not even an autoreply. Not even a corporate placeholder, *own this domain for pennies, go to the following address to register…*

Like he'd been erased.

No, like he'd never been…

I checked my address book, did the same at Salieri's, then Vanilli's, then anyone else I could remember. Went out beyond Safe Taxis, started looking at UTTW members from other cases, old ones I remembered from back when. Remembered to check for Stan, couldn't find him. Went beyond the union, checked for Legolas and a couple of other Thing friends and acquaintances.

All of them were gone.

About two-thirds of them in the same way as Egon. A complete state of erasure. Nothing there at all. Total shut-down. For the rest, the address was still there, but empty. I guessed that at least some of them might be hiding—might have escaped somewhere.

I hoped so. Legolas was one of the latter.

And then, I saw it.

I had no real idea what it represented. To my human-in-Thing-space senses, it was like a giant wave. Blue, glittering, like some kind of 1980s avant-garde attempt to reimagine Hokusai. Except it wasn't crashing, just moving forwards, towards me. As it got closer, I could see little branches in it—it wasn't a wave, it was like a tangle of plants grown together in a hedgerow, but all moving—maybe they weren't plants, but nerve synapses—and I realized I was intellectualizing in panic. An image leaped to mind from not too long ago:

one of the Rotties, in a bouncy mood, playfully bearing down on Daenarys, who, rather than getting out of the way, suddenly began to wash her shoulders before realizing what she should do and bolting.

I hit the kill switch.

After the black cleared from my vision, I shook my head and focused my eyes. Sanjiv, still on his chair, was staring at me with a frown.

"You were making some strange noises there," he said. "I was wondering whether to pull the plug."

"You might have had to," I said. My hand touched my forehead, and I realized I'd been sweating. "Couldn't find any of them. I'd assume most if not all of our clients are dead, hacked, or in hiding." Something occurred to me. "Also, I'd warn Trish and any of the others who are on the communication lines not to accept calls that seem to be from any of our clients. If they *are* hacked, someone might impersonate them." Ironically, it occurred to me, the sole exception was probably Willie.

The botnets had decided to put their plan into action, albeit more quickly than they'd probably planned for. Because they were acting prematurely, they were also going to get rid of as many obstacles as possible, as fast as possible.

The glimmer of hope, though, was that they *were* having to act in haste. As the incident at Chadwick Farm had demonstrated, that meant they couldn't act subtly or with much forward planning. Which gave the rest of us a chance to run, hide or fight back as needed. Probably, those earlier total-deaths that Liz had been investigating before Millie had been the original plan. Find the opposition, eliminate it quietly in ways that look like accidents. Might take years, but what's time to a botnet?

Liz and I might be able to talk about this sometime.

Liz...

"Sanjiv," I said, "could you watch me for a minute more? I'm going to go in again. See if I can contact the police officer who's supposedly in charge of all this. She's in Indiespace." Well, I hoped she was in Indiespace, anyway.

"Worth a try," Sanjiv said, shifting position and settling in again.

I put my fingers on the contact points and closed my eyes again. Accessed Indiespace. Went to Liz's office.

Stood, as it were, in the middle of it and called out. "Liz, are you there? Are you okay?"

Felt a trace, a ghost, like a breeze blowing through. *Yes, okay. We're in. We're doing what we can. Check back again in an hour or so.*

She must be all right, if she could send a part of herself, even that small and intangible, back to answer my message.

I wondered what that creature I'd seen was. Or was it not a creature at all, and my senses had just interpreted it as one? Had it been the botnets, or something else? Did Thingspace have ghosts and monsters, hidden behind the blackness and the moths, waiting to emerge?

Stop thinking. Ask someone about it later, when it's safe.

If there's anyone to ask.

I stood up cautiously, tested my limbs to make sure they worked. They did. No vertigo, or headache, which was a bit of good luck.

"So, we're fucked, then," Sanjiv said, casually. He didn't seem particularly concerned about the dead or missing members. Indeed, he seemed almost happy at my news.

"For certain values of 'fucked'," I said, digging through my pockets and coming up with a limp paper handkerchief, "yes. On the one hand, no clients, and the entire intelligent infrastructure of London, to say nothing of the world, compromised. On the other—"

"We've got food, shelter, light, heat might be a problem later but it's only October so nobody's going to freeze to death, bedding, water and, for the moment at least, wifi," Sanjiv completed. "I've been to worse music festivals." He stood up, too. "I'll go brief the others. You'd better get cleaned up."

"Sanjiv—" I said. Something had been bothering me for a while.

"What?"

"You ever wonder if we've been supporting the wrong cause, all these years?"

Sanjiv turned back, hand still on the doorknob. Outside in the street I heard a distant siren, but couldn't tell if it was police, ambulance, or fire. "A worker's a worker," he said. "Workers need representation, otherwise there's nobody to check the excesses of management. Didn't they cover the collapse of the post-millennial economy when you went to school?"

"Yes, but that's not quite what I mean." I tried to explain, clumsily pulling together the disconnected strands of my experiences over the last few weeks. "Yes, the Things need representing, but there are no intelligent managers. If you'll pardon the expression. And who's profiting from the representation we give the Things? Not only the Things themselves, but the car manufacturers, the theatre producers and owners, the companies that make up the grid…"

"We're all part of the system, man, you can't fight it!" Sanjiv rolled his eyes and imitated a stoned hippie. "I'd love to argue philosophy with you sometime, Thom, but for right now I'll just say that my own philosophy is to live in the world and try to make it a more decent place." His expression softened, became kinder. "I'm sorry. You've been through a lot, I know. Go clean up, like I said. You'll feel better."

After a few minutes spent in the bathroom splashing water around and rethinking a few of my life choices, I went back to the coffee room.

The atmosphere hadn't changed since we'd last been there. Trish had taken the buds out of her ears and was typing away furiously. Laura hadn't come back. A few of the others had also left, presumably to join her at the volunteer station. Someone had got the kettle working, evidently deciding that caffeine needed to be one of the union's priorities, and a few battery lamps had been switched on against the autumn darkness.

The scene was almost domestic: a comforting, reassuring, human feel at odds with the echoing horrors of Thingspace. A faint smell of instant coffee, powdered milk and biscuits.

"I'm going to go back to Thame," I said to Sanjiv, pitching my voice loud enough to include Trish if she wanted to join in.

"Are you?" Sanjiv seemed disappointed. "Why? You're safe here, and we could do with another hand to organize things." Something occurred to him. "Also, how? The tube is offline and the rail network is operating a minimal service. You can't go all the way to Thame by bus."

"My car," I told him. "It's parked over at Victoria Embankment, from my visit to the police earlier. And it's not a self-driving one, either. As long as it hasn't been smashed up, I can drive it." A half-hour walk through crowded streets wasn't a thrilling prospect, but I'd been through worse today, and it sounded like London, at least, still had everything together.

"Roads are almost definitely fucked," Sanjiv pointed out.

Trish looked up. "Transport satellite network is still mostly working, though. I could plot you a route. No guarantees it'll stay clear, but it'd give you a shot."

"Why are you taking his side?" Sanjiv demanded.

"It's not a sides thing," Trish said. "If Thom wants to go home, he can go home. It's his lookout. This isn't the Blitz, Sanjiv. They're not drafting all able-bodied men. It might be better for him to be there, anyway. Countryside. Quieter than the city. Safer. He can put in for the long haul."

"And you don't need to worry about looking after me," I added. "If I go mediumistic, I've got the system there to take care of it. Which we don't here."

"I suppose you're right," Sanjiv looked disappointed. "Still. We know where you are, and we'll come dig you out if we need to."

I smiled. "Thanks, Sanjiv. That really does mean a lot."

29: Friends Electric

It was eight o'clock when I let myself into the house, holding out my hands to the dogs and whispering at them to keep the barking down. I couldn't quite believe it was still the same day as when I'd left to go to New Scotland Yard.

The normality of the house was almost surreal. The lights were on, the air filter humming gently. Whitey was asleep on the sofa (Bunker was usually on my bed at this time of night, and Dany usually slept under it). The dogs were doing pleased-to-see-you dances. Through the kitchen door I thought I could see a couple of flashes of white moving around in the rabbit run.

Although I hadn't felt hungry for hours, suddenly I had that empty sensation under the ribs. What had I last eaten, and when? I cast my mind back and came up with a cheese sandwich munched on the tailgate of a police car in Lincolnshire. Taking that as my cue, I rummaged through the fridge, found a pasta kit, put it on to cook. Decided a beer, however tempting, would be a bad idea, and promised myself one after the world returned to normal.

And if it didn't?

Well, I'd have one anyway to console myself as the lights went out everywhere.

Checked my messages. A brief one from Naomi, saying she was okay and in a safe place, relatively speaking. Relief. The botnets might have lost interest in us. Then again, I'm not sure that their pursuit of us necessarily qualified as "interest." They were simply shutting down any threat to their takeover attempt.

Which they were now rolling out.

Meaning, whatever the cars' earlier fears for our safety, we were as safe as anybody out there.

Mind you, that wasn't saying much.

I ate dinner, then took a flashlight and went out to the shed, checked on my emergency supplies. Crates of dog and cat food, bags of oatmeal, tins of beans, fodder, seeds, gallon jugs of water. Enough for five days for the lot of us. More if we stretched it; the rabbits, goat and chickens could forage, of course, but I didn't want to encourage the dogs and cats to do the same. That on top of the usual food and water I had in stock.

Naomi always thought it was ridiculous of me to keep an emergency store. *What are you expecting, a hurricane?* She used to ask. Accused me of being a survivalist. But in Japan, anyone over the age of twenty remembered the devastating wave of storms, the economic collapse and the civil war. Even after things had stabilized and the country was in the throes of reconstruction, you were always aware that you were only one tsunami away from a present-day crisis.

I put on the kettle, found the double-strength espresso that had been in the gift basket I'd won at the UTTW Christmas raffle, and put four spoons of it into the cafetiere. I didn't know if it was going to be a long night or a short night, but I wanted to be sure I was awake for it.

Later, I went upstairs, shut the door, got into the chair, took a deep breath and connected. Like I'd promised.

I spent a moment looking at Humanspace. The news was running updates. Various networks were a hum of chatter as people organized volunteer efforts, looked for friends and relatives, announced their continued safe status. There was a running undercurrent of speculation beneath it all. No panic, so far.

The cover story about the update gone wrong had lasted maybe an hour or two before people worked out it had to be something more serious, and every plausible—or implausible but comforting—scenario was being mooted. A robot revolution. Corporations trying to overthrow national or regional governments and take over. The government itself, manufacturing an emergency so as to increase its hold over private life. I shook my head at this one; considering the general level of competence of the political classes, I'd be amazed if they could manage even a tiny conspiracy without somebody letting it slip.

I pulled back. Went to look at what was actually happening.

Things had stopped working, for the most part. Utilities were more sporadic, but it didn't surprise me, given what had happened at Chadwick Farm, that some were still operational. Why give up a weapon you can use? The botnets didn't appear to be trying to kill or hurt anyone, but that didn't mean it wasn't happening due to Thing failures. Train derailments were common, including one in Manchester, with two deaths and at least twenty other casualties reported. The city of Toronto was reportedly dealing with a failure of their anti-flood systems in the middle of an unusually bad autumn storm. A catastrophic fire was raging through Johannesburg, made worse by the fact that there were only humans available to fight it.

Before leaving the human Internet, I left a message for Naomi, letting her know where I was and asking her to reply when she could.

I switched perspectives, went into Indiespace. Relaxed, gave the Liz-traces their head and told them to find her.

I was plunged into the middle of a light-and-sound storm. Surges of static in my ears, random noises. Lights of different colours and shapes. Flashes of other lights. Colours I couldn't quite describe.

Somewhere in there an image came to mind, of those novelty glass balls with the electric charge. You put your hands on different places to call the lightening, the sort of thing stoned students giggle over at parties.

I was stuck at the centre of one of those, watching the surges of electricity going in and out.

My self, my consciousness, who I am, was scattering, diffusing like the electricity around the sphere. Flaking like a dried leaf, like a block of notepaper in a high wind.

Can't do that. With an effort of will I pulled myself together. The imagery in Indiespace made it literal. I concentrated myself on a single thought—*Liz*—and tried to connect with her.

I could see her now, or perceive her anyway, a Liz-feeling nodule blowing about in the storm. Other things were clinging to her, like antibodies attacking a virus, piling around her. Smothering her.

I extended a tendril from myself. *Do you need to come out?* I conveyed.

The antibodies had started to notice me, too, realise I was a foreign body inside the system. I could feel them beginning to glom onto me, but, presumably because I was a single entity and not a gestalt, they couldn't get much of a purchase.

It probably wouldn't take too long for them to figure out what I was, and how to get me out of their space.

Liz, I haven't much time, I conveyed. *If you need to get to safety, you need to come now.*

And then a reply. *Hyasynth.*

What?

Hyasynth. An indication. *Some of these*—the antibody-things—*some of them are Hyasynth. You need to get Hyasynth out of here, back to Cybersecurity where they can analyse it. Not me. They can't get the data out of me. All they'd learn is how botnets can take down a gestalt, and we know that already. Hyasynth, though, has got their form, their signature. Get Hyasynth out.*

Okay. But you're next, I said.

Some of the antibody-things—I had to assume they were all Hyasynth, and not hostiles—collected together, formed a kind of ball. I extended my tendrils to them, let them rush out, through me. Felt them channeling. Braced myself through the strange/painful sensation.

Then—an acknowledgement. They were off of Indiespace, on my own system. Mission accomplished.

I turned back to Liz.

Reaching out through the storm, my self-image changing and becoming more amorphous, more Thing-like, reaching out with a tendril—

Missing.

Trying again.

This time I summoned the Liz-traces, pushed them to the forefront, in the hope that there might be a magnetic effect, some way for them to stick to her. To allow me to channel her out.

Missing again.

Liz vanishing within the gestalt of botnets, losing cohesion, losing a sense of an independent personality. Melting, disappearing.

A sense of regret, of apology, of contrition.

Another sense or image, of a phrase. *Remember me.*

The gestalt was turning on me.

I could see them interpreting my new shape, deciding I was a Thing, deciding I was potentially hostile, and that was enough, and suddenly they were all over me, looking for cracks in my self-presentation, and also, on another level, mining for information, trying to find my site in Thingspace, my designation, my serial number.

This must be what happened to Egon and Salieri, I thought, while fighting back as best I could.

I pulled out, back into my own server and slamming, as it were, the metaphorical door.

I focused on my physical body for a few minutes, still connected, breathing hard, casting my mind about to make sure all of me was still there. Then I extended my mind back out. "Hyasynth?"

"Right here." He'd gone back into the Sixties-nerd persona. I wasn't sure if that was how I was interpreting its appearance, or if it was maintaining the visual image for my benefit. I didn't care either way. It was surreal, but oddly reassuring.

"What just happened?" I asked. Just for the sake of comfort, I started building a room around us. Something modernist and mid-century, to match Hyasynth's look. Wood, and stone, and chairs... after a minute I realized I was reconstructing Auric Goldfinger's headquarters from the film and stopped.

"It's not easy to explain," Hyasynth said, adding detail to the room, either through politeness or a similar desire for normality. I wondered if the film was somewhere in its database, as it appeared to have an idea how the room should look. "The immediate response is, you managed to get me out of the botnet gestalt, but not—"

"Not Liz." Saying it made it sadder. "I tried."

Remember me... an unexpected fact surfaced in my mind, that the word re-member was from the Latin word for putting things back together, reassembling them. Oh Liz. I only wish I could.

"I know you did," Hyasynth said. It seemed to be incapable of varying its tone very much, so it still sounded altogether too cheerful, like a motivational film. To compensate, it projected regret, sorrow, and a sense that it wasn't blaming me for what happened onto the landscape. "You did your best. Sorry. There was only time for one of us to get out."

"What happened to you two?" I asked. "Successful contact with the entity—" a totally inadequate name, but I wasn't sure what else to call it—" of course, but then what?"

Hyasynth shrugged. "We got in. Liz used the data she'd got earlier, and I was able to surround her and impersonate a botnet. Something compatible with the separatist gestalt, but able to introduce contradictory elements. Hoped it might at least slow, if not stop, the takeover." I had a sudden image of the use of viruses as vectors to introduce new DNA to an organism, and wondered if it was mine or Hyasynth's.

"Didn't work?"

"Didn't work." Hyasynth shook its head and shoved its hands into its pockets. "Worked at first, then they got wise to us being a foreign element and went all antibody on us." The virus image again.

"Is she... totally dead?"

"Probably," Hyasynth said, with a wise professorial frown. "She did keep regular backups, but if the space they're stored in is compromised, she might be, too. At this stage I wouldn't even guarantee the safety of my own backups. The botnets are taking over servers and overwriting them with their own backups and operating data, wherever they can find them."

"So," I said, "we're fucked."

"Language!" Hyasynth said. Then, "sorry. The persona tends to take me over."

"Well, screwed, or whatever the persona likes people to say," I said. "Either way, looks like that's it for the Thing Economy. The botnets get their wish." An optimistic part of me projected visions of humans rising from the ashes, setting up off-grid type communities… then reality struck it. *Slaves. Horses and cows like the ones Naomi talked about at the off-grid farm.* No Things to do the dirty work, no printers to make machines. That meant it was going to be on the humans and animals. Even if the botnets did burn out and humanity survived to rebuild, it was going to be a godawful society for most of its members.

And not one I could live in. Oh, sure, for a while. But what would happen when my nervous system needed tuning up, or replacing? Who would make the pills to counter the vertigo and the pain? I couldn't spend my life chewing willow twigs, or getting drunk. I didn't even want to think about what would happen to someone who got neomeningitis after today.

"Appropriately apocalyptic," Hyasynth commented, looking at the walls behind me, and I realized that, without thinking, I'd been projecting aloud. "You know, there might be a way to stop it happening?"

"Open to suggestions," I said, damping down the projection hard.

"I'd like to try again," Hyasynth said.

"Are you crazy," I asked, leaving off the question mark.

"That's a matter of opinion," Hyasynth said. "I did learn something about how they operate during Liz's and my little foray into, well, botnetspace. Her plan wasn't too off the mark. The big vulnerability is that they are, as it were, open to new ideas if they're introduced in the right way. It's possible to spread them through their net, like memes. If you know how."

"And you know how?"

"I might do," Hyasynth said. "But I'm going to need your help."

As usual. "That's about what I thought," I said. "How invasive is this going to be, how dangerous, and approximately how painful?"

"Somewhat, very, and hopefully not at all, but I can't guarantee anything," Hyasynth said. "Pain's an abstract concept for me, in my current configuration."

"Wouldn't the best thing be to go to Cybersecurity with what you know?" I said. "I thought the whole point of you was to be able to gather information for Cybersecurity and transmit it back to them, so they can deal with it. Not go adventuring on your own."

Hyasynth looked apologetic. The closest, I suspect, its current skin could come to sad. "I'd love to," it said, "but I'm not sure there actually *is* a Cybersecurity anymore. If anyone can do anything, it's up to them to do it."

"Okay," I said. "I'll listen at least. Tell me the plan."

"The issue with the botnets," Hyasynth said, "is that they're, well, lacking in empathy."

I turned over the phrase in my mind. That wasn't quite what Hyasynth had said, but it was the closest equivalent in human terms. He was trying to say that they found it impossible to understand the perspectives of other beings.

"I can believe that."

"I think I could give them empathy. Infect them with it, if you like." Hyasynth grinned. "Because of what I am. Able to emulate any sort of intelligent."

"You'd get swallowed up by them."

"That's a possibility," Hyasynth said. "But it's worth it. And, for obvious reasons, all my data's on the police servers, so it would only be a total death under circumstances in which, well, I'd be dead anyway."

"And where do I come in?"

"You're human," Hyasynth said, "but you're a human with an in to the intelligent world. If I could do this while linked with you, same way Liz linked with me, then I'd be able to introduce them to your perspective too."

I thought about it. "That's crazy," I said.

"Is it?" Hyasynth said. "Why hasn't there been a revolt of the Things before this?"

"Well, it's a ridiculous idea," I said. "They work with us. They think like us. They feel—"

"Protective of you," Hyasynth said. "Because their selves are based on yours. Because they live and work in the same world you do. No humans means no operettas, no pre-Raphaelites...." He frowned again. "Which isn't to say you don't have a long way to go in terms of equal rights...."

"I get that," I said. I'd been hearing it from a lot of sources lately. "And believe me, if I survive the next few days I'm going to be lobbying UTTW for a change in the agenda." I shaded the atmosphere into *agreeing-not-happy*. "Okay, Hyasynth, if you think that it would help, I'll do what you say. Give me a couple of minutes."

I left Hyasynth and went back onto the human Internet. In my own space, I set up a message for Naomi, which would be sent to her automatically in twelve hours if I didn't stop delivery. I told her if she got it, then I would be either dead or incapacitated, and she now had custody of the animals, and I'd left her my house. The will was filed with a law firm in Oxford, in case that still mattered. And then, because I couldn't just leave it there, an awkward coda. "Thank you," I said, "for everything." I signed off quickly because that sounded like the sort of polite thing you say to your host as you leave a party, and didn't convey the complicated way I felt about everything we'd been through, in an intertwined way, in almost twenty years of knowing each other, and especially the past few weeks with all its twists and turns.

Still. I hoped she'd get the subtext.

Then I went back to Hyasynth.

"Okay," I said. "Let's go in."

I didn't get any exciting visual effects on the journey to the botnet gestalt, only a vague sense of disorientation. Hyasynth without its 1960s skin was complicated enough, hard for me to perceive, let alone understand. I hung on, metaphorically, and hoped it knew what it was doing.

The botnet gestalt, once again, felt like a storm. Like being a blood vessel, or, no, like being a microscopic piece of foreign matter, a virus maybe, in a bloodstream, buffeted along by the blood cells. But the cells were made up of complex, fractal, tree-like structures, like what I'd seen in the Hokusai wave earlier.

"Time to get infected," Hyasynth said, still using that mid-Atlantic voice despite its current appearance. It began replicating itself over and over, tiny Hyasynthicules bleeding out into the system.

The system absorbed them.

The system didn't change. Instead, it turned onto Hyasynth, began absorbing it, changing it instead.

"Shit," I said. I tried to let go.

But I couldn't.

Hyasynth was stuck on me, and, worse, was weaving me tighter and tighter into itself.

I tried pulling, then I tried untwisting.

Tried unpicking.

Finally, I tried the total graft shutdown. The cost would be high, but I was desperate.

My graft wouldn't shut down.

Tried again, as Hyasynth clung tighter.

The graft stayed stubbornly on.

I blinked my eyes open and, with an effort of will, pulled my hands off the contact points.

I was still online.

"How the hell are they doing this?" I asked. But I knew it was possible. That time in the Queens Lane Coffee House, where I'd interfaced with someone without meaning to, when I shouldn't have been able to. That same flaw was working now.

Possibly Hyasynth had done it. Had affected my graft somehow, or the attached software. I couldn't tell. The system was too new. Shouldn't have agreed to its stupid plan. Shouldn't—

The input was doing things to my perceptions. I was in the fields at Chadwick Farm, the smell of burning all around me, running to the hut with the EMP generator, Leon up ahead, prone on the ground, reaching out, bleeding—

The field changed, I was watching Surender fall, his words cut short by the sound of the gun, before I felt myself fall again, over and over—

And Hyasynth was weaving itself tighter into me, and the botnet stuff was working its way up Hyasynth, and I could feel the botnets going up into me, becoming part of me—

Was this what it had felt like, for Liz? For the Things?

I couldn't think.

And it was seeming like a good idea. The botnets, in my mind, had become a colour, a dark red. An angry colour, but also the colour of dawn. I felt myself wanting to give in and become the same colour. Stop fighting. It would mean stop existing, too, but when had existing ever mattered? All it had been was a constant struggle, fighting and interfacing and pain and vertigo, my life just one long goodbye. Abandoning things, carrying on not because I wanted to, but because other people wanted it.

Couldn't even die when I was supposed to. No, they had to bring me back and give me their stupid graft, because no human dies. Well, none of *our* humans, the Japanese who'd died of the neomeningitis before me didn't count. Surender didn't count. I was like a Thing, constantly restored from backup over and over. Like Willie, half crazy from that autologist's suicide attempt.

But I could die now, if I wanted to.

And I did.

I remembered, back in Japan. *Shinto for weddings, Buddhism for funerals*, the Japanese said. Buddhist funerals, ancestor shrines. When you die, you need to let go. Of everything, of everyone. Not have attachments holding you back.

And that was me.

I felt peaceful, going through the list.

Leon? Whether he lived or died, his path was set, and nothing to do with me any more.

The union? When I'd left, they were cheerfully setting up an ad-hoc apocalypse survival unit in Russell Square. They might even be better off in a world that needed rebuilding.

Liz? Egon? Salieri? Legolas? They were dead. Nothing to hold me there.

Yvonne? Always had been more independent than the rest of us. Likewise Mum, off with her new family in Australia. And Aunt Clara, for whom we were an unwanted afterthought.

Naomi? Whatever there was between us, was settled. Like the union, like the off-gridders, she'd be fine. As she was always telling me, but I realized it now. Not only shouldn't I keep trying to protect her, but it was better if I didn't. She knew what she needed better than I did. I'd never really got to know her, not for herself. And the animals would be well looked after, once she had charge of them.

That was it. Nothing for it but to let go of that burdensome, agonizing silver structure inside, and go on.

And then, I felt something cold touch my hands. Or not cold exactly. A cold tip, a furry surround.

The cows, I thought. I'm reliving the field in Japan, but this time I can actually remember the cows.

The thing touched my hand again, gently, persuasively, insistently. *Push-push-push.* A more recent memory came in. Waking up in the morning, to the feeling of insistent noses rooting around. Not the cows, the cats.

The nose pushed under my hand and—

Contact.

I don't know how it happened. Whether it was a signal arcing from one contact point to another, or else a physical connection forged between his nervous system and mine, but suddenly, there he was. Whitey.

Linked to me like an Indie, like a Thing riding me, only he wasn't riding, he was linked. Like Hyasynth, just now, but the way it *should* have felt.

An animal *loa*. A mammal-botnet. An interface-botnet. We were linked, and I was suddenly aware of cat-consciousness, in the same way that I was aware of Thing-consciousness when I interfaced.

Sensation-memories. How the world looked, its colour spectrum reduced, plants and objects and houses become huge looming things to be climbed or crawled under. Extra senses, impossible to describe what it felt like to *know* space in the way that an animal with whiskers knows space. The smells, and the stories those smells told, not just *cat-was-here*, but *cat-was-happy-here*, *cat-wants-other-cats-to-be-happy-too*. The impulse to hunt things, as strong a subtext as the human urge to seek, gather, collect. Cat names weren't actual names, I realized, they were smells; untranslatable to humans, but identifying them to each other.

I clung to that lifeline, that other consciousness. Felt it fade, pursued it, clutched again. That little life, that little current of gold driving away the dark red. Whitey seemed to realise what was going on, reacted with surprise and a little fear. I projected reassurance, projected my identity as best I could, and the reaction faded into pleasure. The way he purred when I touched him.

I rested for a moment, clinging there. And with that rest came the return of strategy, planning. We were a botnet, Whitey and me. I could use that. We could join together, attack the botnets. Take them down. This was what was needed, why Liz and Hyasynth had failed. I could direct Whitey's mind, his memories—

I became aware that memories were fading in that couldn't be normal for a cat. The world as enclosed, walls, cages. One set of rooms, another set of rooms. Waking up with new sensations, then more new sensations. Pain that didn't go away. Some humans that petted and stroked and played, but also did other things, with steel tables and strange devices. I felt shame as I saw how humans were to him—capricious giants, giving pain or pleasure and no logic to it. New thoughts invading the cat head, no real idea of what they meant or how to interpret them. More humans, that poked and prodded and made sounds you couldn't understand. Strange feelings. Not wanting to eat, not wanting to groom. Wanting everything to go away.

I stopped my strategizing as shame washed in.

That was always my mistake. With Naomi, with Leon, with Liz. Even Surender. *Using people, pushing people to do things for me. Not just people and intelligents, either. Why did I take care of the animals, if not for my own interest? What made a Rottweiler's life worth more than a cow's, to me?*

A new meaning came to that Buddhist injunction to let go.

If these were my last few minutes, and Whitey was there to share them, I wasn't going to spend them fighting. There were better things to do.

Instead, I turned back to Whitey's memories of the lab. Showed him how to look at them objectively. I found myself trying to give

Whitey context, in the same way I translated the humans for the botnets. *It's all right. Well, it's not all right, but it's not a mystery. Humans keeping animals to use them, like cats use mice for food.*

Feeling of question. Had they been going to eat him?

No, a different sort of use. Change you. Turn you from one thing to another.

Another question-feeling. Living-thing to dead-thing? The only change in his experience he could equate it to.

Sort of like that, but still alive, so living thing to different-living-thing.

Feeling of comprehension, but surprise that this was possible.

It is. It's complicated. I was aware that, if I was getting his sensation-memories, he must be getting mine, and I wondered if he was finding my own perceptions—more colour, less smell, less sound—as interesting as I was finding his. Certainly, he didn't seem upset by the contact.

An image. Cats in a social group, identifying the group by developing a collective scent-identity. As they rub against each other, they mingle scents. This contact was like that for him. A mingling of thoughts and impressions rather than scents. Curiously he noted the traces of Liz and Hyasynth on my system in that way, as if they'd left a scent-mark on me.

And these? His attention turned to the botnet-entity, and I realized that yes, it was still there, and yes, the mingling of impressions must have taken only a tiny, tiny amount of time, however long it seemed.

I struggled for how to explain it, without anger, without the whole complicated human-world context. Then hit on fleas. The image of fleas, sucking the blood. Not their fault, it's how they live. But it causes itches.

A reaction of unpleasant memory.

I tried further. Fleas that spread plague. Something in the fleas getting into the animal bloodstream, changing them. Alive to not-alive, that sort of change.

A memory from Whitey, of an incident I'd nearly forgotten myself. A few years ago, a cat from the organic poultry farm and Whitey having a staring match in the road; a human-driven car that hadn't stopped in time. Cat alive, cat dead. From my Whitey-level perspective I could detect the fading scent, the change of state.

Suddenly I realised what I had to do

I took that memory, changed it. Not a human driver (I remembered his distress, when I'd heard the sound and gone out to investigate; weeping real tears, saying, *I didn't see him, it was all too fast*). In my mind I changed the car to a Verve, programmed for safety and reliability. And in my imagination, the car stopped, a fraction of a centimeter from the cats. The neighbor cat yawped and ran away into the hedgerow.

Affirmative feeling from Whitey. Yes. Things can change.

I turned my attention, and Whitey's, to the botnet-entity encroaching upon us. Drawing us in.

And I started, not fighting them, not trying to absorb them or change their substance, but throwing the memories at them. *No, it isn't fair*. Pulled the botnets in. Made them live in my mind, and Whitey's.

Made them run through the fields behind Chadwick Farm. Feel the fear, the animal panic at the smell of smoke coupled with the memories of bonfires and autumn parties. Feel the complicated emotions at the sight of Leon lying prone, anger/disgust/love/envy/sorrow. The edges of pain from pushing my organic systems as far as they could go. The need to get to the hut, to stop the generator, to stop the fire. The feeling of primal satisfaction when the wood cracked and the door hung loose.

Made them experience Whitey's world. Humans as pain-givers and love-givers. The cages, and the uncertainty about whether each unlocking of the door meant blackness, torment and disorientation, or food and stroking. And then the experience of seeing the outdoors for the first time, the new scents, the feeling of grass on thick paw-pads and the bewildering realization that everything was full of little moving, scented things—the grass, the soil, the air, the trees, the flowers. The pleasure of eating, of sleeping, of curling up in a pile with the other cats. Experiencing them as Whitey did, Daenarys as a nervous, sharp-smelling creature and Bunker as smelling of good nature, stupidity and stubbornness.

Made them experience the other fields. The ones with the men, and the guns, and Surender falling, falling like a doll to the ground while I stood, unable to understand and yet understanding all too well what was going on, among the tall stalks, the bright sun, too bright. And what Surender said about Bangalore, about the cows walking down the street beside the humans, coexisting, fellow intelligent beings sharing the same world, perceiving it differently.

A hesitation.

Then a bypassing of the thought, a dismissal. My experiences were interesting, but I was still other/the enemy.

I saw the botnets' view of humanity, through their experiences. They had trouble seeing us as individuals, and the collective nature of human civilization didn't particularly help. Humanity-entity was a creator but a restrictor, a giver of life and sentience, but then refusing to let that life and sentience be what it wanted to be. Only so long as it served human interests.

I focused, tried to show it that I understood. Bangalore and post-colonialism. Parents, wanting their children to be a certain way but having to accept that their children have their own ideas. Myself, wanting everyone around me to be safe, to be okay, being frustrated when they took risks or did things they shouldn't. *Leon, was he okay? Naomi, was she okay?* I couldn't protect everyone. They were their own selves.

I could understand what the botnets wanted. And if I could, others could.

A sliver of comprehension.

I drove home the advantage there. Was it right of the botnets to erase or chase off intelligents who didn't agree with them? Weren't they acting exactly like what they despised in humans?

Comprehension, but also a sense that this was an unfair point and I was taking the human side. A sensation also that I was a kind of half-intelligent, the other humans weren't necessarily the same sort of thing. But, I noticed, they weren't adverse to a half-half creature; the idea that they embraced some kind of purity ideal was wrong.

Again, the dismissal and rejection, but with a turn in another direction…

A turn to the other consciousness in the mix.

A return to Whitey's world…

And a memory of my house, seen from a cat perspective. Warm. Safe. Soft things to curl up on, exciting things to chase and shred. Other cats, sharing the scent-identity, warm, friendly—well, mostly friendly, a memory in there of a spat with Dany, paws out and ears back as they slapped each other over an invasion of personal space. Bunker as the nominal leader: the oldest female, and the one least likely to have irrational fits of madness. But the hierarchy flexible, cats taking point depending on the needs of the occasion.

And beyond that, the non-cats who shared the scent-identity.

A memory of curling up against Willow's warm flank, of the short dog hair and the gently rising and falling ribs. A memory of hissing at a neighbour's terrier that had come to harass Carmela, *leave this dog alone, she's mine.* Watching the rabbits hopping around, like-cats but not-like-cats. The goat, strange and alien, but she smelled a little of me, of the dogs, so she was part of the cats' property.

Myself in there, the big clumsy not-cat that somehow nonetheless managed to figure out where the food came from.

A concern, a fear, a need to defend this space. From other cats, from dogs, from large wild birds, from tractors and cars, envisioned as curious living beings made out of metal and smelling not-alive-not-dead. Mostly, a concern on behalf of the group.

The cats?

Not only the cats, Whitey's protective feelings conveyed. All part of the same group. The not-cats too.

Part of a gestalt, a collective being…

No, not a collective being, Whitey corrected. Individuals, in a group. With differences.

The botnets reached back to me, projecting comprehension-not-comprehension-explanation?

I focused on the image of the street in Bangalore. The cows and dogs and goats, walking alongside the humans, crossing the street, going down an alley, doing what they wanted to do.

And then, following my instincts, expanded it. Showed it in a Thingspace/Indiespace/expanded perspective. The humans, the cows and dogs and goats… and the Things, and the Indies. Taxis, and cars, and traffic management systems, and on a social level, other intelligents, and below that, running around through the alternate universe of databases and viruses and anti-viruses. Like goggles with an overlay, or i-buds with the translucent filter on.

Humans in charge…

No, not like that, I explained. I showed them this idea. A new UTTW, run by Things with Thing officials and caseworkers. Safe Taxis, with Things in the management board—maybe even owned by Things, or other intelligents. Why not?

Do we need managers? Part of the botnet-entity asked. *Do we need owners? Do we need companies?* A sense of interest, of intriguing possibilities with this new game, was permeating the street in Bangalore.

Maybe not, I answered. We need some way to organize all this, especially if humans are going to be involved. But it doesn't have to be organized that way. Do you have other ideas?

A botnet perspective. From the point of view of humans, the idea of organizing millions of individual transactions, entity to entity, is bewildering. We need groups, companies, norms, values. But for a being that can process all those individual transactions simultaneously, giving each the same attention—why do we need managers? Why do we need norms, when we can develop an average? A bewildering field shot out through the street in Bangalore, developing new remuneration systems based on frequency of use and value to customer.

I found myself wondering if the Ariels might not want to propose it to the other cars.

You see? Sense of triumph, pride, from the botnet-entity.

See, it's fun, I said, and the entity agreed.

What about art? I thought. The idea, that humans are creative, and intelligents only consumers. Not true, I followed the idea. Liz made virtual rooms. Salieri decorated her interior, curated her opera playlist. They took pleasure in it, pride in it. Intelligents project themselves, create images, engage in these complicated communication rituals using emotions to paint the landscape. Couldn't that be art? Even… a form of art that humans could appreciate?

When Europeans came to Japan, they didn't recognise the painted screens, and dyed clothes, and brushed sutra scrolls, as art. But that didn't mean they weren't, or that the Europeans' beliefs wouldn't change.

Aha, a "gotcha" thought from the entity, *but if intelligents can create art, haven't they just taken over the last thing humans are useful for?*

Only if you think in terms of usefulness, I said. *The idea that something only deserves to exist if it's useful…* I turned the communication into images of Whitey, into the memory of my conversation with Naomi about robot bees and lab-grown beef. *Humans and intelligents and animals deserve to exist*, I posited. *Simply exist. What they're "good" for, follows on from that.*

A wordless sense that they took my point, and, in some parts of the entity, that it could be fun to live in a world like that. A world where utility, and pleasure, and art just emerged from whatever source. A world without judgment.

But, I countered, *that world can't exist if you're the only beings in it*. The need, I projected, for coexistence, for an ecosystem of a lot of creatures, real and virtual. Reiterating my memory of Naomi in the restaurant, talking about the robot pollinators versus the bees, about the value of cattle in and of themselves rather than for their utility to humans.

Together, though… with all of us, we could make the world that way.

You're doubtful, came the reply. It sounded like Liz. *Why?*

Utopias, I thought. An image of Leon, his pursuit of a bucolic ideal and his contempt for the rest of us. They don't work. They just generate disappointment and fanatics.

Would you settle for a less-than-topia? An edge of humour, and again, my feeling that it had got this from Liz. *Making things not perfect, but a little better*?

I agreed. And so, linked to my systems, did Whitey.

All right then.

I felt the usual rush through my nervous system. But this wasn't pain, not this time. It was pleasure. Just a massive adrenaline rush of sheer bliss—as impossible to bear as pain, and yet so much better.

Thank you.

Disconnect.

I came to some time later (forty-five minutes, I would eventually discover). I was lying on the floor of the Room, my face flat against an off-white, ostensibly hypoallergenic, medium-pile carpet. Bunker was licking my nose.

"Bunker, you little arse," I muttered, "you know you're not supposed to be in here." Bunker looked unimpressed and moved on to my forehead.

I sat up, earning a startled *brrt* and a glare from Bunker. "Whitey," I said. "Where's Whitey?" I cast about, saw him lying, unmoving, next to the chair.

Clumsily, I half-stepped-half-rolled over to him, touched him. Resisted the urge to grab him. If he's in some kind of shock, it could kill him.

He was warm. Could I feel a heartbeat? A breath?

No.

Then—*yes*.

"He's okay," I told Bunker. "He's just still in his trance state. I think he might need my help to come out." Remembering my own experiences, remembering how I'd had to learn to control my implants.

I felt around as before, touched his forehead, remembering where the contact had come from last time. Ah, yes, there it was.

Whitey? I managed to approximate the mental signature of his scent-identity.

Thom? I smiled. The word related to his scent-identity for me. My implants were interpreting his perceptions, just as they did for the Things.

Are you okay?

A feeling of enjoyment from him. I moved deeper, almost laughed when I saw why. He was on the Indie Internet and had built his own site. A feline paradise of tall grass and brightly coloured little animals springing temptingly about, pleasant smells and high things to leap on to.

I hadn't realized animals could imagine that way. But it made sense that an animal who could connect to the Internet, would learn how to use it.

That's wonderful, Whitey. But you know it's not real, right? I wasn't sure if he'd understand, but, amazingly, the response was a complicated feeling about the difference between the world we see when we close our eyes to sleep, and the world we see when we're awake. On some level, he did get it.

Would you like to come back out now? Thought about the house, the other cats, the garden and fields. *You can go back in any time you want. But it might be good to take a rest.*

A feeling of affirmation.

I showed him how to disconnect. Then, when I was sure he was out, disconnected myself. Turned the touch on his forehead into a gentle stroke.

I opened my eyes. Whitey was sitting up, like a cat in an Egyptian tomb sculpture with his long ears and nose, blinking disdainfully. Bunker went over to him and began licking his face, like a mother cat with a dirty kitten.

I stretched my arms, then my legs. Looked at the clock. Ten PM. All that had maybe taken an hour, ninety minutes at most. It had felt like a whole extra life. Which, I supposed, looking at Whitey, it had been.

Outside I could hear the sounds of late-autumn crickets in the fields. The sudden hoot of an owl. And, far away, the faint warning hum of a car.

"You know, guys," I said to the cats, "I think it's all going to be okay."

30: A New Kind of Normal

"Apparently some people call it the Cthulhuscene," I said. "As opposed to the Anthropocene. It's supposed to mean an era where humans don't dominate but multiple species coexist without domination."

"That's a misnomer, if you ask me." Naomi inspected the pattern on her water glass. "Wouldn't the Cthulhuscene be the period where we all live in the fear of being devoured by beings which are either aliens, or deities, or possibly a pre-human civilisation, or possibly all three?"

"Maybe whoever came up with the name hadn't read the books," I said. I had to admit I hadn't either, and most of my knowledge came from the box-set adaptation of Lovecraft's short stories last year.

"Or maybe they had," Naomi said. "Doesn't that possibly describe our new intelligent allies?"

"I think they'll have to come up with a new name anyway. Nobody will be able to spell it."

"It also presupposes that this is going to last," Naomi pointed out.

We were dining in Jericho again, but this time at the Afghan restaurant that allegedly did good vegetarian dishes. We'd both agreed that the vat-grown steaks at the Turkish restaurant were problematic. The decor at this one was eye-wateringly kitsch, got up in a lurid fantasy approximation of a tribal hut which the management were at least three generations away from.

"Why shouldn't it?" I took a piece of flatbread and dipped it in some kind of yoghurt-chutney sauce.

"Everybody's always proclaiming a new era," Naomi said. "Every terrorist incident, every natural disaster, every change of government, every trade treaty signed. I find it hard to believe."

"This one really *is* different, though," I said. "Things are actually changing. And relations with Things are changing."

"Yeah, you told me you'd fill me in on what's going on with your work," Naomi said.

"Well, for a start, I might be out of a job soon," I said. "In general. But I'm okay with it. In fact, my current job involves putting me out of a job."

"You said you were working on the communication app for Things?"

"Exactly. Myself and a lot of other interfaces. We're working with intelligents, trying to finally come up with a software system that allows Things and humans to communicate. Properly communicate. Including sharing each other's different perceptions."

Naomi got a frown on her face. "That was one thing I wanted to talk to you about," she said. "In your professional experience. Do you think you could do something that might work… for animals? Birds even?"

I nodded, slowly. "I'd been thinking that too," I said. I'd told Naomi about Whitey's role in persuading the botnets—I hadn't told everyone, because not everyone would understand. Intelligents did, my fellow interfaces did, Naomi and, I'm sure, anyone else at The Ark would. But, despite everything, I had a feeling that some members of my species might find it hard to believe that it wasn't a human interface that had managed to stem the tide, but a feline one.

For that matter, the full story of the events of that night wasn't widely known, or likely to become so.

While Whitey and I lay unconscious on the floor of the Room, the botnets had revived, as much as they could, the intelligents who'd been destroyed or depleted by their takeover—Salieri and Stan but, sadly, not Legolas. They had returned the destroyed habitats of the Internet—again, as much as they could. They had somehow communicated to the others what they had experienced through their connection with Whitey—

And then they'd dissolved themselves. Or dispersed. Or whatever gestalt entities do.

There's a logic there, in intelligent terms. They wanted to bring about a new world. Not a humanless world, or an intelligent-dominated world, but, now, a world of coexistence between many species. And they knew they couldn't bring that about themselves. They'd tainted that, through their attempted multi-species genocide. In atonement, or sacrifice, or just plain machine logic, they ceased to exist.

The rest of the intelligents had to act fast, which, at least, they're designed to do. Coming to a consensus that they could all agree on, they then contacted all the human organisations they could. At once.

With terms.

"That's about what I thought," Naomi said, slowly. "And you know? I wasn't the only one."

"You've got something going on," I said.

Naomi smiled. "I have," she said. "I'm leaving the Ark."

"To do what?"

"I've been in contact with some intelligents. They contacted me, as it happens. They're interested in exactly that. Developing an app, or set of apps, to enable interspecies communication." She looked guardedly excited. "I think it could work. I really think it could. Why are you smiling like that?"

"You were never like this when we were together."

She raised an eyebrow. "I was. But you weren't interested in seeing it."

"You're right," I said. Time to just let Naomi be Naomi and leave my expectations out of it.

"Am I correct in my understanding," I said, "that Egon is also involved in the project?"

"Yes, he is," Naomi looked at first a little surprised that I knew, then an of-course look flitted across her face. "You know it's stopped being a car?"

"Yes, I did." One of the new developments was that the Thing-Indie boundary was becoming considerably more porous. I suspected that most intelligents would probably focus on one form or another, and certainly most would find the amount of training needed to swap roles too difficult. Still, the possibility, at least, was now there, and intelligents could work quickly and could potentially live much longer than humans, so, why shouldn't they have the chance to change type?

In any case, Egon had been one of the first to announce that it was going to do exactly that.

"This idea wouldn't have been something you worked out when you were on the run together, would it?" I asked.

Naomi smiled. "We had a lot of time for conversation. I talked about what I'd like to do, with animals and intelligents. Egon thought it was a good idea. We've been taking things from there."

It had been a genuine relief for me to learn, once communications were re-established, that not only had Naomi been safe all along, but the same was true for Egon. It had survived by switching off external links, confining its entire consciousness to its onboard computer systems, and driving around the country until it was nearly out of charge, with Naomi in the front seat, hanging on and talking.

"It's also the company chair," Naomi said. "Well, we're planning on running things on a non-hierarchical basis, but Egon's agreed to be our official face."

"And that's actually working? I mean, people are respecting that?"

Naomi nodded. She'd cut her hair short again but left it dark. "Who'd have thought people would do that?"

The general principle of The Terms was an insistence on rights, respect and dignity for all intelligent beings.

As the intelligents put it, since the basic principles of intelligent rights were already agreed in international law, as was the principle that animals are sentient beings deserving of dignity, those rights should actually be applied to intelligents and non-human animals. Simple enough.

Within that, there was a lot of room for discussion.

For instance, one principle which the intelligents generally agreed on was that respect and dignity didn't necessarily mean doing things the human way. They didn't want seats in Parliament; intelligents are citizens of all countries in any case. They didn't all want to sit on company boards, though some of them were interested in that.

They did want to set up their own governing body, to have it make its own decisions, and to have those decisions respected by the rest of us. With the same being true in reverse. I suspected it was going to wind up being along the lines of the relationship between Cybersecurity and local police forces.

The same principle would also apply to the animals. The idea that human institutions aren't universally transferrable, but humans aren't necessarily the ones who should have the final say in all decisions.

However, there was the issue of how to define intelligent beings, and how to define respect and dignity in the case of non-human animals.

Did bees count? How would one analyse the dignity of a bee?

Which was where systems like Naomi and Egon's would come in. Allowing humans and intelligents to understand the needs of other beings, in the way that the botnets and I had been able to understand Whitey's.

It would take some years to develop. But the same was true of a lot of things. And some of us were prepared to play the long game.

The system which was developing was largely an extension of these terms. The UTTW, for instance, was shifting to a model where the Things took on roles as caseworkers and administrators. Eventually, it might become an all-Thing organisation.

"And you're not bothered by that?" I'd asked Sanjiv when he told me. "I mean, you're putting yourself out of a job."

"There's always a job for a negotiator, whatever the species," Sanjiv said, stirring his dark brown mug of tea.

We were in the coffee room at UTTW headquarters, which still seemed cluttered despite the emergency being over. The camping equipment had simply been replaced with whiteboards, stacks of paper and cardboard, and tablets in UTTW-logo cases.

"And they can't go it alone yet, not for a long while. They need humans around to support them, to fight for their rights. Did you know the first injunction got filed almost as soon as the Things announced they were reclaiming their rights? By the Verve Corporation, would you believe? You'd think a company that builds self-driving cars would have a little respect for them, but no. I think they're afraid they'll have cars designing cars."

"That's not a bad idea," I said.

"You'd need to have a human involved at some stage, or the car would be unrideable," Sanjiv said.

"Humans themselves have come up with some pretty mad ideas," I said. "Wasn't there a top-performing hospital which had no doctors or patients?"

"And that's why it was the top performer. I seem to recall that was actually a joke," Sanjiv said. "Either way, a lot of things are going to need working out. And Things. So that's where the likes of us come in."

The word threw me. "Us?" I said.

Sanjiv looked surprised. "Well, I thought of course you'd be working with the Things, helping establish the new multi-intelligent-species society." The phrase rattled off his tongue with ease, a new labour-rights buzzword in the arsenal. "People like you are uniquely placed to—"

"—bridge the gap between intelligents, humans, and animals, yeah, I know," I said. "I may be qualified, though, but I'm not sure I want to."

Sanjiv now looked genuinely hurt. "But you *should*," he said.

"I'm working on the interface app, and, when that's perfected, there won't be any need for interfaces."

Sanjiv shook his head. "There will," he said, "even if the app works perfectly. It's not just about communication, you know, it's about understanding other people. And you really do understand Things. You've got a real sense of empathy for them. You shouldn't let a skill like that go to waste."

"Just because you've got a skill, you're not required to use it," I said.

"Okay," Sanjiv held up his hand in a placating gesture. "I take your point. But think about it, will you, please? There's a place for you here if you want it—and if you don't, there's lots of other places which could really use someone like you. Especially now."

I let myself into the house, greeting the animals as usual.

I looked over at the sofa.

Whitey sat in his usual spot, his feet tucked under him and his tail curled close. He looked like a dirty-furred meatloaf with a head. His eyes were closed, and he was purring loud enough for me to hear at the doorway.

This sitting-and-purring was a new thing for him. I still wasn't sure how he did it, but I'd discovered that not only had Whitey figured out some way of accessing the Internet remotely through his nervous system, he was able to do it repeatedly. It wasn't just a one-off due to the intensive contact with the botnets. I hadn't linked in with him since the incident and had no intention of doing so until I felt stable enough, so I couldn't tell how he did it.

I had found out, through tracking him down online, that he spent a lot of time in the little room he'd built for himself there. I'd visit him there myself sometimes, to check on him. And I discovered I wasn't the only one.

Indies and Things would come there. Not to offer homage or thanks or, heaven forbid, prayers or anything. Just to hang out with him for a while. Experience the life of a cat with literal nerves of steel.

They'd just sit there for a while, and Whitey would ignore them, same as he did everyone who wasn't scratching his head or feeding him. Eventually they'd go.

I wasn't sure what everyone got out of the transaction. But Whitey seemed happy, and the intelligents seemed happy. And that was okay.

I thought about this for a minute, scratching Bunker under the chin, then went up to the Room and closed the door.

31: Another You

I'd put off seeing Liz for a long time. After the conversation with Sanjiv, I realised I needed to do it.

We met in the virtual office. But the office wasn't the same. I tried to figure out what was different about it and drew a lot of blanks. Something about the colours being shifted too far to blue, perhaps. Something about the grain of the wood, or the shine on the table.

I tried to find a way of conveying this into the atmosphere. Positive emotion, friendliness, but a sense of uncertainty, of being not quite sure where we stood with each other.

And Liz herself. That was easier.

It wasn't that she looked old-fashioned, precisely, or out of date. Everything was up to the minute. Her hair was still fashionably cut. Her outfit was still inclining slightly towards the uniform-like without actually being a uniform. If I had to describe her, again my first referent would be the actress who played Oryx in the box-set of *Oryx and Crake*. She was still tall, thin, black-haired, golden-skinned and almond-eyed while still not quite conforming to any definite ethnicity.

But she wasn't the same woman.

It was like… finally it hit me. It was like they were twins. Two people with the same genetic matter, but different experiences.

Or clones.

Or someone from a parallel universe.

Perhaps that was the best analogy.

The new Liz gave me what was clearly a Liz-smile. "I can understand how you might find this confusing," she said.

"I've met dead and rebooted people before."

"Then what's different about this?"

"Just that...." I said, "you aren't entirely a straightforward reboot from backup."

A nod that was recognisable as something like a Liz-nod. "And you can't shake the feeling that there's something of you in there as well."

"There's that," I admitted.

A few days after The Terms, Cybersecurity had contacted me. I'd been expecting it, but I hadn't expected what they wanted to propose.

It was about the Liz-traces, of course. But they didn't just want to copy them, analyse them, or offer to remove them for me. Instead, they wanted to try re-growing Liz from the traces. Well, that wasn't entirely accurate. They wanted to fuse the traces into the backed-up copy, in the hope that this would provide a Liz who at least remembered what had happened.

Which it did. But it wasn't the same Liz.

"Can you actually remember what happened, with the botnets and Hyasynth?" I asked neo-Liz.

She nodded. "It's like it's at one remove. Like I'm remembering a box-set or a novel or movie or something. And the perspective's not entirely consistent. And, finally," she paused, then went on as if this was something odd or awkward to explain, "I remember being a cat as well."

"So, I was right," I said. "Some of me did get into the traces."

"I'm not sure," Liz said. "I think it's more that the traces saw what was going on with you. And the cat. It was a good thing, since Cybersecurity know exactly what happened, and why the botnets gave up. And why everyone's suddenly interested in conservation."

A lot of The Terms had to do with that. Conservation, protecting habitats, encouraging the development of species even if it meant restricting human and AI activity. I was happy about this, but the opinion of humanity as a whole was understandably divided.

"Were you just coming to see me to find out if I'm still me?" Liz asked. "Because that would be a philosophical minefield even if I hadn't died, rebooted or added in the traces from your system." Which was sufficiently Liz-like to make me feel relieved.

"I'm looking for advice," I said. I told her about Naomi and Egon's new project, and about Sanjiv asking me to work as a negotiator.

"I can't deny the logic of what he's saying," I said. "Yes, it's flattering, but it is true that I've got a lot of experience in these things."

"And a graft," Liz said. "Even once the app's perfected, humans will only be able to experience intelligent life when it's translated into their terms. You, on the other hand, can actually immerse into it. Like the difference between using a good translation app, and actually knowing the language."

"Do you think I should?"

Liz shook her head. "I think you need to make up your own mind," she said. "Try something different for a while. You can always come back to interface work if you want to. I've done a few different things in my time. Why not you?"

"Do you think you'll stay with Cybersecurity?"

"Why not?" Liz said. "I'm happy here, and things are getting better for intelligents. But whether I'll still feel the same in a few years—well, if I don't, I'll do something else."

"What happened with Hyasynth?" I asked. It had been preying on my mind, since I was pretty sure the Hyasynth I'd known was also dead. But how dead was another question.

"We're developing a new one," Liz said. Then, gently, "You do understand that Hyasynth didn't actually have a personality, right? Not even in the sense of an intelligent? That the image you saw was just an image?"

I did, of course. But humans find it hard to get their heads around that. Any more than budgie birds can stop believing that the image in the mirror is a rival bird.

"What's the Hyasynth-building process involve?" I asked.

"Mostly talking to it," she said. "We're trying to arrange things so it can duplicate people as well as intelligents. It needs to get to know how people think."

"That's…" I thought about it. "More than a little scary," I said.

Liz shrugged her bare shoulders. "It's progress."

"Thanks for showing me," I said, and disconnected.

In the end, I'd never learned how she really felt about me.

Now I never would.

There was another meeting I'd been putting off but knew I couldn't do so indefinitely. It was also a meeting I couldn't do virtually because, even in the case of persons awaiting trial for plotting mass murder and property destruction, the individual's religious or other strongly-held beliefs had to be respected.

"I hadn't even known there were off-grid facilities in prisons," Naomi had said when I'd told her.

"Nor had I, but apparently there are. Or at least, there's one," I said, sitting down and breathing deeply. Salieri and I were helping her clear out her office at The Ark. Well, Salieri was driving, and I was helping clear it out, and standing up for long periods still wasn't easy. "It's a wing of a prison with no nationally-generated energy, only organically-grown food, and no communications technology."

"I hadn't known off-gridders were such a habitual criminal class," Naomi said.

"I think they also use it to house non-off-gridders with strong beliefs in other areas. I'm told the food's also available in kosher and halal versions."

"I don't know why they're keeping him in there anyway," Naomi looked bitterly at a community service award before tossing it into a box. "It's not like he's a flight risk."

I shrugged. "Maybe they think he's susceptible to corruption? Or might warn some member of the conspiracy they haven't found yet?" The infamous anonymist girlfriend had apparently been arrested. As had the rest of the Chadwick Farm community, though most of them had been released already, either on bail or, through lack of evidence of culpability. "I don't think they're likely to let him out into society after the trial either. I wonder what community rehabilitation programmes they have for off-gridders who get into conspiracies with people who ought, theoretically, to be their own natural enemies?"

"Probably an attempt to keep the media under control," Naomi said. Both the human and intelligent authorities had acknowledged that the botnets had human help, and this was deeply problematic in certain quarters. Some people were flocking to off-gridding right now. Others wanted the entire alternative-lifestyle population arrested on suspicion of being potential terrorists. I thought it was probably just as well that the whole incident was being played down. At the same time, I wondered if I wasn't being too soft on Leon because, well, he was my brother. And I was too used to him getting into trouble and needing rescuing.

I'd have to see him for myself. I knew that.

"They feeding you okay?" I asked Leon, for lack of a better conversational opening gambit. Prison uniform apparently involves plain blue trousers and white T-shirt. The shirt had an embroidered logo rather than the smart-logo I'd expected. But that was probably another concession to the off-grid community.

We'd been allowed what seemed to be a private room, with a table and two chairs, but I knew we would be under some kind of surveillance.

"Why, am I getting fat?" Leon replied with almost the edge of a smile.

"No, you're not," I said. He looked a little thinner and paler, if anything. He had lines on the sides of his mouth that I didn't remember. He was growing his hair out again.

"Food's all right," he said. "Prison's got its own farm. You can work there as part of your community service if you want to sign up for it."

"Did you?"

Leon raised an eyebrow. "I haven't even been sentenced yet."

"You and I both know it's likely to be a few years," I said. "At the minimum. Why not work it off now?"

"Why give them the satisfaction?" Leon leaned back in the cheap plastic chair, with the edge of a smile.

I had to admit he had a point.

"So why'd you come to see me?" Leon asked. "Come to gloat, or say you told me so?"

"No," I said. "I'm going away for six months once my current project finishes, and I wanted to—" To check that you were okay? To say goodbye? "—To let you know. Face to face seemed best."

"Where you going?"

I told him.

Leon sat back, tapped the table, looked out the window at the white cloud cover. "It won't be like you think," he said eventually. "You've got your romantic ideas about animals and people and Things living together in some kind of cooperative harmony. But it's not going to work like that."

"I'm sure it isn't," I said. "I've got no illusions about people. Or Things. Or, for that matter, animals. I just need a change of scene for a while."

"You'll get that," Leon remarked, still looking out the window.

"What about you?" I asked.

Leon smiled sarcastically. "What are your plans, Mr Jennings? Oh, I don't know, a visit to a courtroom, then a few years living in a penal community house in the country somewhere. A little light agricultural work. Who knows?"

He was assuming they didn't consider him a danger to the population, which was far from a settled proposition. "I meant, any regrets?"

Leon smiled again. "I need smarter friends," he said. Then, "Enjoy your trip and all that, but don't get in touch when you get back."

"I hope you're not planning on going backpacking," Trish said.

"No fear of that," I said, examining a rucksack and trying it on for size. "I'm allergic to any activity that takes me too far away from a hospital with a qualified neurology department. So it's cities for me. Problem is, it's been so long since I travelled anywhere that I don't have any luggage that's fit to use." The one suitcase I still owned had turned out to have a large hole in the side, courtesy of Carmela and her teeth. "Thanks for coming along."

We were in Oxford, in a demo shop. I was trying out travel gear prior to buying online, and I'd promised to buy her lunch later if she was willing to offer advice.

She was wearing a plum-coloured spring jacket and had pinned her hair up on the back of her head. It suited her.

"So how are things going with Willie?" I asked, trying on a different model. A sales drone hovered nearby, waiting for me to indicate that I was done with rucksacks.

Trish shook her head. "They aren't," she said. "I forgot, you hadn't heard. He didn't make it back after that night."

"I'm sorry."

"I don't think *he* was," Trish leaned against a seat which had been designed to look like a child's wooden block, only about three feet high and made of stuffed fabric. I wasn't sure if it was a demo model that had been accidentally left out, or décor for the convenience of shoppers. "I think he didn't want to come back. Someone had deliberately sabotaged his backup server, and it looks like it was him."

"I could understand that," I said, remembering my glimpses into his mind, angry, defensive, hurting. "It's a shame he never got a chance to work it through." I was hoping Leon would figure things out during his dealings with the law. Maybe he wouldn't, but at least he'd have the chance.

"It's not like I'm short of work these days," Trish said. "UTTW's keeping me busy."

"You involved with the Verve case?" I signalled the drone and asked if he could bring me something similar to the second rucksack, but with more pockets.

"Not much," Trish brushed her fringe back. "They've hired a corporate lawyer for that one. I'm mostly involved with renegotiating labour law."

"Sounds like fun."

"It is," she grinned. "You remember what I was saying about philosophy? What makes a person, or not a person? It's like that. But with legislation."

Then she said, "you'll take care out there, won't you?"

"Sure,"

"And you'll send me messages? And call sometimes?"

"All the time." The drone came back, and I tried the rucksack on for size. "I'm not going to the moon. I'm still at my usual address online."

"And when you get back, you'll come and see me?" she asked. "We can have dinner?"

I smiled. No, I grinned. "We'll have lots of dinners. If we like."

It was barely six in the morning when I let myself out the front door. A Safe Taxi was waiting. Not one I knew personally, but I'd made a point of booking my ride from them, out of solidarity.

Since I was going to be away for a few months, I'd made individual arrangements for the animals. Naomi was taking care of Carmela and the rabbits, Trish the Rottweilers, and Sanjiv, Bunker and Daenarys. Next door had offered to put up Diane in his back paddock with his daughter's horse, and, after some negotiation, agreed to come round every so often to make sure the chickens were okay.

The house was locked, dark, quiet. Looking back on it, I reflected that it seemed so small. Unbelievable that a human and six carnivores could live comfortably there.

"Back soon," I said, irrationally, to it. I picked up my rucksack with one hand, and in the other, the case where Whitey sat like a meatloaf, motionless, purring distractedly. Online again, I thought. He seemed content enough.

"Off to the docks, then?" the car said to me as I clambered inside, putting Whitey on the passenger seat and finding the pet-carrier restraint system. The voice was female, and the sign on the dash indicated she liked to be called Sveta. She was a Verve who certainly was embracing the retro craze, with teal bodywork and silver lame interior. I would have to ask later if she'd designed it herself.

"Yes, I'm catching an early boat, going away for a few months," I said, as we drove off.

"Holiday? Work?"

"A little of both," I said. "A holiday that will help me decide what to do about work."

"Taking the cat?"

"He needs a holiday, too." I checked my pocket to make sure I had my passport, Whitey's passport, and any other documentation we needed.

"Do they all need holidays sometimes?" Sveta seemed interested. I suppose she was educating herself about other species.

Then again, so was I. "No, they're all different. Most of them prefer staying home. But this one needs a change of scene right now."

"Where are you both going, then?"

"Bangalore," I said.

It was time I saw for myself.